LINEAR TACTICAL: OAK CREEK

HERO'S
FLIGHT

HERO'S FLIGHT

Dedicated to my youngest cousin Kingslea and her dear husband Michael —two of my favorite people. How I admire your vision, perseverance, and spirits of adventure!

Chapter 1

"Five minutes out. Everybody hang on." Derek Bollinger's hands were light on the cyclic and collective controls of the utility helicopter he was piloting, despite the direness of the situation.

Quick affirmative responses from the other members of the Teton County Helitack team came back, but acknowledging them was secondary. Derek's eyes were focused on his target—and the rapidly approaching storm they were trying to beat.

The call had come from a climber in trouble. The guy was a skilled alpinist, but even the good ones could make mistakes. One of his anchors had failed, and he'd fallen over thirty feet down the side of the mountain.

Frankly, the man was lucky his line hadn't snapped. If it had, this mission would be a body recovery and not a rescue.

Lightning flashed just behind the cliff they were flying toward. This might *still* be a recovery mission if they weren't careful.

Derek's mind was entirely focused on bringing in the S-70 Firehawk, a civilian version of the UH-60 Black Hawk helicopter used in the military, as quickly as possible. Barely half an hour had passed since they'd gotten the call, but they were on the clock in more ways than one.

The climber's leg was broken. He said he was fine, but it was hard to assess your own injuries when you were dealing with pure adrenaline and survival instincts.

That was definitely something Derek would know.

Having a broken leg and being stuck on a nearly sheer cliff face were bad enough. The weather was what made this a true emergency. A thunderstorm that turned the sky black was moving in, and even helitack professionals couldn't perform this rescue in the middle of a storm.

The helicopter had to be too close to the cliff face to get to the climber, and the wind from the storm made that especially dangerous. Hell, these mountains were already a minefield of unexpected air movement thanks to heat fluctuations and a dozen other reasons on any given day.

Derek was a good pilot. It was the only thing he considered himself good at. The rest of his life? Shambles. But here in the pilot's seat, everything made sense.

Still, even a pilot of Derek's caliber couldn't control the wind. Attempting this kind of operation in bad weather put everyone at risk, including the climber. Which was why Derek had the stick pushed forward, pressing the limits of speed. They needed every second they could get.

"Sam, Scarlett, you guys ready?" he said into his comms unit.

"Yeah," Scarlett Collingwood said. "Everything's prepped. Ready to throw."

"Ready to rappel," Sam Dempsey replied a moment later.

The mountain's cliff wall rose up in front of them, and Derek noted the red smoke that marked the climber's location. Pulling up on the cyclic stick in his hands, he eased the helicopter to a hover in the air. "We're in position, Sam."

Derek glanced back at the other man once, seeing the gear he carried on his back. A litter, to be used to transport the climber, was the biggest part of it, nearly as tall as Sam's body. Sam and the stretcher would have to be lowered down before Derek got them close to the cliff wall.

Derek didn't have to watch to know that Sam and Scarlett were both checking Sam's connections one more time.

"Rappelling," Sam said a moment later, slipping backward out the copter's doorway. Even while they were connected to a rope, the sight of someone disappearing over the side into nothing could be nerve-racking.

The line extended, and Scarlett stopped it when Sam was far enough down.

"Good, over?" Derek asked.

"Good," Sam replied.

"Comms are yours, Sam."

Derek pushed the cyclic forward again, this time maneuvering the helicopter lightly while approaching the mountain. The climber was a good thousand feet off the ground. There was a ledge for him, but not much of one. If he'd been exposed to this storm before they had a chance to rescue him, he probably wouldn't have survived.

"Higher," Sam said.

As Derek pulled back on the stick, they rose slowly. The body of the helicopter tilted, one of those damned heat pockets knocking into them. Derek cursed under his breath, correcting against the movement.

"Higher," Sam said again calmly, and Derek did as he asked. "Good. Scarlett, wave and throw."

"Roger that," she echoed.

A moment later, she lowered a weighted bag Sam would throw to the climber. Derek noted several unique points on the rock wall beside them to make it easier to return.

In a flight rescue, the helicopter could only get so close to a cliff wall—it was on Sam to get to the climber. Sam threw the weighted line, and the climber caught it.

"Connection established." Sam's voice was calm, as if he weren't currently in one of the most dangerous parts of an already dangerous mission.

Derek had to let Sam do his job, and he narrowed his focus to the task in front of him: making sure the helicopter *did not fucking move.*

The seconds slipped by, and he concentrated on feeling the bird around him. He'd always been able to do it while he flew. Something about being in the pilot's seat—whether in a helicopter or an airplane—made him one with the machine around him.

In his hand, the stick shook. Winds from the storm were coming, the first brushes of them making the air a little more uneven. They were okay for now, so Derek said nothing. Sam and Scarlett needed no distractions.

"Down and locked in," Sam finally said. "You're free, Derek."

"Roger that." Immediately, Derek eased the helicopter back from the mountain wall, to give Sam a chance to help the climber without being buffeted by the rotors. The short-haul line still hung out the side of the helicopter, where it would stay.

Sam's and the climber's forms were smaller, but Derek could still see them. His friend would move fast. Derek had known both Sam and Scarlett most of his life and had been working with them on the helitack team for almost a year. They were the best at what they did.

Right now, Sam was drilling safety lines into the rock for both he and the climber before setting up the litter and getting the climber into it. All Derek and Scarlett could do was wait and watch the storm rapidly approach.

This was going to be too damned close.

Because the climber had experience, and in spite of his pain, it took only seven minutes before Sam radioed for a pickup.

"Ready," Sam said.

"Roger that. On our way."

Derek returned to the cliff, edging as close as he dared and aligning himself with the markers he'd noted earlier. Once again, there was no room for error.

"Almost perfect," Sam said. "A little lower, and slack."

Scarlett let the short-haul line out farther so Sam could catch it and then attach both himself and the litter to it. There wasn't time to get them into the helicopter itself. They'd be hanging as Derek flew them out.

Not a gentle ride, but better than dying.

"Ready to attach." Sam's voice was still calm.

As was Derek's. "Roger that. Go." He adjusted to make sure he was ready to compensate for their weight.

"Tension," Sam said.

Scarlett pulled in the line until it was taut and locked it. "Locked, Sam."

"Releasing anchor."

This was it; Sam and the climber were removed from the cliff wall. Only their attachment to the helicopter kept them from plummeting to their death.

The extra weight momentarily dipped the bird, and Derek leaned into the movement with the stick to catch their momentum. As he turned them, his heart dropped. The storm had flanked them, curling around the way they'd come from, and it was too close.

Wind slammed into the side of the copter, throwing them back toward the cliff.

"Fuck." Derek was barely able to readjust enough to keep the rotors from clipping the rocks and sending all of them to an early grave.

"Derek," Sam said.

"Hold on." The words were said through gritted teeth. "Storm's on us. Gonna be bumpy."

"They're spinning," Scarlett said into the comms unit, her voice just as calm as his and Sam's. "Momentum's going to take them into the cliff."

Derek wasn't going to allow that to happen.

He wrestled the helicopter under control and got them away from the cliff just in time. Another rogue wave of air— heat reacting to the incoming coolness of the storm—lifted them quickly.

The first signs of rain pelted the windshield, and the stick shook in his hand. "How's our friend doing, Sam? How fast can I go?"

Wind whipped through Sam's comms. "He's good. Go."

Derek didn't hesitate, pushing the chopper forward, directly into the edge of the oncoming storm. He could go out and around it, but that would mean going over the mountains, and with the air shifts right now, that was almost as dangerous.

He shook his head once. Flying into the storm wasn't ideal, but he could do this. His mind snapped into crystalline focus. Flying was the only place his mind was this sharp.

Behind him, he heard Scarlett strap herself in. "How's the line?"

"It's good." Her voice was tight. Underneath the necessary calm was fear. They were lucky they'd even been able to get the climber out in time. One minute later…

Derek shoved the thought out of his head. They weren't out of danger yet. He leaned into the headwind, the rotors fighting the unevenness of the increasing wind.

Vaguely, he heard Scarlett talking on the other line to base camp. They needed an ambulance for the climber once they landed.

If they landed.

No. Fuck that.

A gust of wind picked up, hitting them like a battering ram from the right, tilting the chopper too damn far. Neither Sam nor Scarlett said a word on the comms unit, although they had to know how dire the situation was.

The stick fought Derek, but he won, righting them, trying to compensate for his charges now swinging below him, at the same time as the wind. They were far enough from the mountain, so he lowered his altitude as much as he could. Sam and the climber would be just above the tree line, but the winds were better. Rain pelted them, and lightning flashed too close for comfort.

Derek's knuckles were white on the stick, but his head was clear. He had this. He'd weathered worse storms than this, both figurative and literal.

And the flight ones, he'd always come out of whole.

Still, when the landing zone came into view, flashing lights from emergency response vehicles visible, he blew out a breath of relief. But he didn't dare lose focus now. The storm was still surrounding them, and he wasn't about to drop his guard at the last second.

They hovered over the pad, and Sam finally spoke. "Counting you in."

With a gentle hand, Derek descended as Sam counted down the meters.

He held steady while the first responders swarmed in and got both the litter and Sam and cleared them from the pad.

"Line clear," Sam said.

Scarlett hit the retraction crank, and Derek descended the rest of the way as the line spun back onto its coil.

Only once they reached the ground did he breathe in a deep sigh of relief. Every muscle in his body was taut, and he squeezed and released his fists to try to let some of the tension out.

He could think of about two hundred things that could have gone wrong, and if he were honest with himself, they had come way too fucking close with that one gust of wind.

He pushed it from his mind. The last thing he needed was one more factor to fuel his nightmares. He had enough of those already.

A hand came down on Derek's shoulder, and he jerked.

Scarlett held up her hands, one eyebrow raised, and he shook himself loose from the fight-or-flight response that gripped him in its ugly fist.

"Good job. Although, not going to lie, that was…terrifying. I'm glad it was you. Any other pilot? Not so much." She shrugged.

"Any other pilot would have done the same. Everyone here."

"Yeah." But she didn't sound convinced. With one more nod, she grabbed her gear and exited.

Derek shut down the helicopter and leaned his head back against the seat, willing his mind and body to ease from the adrenaline. At the same time, he didn't want to lose the precious clarity time in the air granted him. Even in dangerous flights like this, being in the sky was the only thing that felt right.

The storm was well and truly here. Derek unclipped and got out, jogging through the rain back to the helitack headquarters. He could have taken alternative paths indoors, but the icy cold water kept the clear feeling going just a little bit longer.

I'm glad it was you. Any other pilot? Not so much.

He shook his head, Scarlett's words echoing in his mind. He wouldn't think about the what-ifs, but he would choose to be grateful.

Today, he helped save someone's life.

Today, for once, he'd done something good.

Chapter 2

The ceiling above Derek's head was a good blank space to project his thoughts on—a tool he'd learned about in therapy. He was supposed to use it to help fight some of the demons screaming inside his mind. By focusing on the ceiling, he could quiet them for a while.

He'd found the practice to be mostly bullshit.

But today, combined with the release flying had given him, as it always did, his subconscious was somewhat quiet.

It was still relatively early. After a shower and some food he barely remembered eating, Derek had retreated into his room here at the helitack base camp.

The storm made it feel like it was night, but it wasn't. Absently, he wondered if it finally made him an old man at thirty if he went to bed at seven p.m.

Probably.

A knock came at the door.

Everyone on the team here at the helitack base camp had their own room. Nothing big or fancy, but a little bit of privacy since, during the worst of the fire season, teams might be on duty for weeks at a time.

The rest of the compound was made up of group spaces: kitchen, common room, game room, gym. If Derek concentrated, he could hear the sounds of people relaxing. The faint clang of weights in the gym and cursing from the guys playing some kind of video game out in the common room.

It reminded him of being in the military. Before…*everything*.

The knock sounded again, and he realized he'd gotten lost in his thoughts.

"Yeah?" He sat up.

The door opened, and Sam stood in the doorframe, also freshly showered. "Mind if I come in?"

"Sure."

Sam crossed to the chair in the corner to sit. He settled in like he was prepared to be there for a while—which probably wasn't a good sign.

"How are you doing?" Sam asked.

"I'm fine," Derek said. It was the truth. Mostly. He was fine. Breathing. Alive. His brain was relatively calm.

Sam shook his head. "That mission was…" He searched for the right word. "Stressful."

"Understatement of the fucking year," Derek said, relaxing. If Sam wanted to talk about the rescue, that wasn't a problem.

He'd known Sam for a lot of years. Sam hadn't grown up in Derek's hometown of Oak Creek, but he'd been around nearly every summer when his family had come to visit. Sam had always been quick to jump into whatever shenanigans Derek and his three brothers were currently involved in.

But now, things were a little different. Sam was the helitack team leader, and Derek wasn't currently sure if he was talking to his friend or his boss. Though Sam was smiling, and there was no awkwardness, Derek suspected the latter.

Sam leaned back in his chair. "I wanted to make sure you

were okay after something so intense—and to both let you know that your piloting was top-notch and to thank you for it."

"We got lucky," Derek admitted. "A lot of things could've gone wrong."

"I don't believe in luck," Sam said. "I believe in preparing as much as you can and trusting that training in the moment. Which is exactly what you did—what we all did. Did I throw my guts up as soon as we got the climber in the ambulance? Yes. Do I ever want to come that close to being a splattered bug on a mountain windshield again? No."

Derek snorted a laugh.

Sam grinned. "But it was your skill that got us out of there safely. Climber is resting well at the hospital and is going to be fine."

Derek nodded. "Great."

"You did good, Derek."

Derek just shrugged. The Air Force had made him a good pilot then he'd honed the skills further in the past year he'd spent here as part of the Teton Helitack team.

Piloting had never been his problem. Flying damned near anything came as naturally to him as breathing.

"The big fire season is over now," Sam continued. "Things are slowing down. We'll have a lot less to do, today's drama notwithstanding. No more crazy hours. Everyone will have scheduled time off."

Derek already knew all that. "Sounds great."

Actually, it didn't sound great. Sounded liked Derek would have a lot more time on his hands, which wasn't necessarily a good thing.

Sam shifted in his chair. "Team is heading to Oak Creek tomorrow night."

Derek's whole body stiffened. He knew the team went to Oak Creek as often as they could, although, with their schedule, those trips had been few and far between in the past few months.

The small Wyoming town was a little less than an hour away and boasted the Eagle's Nest, the closest bar to helitack HQ. It was a great place—friendly, comfortable, the quintessential small-town bar where everyone felt welcome. Derek should know; he'd been running around the place his whole life.

Right up until eighteen months ago. He hadn't set foot inside it since.

Sam kept going. "You should come with us. You're from Oak Creek, for crying out loud. What do you say?"

The words felt like they stuck in Derek's throat. "I'll think about it."

Leaning forward on his knees, Sam sighed. Derek knew the sound. It was one of resignation and frustration. This wasn't the first time he'd been asked to go, and it wasn't the first time he'd said he'd think about it so he could let them down easy.

"I'm going to level with you, Derek." There was no anger in Sam's voice, but Derek could hear the steel of a team leader. "You're the best pilot we have. Hell, you might even be the best pilot I've ever worked with, and I'm not the only one who thinks that."

Derek looked past the compliment to the word that lurked behind it. "But?"

Sam stared at him for a long moment, like he was trying to figure out how to say it. "But you're not a team player."

"Because I don't want to drive an hour there and back to drink beer in a town I've lived in my whole life?"

"No. We'd love to have you come with us, but that's not why."

"Why, then?"

"Because you keep yourself separated from the team. Take today, for instance. What you did was incredible. Everyone wants to talk to you about it—clap you on the back. But no one knows how to do it."

"I'm just taking a little downtime in here. Decompressing."

Sam scrubbed a hand down his face. "Which is completely understandable, and nobody would think twice about it if you *normally* interacted with the team. But even after nearly a year, no one feels like they know you well enough to come in here and shoot the shit with you for a few minutes."

Derek let out a sigh. What Sam was saying was true. Derek had deliberately kept himself apart. "I have my reasons for flying solo, Sam."

"Hell, I know that, man. Scarlett does too. We both know you have your reasons for staying out of Oak Creek, and we've tried not to press."

"Thank you." If they had pressed, Derek would've had to leave.

"And we won't. But my priority has to be this team. Your distance has the potential to form a crack in our formation. If people don't think they know you, they won't feel like they can trust you, regardless of your skills. Out on a mission like today's, that lack of trust could be deadly."

Again, Sam wasn't wrong. Silence dragged out between them.

"Right now, you're here in your room instead of hanging out with everyone else. Why?"

There wasn't a reason. Even the truth—something Derek had no interest in sharing—shouldn't really affect his interaction with the team.

"It's not just tonight," Sam continued, voice calm as ever. "It's all the time. The crew needs you. Not just as a pilot, but as an actual member of this team."

"I know—" Derek cleared his throat. "I know I keep my distance. I have my reasons."

Sam nodded. "But like it or not, the team naturally looks

to the pilots for leadership. I need you to try to connect with everyone else. If you don't want to go have beers with everyone, fine. But at least here, I'd like you to try."

Slowly, Derek nodded. "I hear you. I'll come out and do my best tonight, and I'll try to be better about it in the future."

"Good."

Derek held out a hand as Sam stood. "I'm never going to be the life of the party."

Sam shook his hand. "That's not what I'm asking for."

"And Oak Creek… I can't. It's not an option. If you want me to do something else, I will. Put me through team-building hell for all I care. I'll catch a hundred trust falls. But I can't go home yet." Couldn't go home *ever*.

Sam looked at him, assessing, but finally just clapped him on the back. "When that changes, I've got your back."

It wouldn't change.

Derek nodded. "And I do understand about the need to have a strong team, Sam. I was in the Air Force long enough to know that one person can erode the morale of the whole crew if you're not careful. I'll make sure I'm not that."

Sam smiled and turned toward the door. He pointed at the small desk, where two phones were charging. "Two phones? You have some kind of secret life we don't know about?"

Derek forced himself to laugh. It was closer to the truth than he wanted to let on. "I got a new one, but I'm still in the process of switching everything over."

Derek followed Sam out into the common room, his chest tightening. It wasn't overly loud out here, but it was still more than the relative silence in his room. For now, it was bearable. He'd muscled through worse, and thanks to the flight earlier, his mind was in decent shape.

He could do this. These were his friends. No one here meant him any harm.

"Whoa," Eric, one of the younger team members, said. He

stood at one end of the ping-pong table in the corner and had his hand on his chest. "Is that Derek coming out of his room, or am I seeing some sort of apparition?"

The room got quiet. This definitely wasn't what Derek had wanted.

It was Scarlett who saved the day. "Don't pay any attention to that dumbass. He got a word-of-the-day calendar and is trying to make himself smarter for the ladies."

Derek snorted a laugh. "Well, congrats. You used the word correctly."

Eric made a grand bow. "Ping-pong, ghost?"

The others in the room were now watching the exchange with amusement. But no one was upset with him. If anything, people were smiling because he was here. That was…good.

Different.

"You're on."

The guy opposite him, Justin, grinned. "This, I have to see."

Scarlett sat at the community table, a bowl of cereal in front of her, and laughed. "Eric, I can't describe to you how royally shit on you are about to get."

Eric rolled his eyes. "I think I can take him."

"Don't say I didn't warn you." She smirked then stuck the spoon in her mouth.

Scarlett had been one of Derek's friends in Oak Creek growing up. She knew the hours they'd all spent at the arcade, playing all the classic games, including ping-pong. Derek had been one of the best. Definitely practiced enough to stay better than his brothers.

He picked up the paddle, and they went to work. Derek fell into the muscle memory from all those years ago and beat Eric quickly. That turned into the others wanting a try. By the time he'd handily beat everyone who had a chance to go against him, hours had passed, and people were drifting off to bed.

Derek was tired too. A *good* sort of tired.

Sam nodded to him as he headed back to his room. Mission accomplished. Derek was now much more approachable to everyone.

His eyes snagged on the two phones when he entered his room, and he paused. The second phone, he hadn't charged in a while. Normally, he barely charged it at all, just plugging it in once a month in order to check it then letting it die again. If it was dead, he couldn't be tempted.

Only one person still used that number.

But the phone had fully charged while he was playing with the team, and it now called to him like some sort of beacon. It wasn't the first of the month, the day he always checked, but…

Sitting down on his bed, he reached for it, unable to resist tonight. He just needed to see.

And what he saw were messages—texts and voice mails. All from the same number.

Becky.

He skipped the text messages and went straight to the voice mails, needing to hear her voice. He listened to the oldest first, from nearly a month ago.

"Hey, Derek." She cleared her throat. "I know you're probably somewhere…dangerous or exotic that I can never know about. Maybe you're in the Middle East, complaining about how much sand is in your shoes. Maybe you're somewhere so cold not even you and I together could warm you up, I—"

A long silence filled the space, and Derek closed his eyes. She thought he was in the Middle East. It was one of the places he'd been. Not anymore.

"This was a mistake," she whispered. "I don't want to bother you or anything. I just hope you're okay. I miss you."

Derek ignored the spike of pain in his chest and skipped to the next message. Missing him was a small price to pay. He was doing the right thing. The *only* thing. A message from her wasn't going to change that.

This time, she was drunk. Derek knew Becky well enough to hear it in her voice without her having to say the words.

"I'm at the Eagle's Nest, and all I can think about is you." She sounded somewhere between sad and angry. "I need you to call me back. Right now. Or I'm going to start dancing with other guys."

He shoved aside the brief flash of jealousy. There was nothing to be jealous of. He and Becky were done.

Next message. "Are you fucking kidding me, Bollinger? We need to talk. I know you're off doing something important, but you can take time for one phone call. Just one. Are you going to ignore me forever?"

A laugh almost burst out of him at that. *Ignore her?* The last thing he was doing to Becky Mackay was ignoring her. He was protecting her. His thoughts were beginning to slip, and he needed to shut the phone off and pull everything back. Stop himself from becoming mentally derailed.

But he didn't, flipping instead to the next message.

That was a mistake.

Becky's ragged breathing came through first, and everything in the room shifted. He was right back in that Vegas hotel room eighteen months ago.

Becky was crying, broken sobs he wanted to stop but couldn't. He couldn't seem to do anything.

Couldn't disconnect the call.

Couldn't stop her crying.

Couldn't separate the past from the present.

"Why, Derek?" Her voice sounded so small and so broken. She sobbed again. "How could you do this to us? How could you?"

Her voice broke, her pained cry filling his head.

Darkness. Sobbing. He looked down to find blood on his

hands. *Her* blood—bright red against his skin, marking him for the monster he was.

How could he do this?

She was right. He was the one who'd broken them beyond the point of repair. He'd destroyed everything good in his life.

Lunging away from the sound of her voice, Derek blinked and found himself back in his room at helitack. There was no blood on his hands. No crying Becky on the floor with her arms up, blocking her face.

Not there. But yet, *always* there.

He blinked, trying to get his ragged breathing under control. He had destroyed everything, so he was trying to fix it the only way he knew how.

Listening to her voice wasn't helping with that mission. Hearing her just made it harder to stay away. He shut off the voice mail without listening to the rest.

Putting on the heaviest boots he had, Derek crossed back to the nightstand and grabbed the phone, dropping it on the floor. The screen shattered, but it wasn't enough. He crushed the phone under his foot, over and over until he was sure the little piece of technology would never work again.

He couldn't hear her anymore.

But that wouldn't stop him from knowing what he'd done, what a monster he was.

That would never go away.

Chapter 3

"I am not taking no for an answer."

Becky Mackay looked up at Lilah Collingwood standing in the doorway to her office, hands on her hips.

This lecture had been going on for quite a few minutes now, her friend's attempt to keep Becky from drying up and becoming a spinster.

Becky wanted to roll her eyes but knew that would just prolong said lecture. "And what if I told you I already had other plans? Eva is supposed to come by, and we were going to have a relaxing dinner together."

Eva Dempsey was the new vet tech Becky had hired in the past few weeks. The quiet woman had become a good friend.

"No. Because Eva—I like the gal, but she's as boring as you—will leave early, and your plans will become you sitting on your couch eating ice cream and watching documentaries."

Becky sighed. "It would be cookies from Fancy Pants, not ice cream."

Lilah lifted her hands to heaven as if begging for help. "You're wasting away, Becky. People want to see you. Human people. Your friends."

Becky almost argued that with the number of cookies she'd been eating, she wasn't anywhere near wasting away. But again, no need to prolong the come-to-Jesus she and Lilah were having.

Or, more specifically, the come-to-the-Eagle's-Nest. The bar had been sending out text advertising: *You're not going to want to miss what happens at the Eagle's Nest tonight.* Evidently, that had been enough to send Lilah on the girls' night out rampage.

"Lilah," Becky begged. "Do you really want to drag me out just so I can sit in the corner and watch you dance?"

It was Lilah's turn to roll her eyes. "Of course not. Ella will be there, and we'll make Eva come. We'll all dance. Drink Tokyo Teas. Or we can try something my parents were telling me about. An Electric Smurf."

"What the heck is an Electric Smurf?"

Lilah leaned against the doorframe. "Apparently some sort of bright-blue drink from back in the day. Is it delicious? Yes. Does that make you drink far too many of them? Also, yes. And does all of that lead to you waking up with the worst hangover of your life, having made bad decisions? Triple yes."

Becky grinned. "Sounds like a real winner there."

Lilah laughed. "Evidently half the marriages in Oak Creek can be directly traced back to Electric Smurfs in one way or another."

The smile fell away from Becky's face, but Lilah didn't seem to notice. She truly, genuinely, wasn't sure she was up for a night on the town.

But then again, was she ever going to be?

She hadn't been out in over a month. Hadn't had the stomach for it since calling and leaving Derek that last message.

The one where she'd been so upset. So pathetic. Asking how he could do this to them. Then finally begging him to call.

Just for one minute. Even if he couldn't say anything, she needed to hear him breathing.

She told him if he still cared for her at all, he would call.

Derek hadn't called. She could see he'd accessed the message, but he hadn't called.

It had taken two days before she'd even been able to get out of bed. Even now, weeks later, she still rubbed at her chest sometimes, trying to ease the phantom pain there.

Derek hadn't cared enough to call. Hadn't respected her enough to say directly to her that it was over. Had just let his unspoken words do it.

After all they'd been through, she couldn't believe it had come to that.

Lilah picked up that something was wrong with Becky and rushed farther inside the room. "Whoa. Hey, Bec, listen. We don't have to—"

No. Screw that. Becky was not going to sit around having a pity party for herself anymore.

Derek hadn't called. They were over. It was time to move on with her life.

She held out a hand to stop Lilah's progress. "If I say yes and go, will you promise not to ask me again for…a month?"

Lilah narrowed her eyes. "When was the last time you went somewhere other than to spar with me, the grocery store, or do something with your vet business?"

Way too long. "I don't know."

"Bullshit," her friend muttered under her breath. "Fine. If you come out tonight, I swear on my life I won't bug you about it for another two weeks."

Becky laughed. "I said a month."

"And two weeks is my counteroffer." Lilah walked the rest of the way over and pulled her in for a quick hug.

The woman was tough, a warrior, and Becky knew the gesture didn't come easily. So she appreciated it all the more.

True to form, Lilah pulled back after just a second. But her blue eyes were alight with concern. "In all seriousness, we do miss you. We're worried about you."

"I'm fine."

"Once again, I say bullshit."

Becky studied her, unsure of what to say. Of all the people in Oak Creek, Lilah was the one closest to knowing the truth since Becky had been training with her for more than a year. Lilah knew Becky had demons but had never pushed to get her to talk about them—probably because Lilah had demons of her own she didn't talk about.

Becky squeezed her friend's arm. "You see me every week, and you know how I'm doing. I'm okay. Promise."

The look in Lilah's eyes made it clear she didn't believe her. That was okay. Becky wasn't ready to talk about it, because the one person she actually needed to talk to about it wasn't answering her calls. Or her texts. Or her emails. Nothing.

For eighteen months, the person who meant everything to her had refused to talk to her at all.

Lilah took a step closer. "Whatever it is, you know I'm here for you, right? I know I'm not the best at girl talk, but I can listen like a champ."

Becky nodded. "I know."

"Good." Lilah winked. "I'd hate to have to beat it out of you."

Becky laughed, but she smirked at her friend. "Not so easy to do that anymore."

"That's sure as hell right. You're my best student."

Out beyond the office, the small bell attached to the front door of the vet clinic rang. "I need to see this patient."

"But will you come to the Eagle's Nest tonight?"

Becky closed her eyes. "Okay. Although I don't promise to stay the whole time."

"That's okay. Baby steps. I'll take it."

Her friend disappeared out the door before Becky could respond. Walking the ten feet to her office already had Becky regretting her decision to go out tonight, but she pushed it down.

She could go have a good time with her friends this evening. Her broken heart would still be there tomorrow.

Closing her eyes, Becky pushed aside everything else and put on a smile for her patient.

"Hello there, Buttercup." The excited golden retriever jumped up to see her, making her laugh. There were some clients who always brought a smile to her face. Buttercup was one of them.

The appointment was just a checkup, so it went fast. Becky lost herself in paperwork and appointments until the workday was ending. Eva popped her head into the office from her last task.

"Um, I'm going to head to my place really quick and clean up. I'll see you over at the Eagle's Nest."

"You don't have to go if you don't want to, Eva," Becky told her. The other woman was reserved and tended to keep to herself. They'd been able to talk her into one other girls' night out, but she hadn't been completely comfortable. "I know we'd planned a quiet dinner at my place."

Eva smiled softly. "I know, but...I think I want to go. It will be good to get out for a little bit, and I should try to make more friends."

Eva's eyes were filled with something Becky recognized —*longing*. Theo Lindstrom would probably be there tonight. Becky's quiet new assistant was definitely smitten with the man who ran Linear Tactical. And he was equally smitten with her.

"As long as it's what you want."

Laughing, Eva pulled her hair back into a ponytail. "I

could say the same about you. How about this, if either one of us seems like we're drowning, we'll pull the other out. Fair?"

Becky nodded. "Fair."

"Okay. I'll see you in a bit." Eva grinned before she left, and Becky sighed.

It would be fine. One drink wouldn't do her any harm, and then she could slink back into her comfortable cave where the grief couldn't hurt her as much. The carefully constructed shell she'd built where things didn't remind her of Derek every single second. It was a painstakingly orchestrated dance with steps she now had memorized.

She had plenty of memories at the Eagle's Nest, but Lilah was right. If people didn't see Becky was alive and well, the poking and prodding would only get worse. One drink seemed like a decent price to keep everyone off her back.

She winced, immediately feeling the guilt of the thought. Her friends and family here in Oak Creek genuinely cared about her. And there were days she wished she could tell them everything so they could understand why she needed to withdraw.

But she couldn't do that.

Without proper context and Derek here to explain, it would ruin his reputation, and she couldn't stand the thought of that. And like hell was she sharing their business with anyone else before she had a chance to talk it through with him.

If he ever decided to come back or answer the phone.

The pain knotted her gut again, and she had to deliberately stop herself from wrapping her arms around her stomach and curling into a ball.

It would be so easy to fall into the spiral of thoughts that plagued her every time she was alone. A hundred different paths to ask herself why she was alone and why the one person she wanted here was the person most absent in the world.

Becky was tired of the spiral. Tonight, for one night, she resolved not to think about Derek and the way her heart ached. She could do that for herself.

Was she ready to let it all go? Hell no.

But the promise of a break from it already felt like a breath of air she desperately needed.

She took a deep breath and stood up straighter. She would go out and have a good time without feeling guilty about it.

A quick shower and a change of clothes later, she pulled up to the Eagle's Nest, and despite her resolution earlier, she was still a little nervous. It really had been a while since she'd been around people.

Lilah lifted her arms in victory when Becky stepped through the doors, tilting her head back and whooping. In spite of herself, Becky laughed. Lilah sat with Ella O'Conner, one of Becky's other closest friends, who owned Fancy Pants bakery. Both women held blue drinks in their hands.

Before Becky could slide into the booth, Ella stood and embraced her. "It's good to see you."

"You too." Becky found she wasn't lying. It really was good to see her. And Lilah. And the whole Oak Creek crowd. It was good to be out in a setting that wasn't her home.

Sometimes it took someone forcibly dragging you out of your comfort zone to realize how far deep you'd put yourself in there.

"Let's get you a drink," Lilah said, pushing out of the booth.

Becky laughed. "Fine, but I'm not going into Smurf territory tonight."

Her friend made a face. "Party pooper," she muttered under her breath. "What would you like?"

"Umm… I don't know. A cosmo."

"One cosmo coming up," Lilah said, taking off for the bar like she was afraid Becky would change her mind.

Eva walked through the front door, then beelined toward their booth, trying to be as invisible as possible. The woman was painfully shy.

Still, Becky was glad Eva had come as well. They both needed it more than they'd admit.

"Let me go tell Lilah we need another drink for Eva," Ella said, getting up and hustling over toward their friend at the bar.

Becky took the opportunity of being alone with Eva to tease her a little about the blossoming romance between her and Theo Lindstrom, the manager of Linear Tactical. Becky had known Theo for decades and had never seen the normally stoic man so infatuated.

Eva tried to deny it, but Becky could see the truth. Could see it in the man's eyes now as he stood across the bar, his gaze only on Eva.

"Theo tends to keep to himself, but you are like some sort of magnet for him. If you're in the vicinity, he can't keep his eyes off you," she told Eva. She'd been seeing it happen for weeks now every time Eva and Theo were together.

As if they were in some sort of romance novel, Theo made his way through the people toward their table. Eva stood up as he approached, evidently caught in the same trance as him.

"Dance with me, beautiful," Theo asked softly as he reached them. Eva blushed before nodding and taking his hand, letting him pull her out onto the dance floor—the two of them beaming at each other.

Becky's heart twinged with pain. Theo and Derek had been best friends for as long as she could remember, and seeing Theo made her think about that same look on Derek's face.

For her.

She was never going to see that look on his face again.

"Holy shit!" Ella said with a squeak, looking out at the

dancing couple as she and Lilah came back with the drinks. "Did you see that? That was some next-level hotness right there. Swoon!"

Lilah grinned. "Those two have it bad for each other."

The women slid into the booth. Ella pushed a glass toward Becky, and she took a sip of her drink, shoving the thoughts of Derek away. Tonight—*just for tonight*—she wasn't going to let the pain in.

"Becky, what did Lilah threaten you with to get you to come out?" Ella asked, eyes sparkling with amusement from the other side of the booth.

Becky took another sip. "That she wouldn't ask me to come out again for another month."

"Hey, I only agreed to two weeks," Lilah set Eva's off to the side. Then she sighed as she sat. "Becky drives a hard bargain."

Ella laughed. "I thought she might try to take away your weekly Fancy Pants cookies or something."

Becky's eyes got wide. "Death before that."

"Keep going, and I might be convinced to let you try the new recipe I'm working on early. A red velvet surprise."

Becky stared at her, afraid a little drool might be coming out of her mouth. "Red velvet? Can we leave here right now and go taste test?"

"No, we most certainly cannot," Lilah crossed her arms over her chest. "Tonight is for drinking and dancing and forgetting about our problems. Let's get to it."

Becky nodded. Damn it, Lilah was right. "We have a designated driver?"

"Yeah." She pointed toward the bar, where a familiar man lounged at the end, eyes glued to his phone. Her heart stuttered again. Bear, Derek's brother. It wasn't uncommon for him to offer to drive friends home if they needed it.

But damned if it didn't seem like the universe was

conspiring against her and her plan not to think about Derek. The ghost of him was everywhere.

"Good." Becky lifted the cosmo to her lips and took a long sip, deciding then and there she would have a good time, even if she needed to dive headfirst into an Electric Smurf to do it.

Ella's eyebrows rose as she watched Becky throw back her drink. "Something we should know?"

"Nope. I'm here with y'all, and I'm ready to have a good time."

Lilah and Ella exchanged glances, then both nodded.

"Hell yes," Lilah said, slamming a hand down on the table. "Let's do this."

A couple of hours later, Becky was the perfect amount of tipsy. The drinks had been flowing, and the minutes flew by as she danced with her friends. Despite the message she'd left Derek a few months ago threatening to start dancing with other guys, she hadn't worked up to it yet, and tonight was no exception.

Opening that can of worms in her head was good for no one.

During a slow song, she plopped down on the edge of the booth, laughing. "They need to get the fast songs back on, stat."

"Nooooo." Ella fell over sideways onto the booth seat. "I need a break. I'm not in as good a shape as you two. Occupational hazard."

"Stop." Both Becky and Lilah said it at the same time. Ella was always so concerned about the extra few pounds she carried on her frame. She thought of herself as fat, but nobody else thought of her that way.

"Don't talk about my friend that way. You're beautiful," Lilah said.

Becky was about to back Lilah up when the door to the bar

opened, and a group poured in. A whole bunch of cheers went up, and people rushed over to the newcomers.

Lilah stood up, grinning. "Oh yeah. It's the helitack team. Let's get my twin in on our dancing action. I haven't seen her since the last time they were in a month ago."

Becky clapped. "Yay, Scarlett's here. Now it can be a real party."

But the high of her buzz was starting to move more toward sober and tired. Becky would probably only stay for a little while longer. Scarlett being here would keep the other girls occupied.

"Oh my God," Ella suddenly said under her breath.

"What?"

Her friend nodded toward the door, and Becky looked.

Everything in the universe froze as she saw Derek walk through the door of the Eagle's Nest.

Unadulterated joy spiraled through her system at seeing him safe, unharmed, and smiling—albeit stiffly—at the locals who were trying to get to him and shake his hand or pat him on the back.

He looked good. Fit and tanned. His thick brown hair tousled like he'd run his hand through it multiple times. His posture was rigid, but that wasn't necessarily unusual.

She couldn't see his eyes from here, but she knew the blue in them would nearly knock her to her knees the way they always had.

Derek was *here*.

She stood, unable to stop herself, her orbit already shifting toward him.

And then she froze as her mind took in what he was wearing.

A helitack uniform.

Helitack.

And the way he'd just walked in with everyone, it was

apparent this wasn't his first day as part of the team. He was their buddy. They had an ease with him that bespoke of familiarity and...*time*.

Betrayal and heartbreak cracked through her. She clasped her hands in front of her to try to stop their shaking.

Derek Bollinger was here, exactly like she'd been hoping and praying for over the last eighteen months. The man she'd just given up hope on ever seeing again.

Her husband.

Chapter 4

"Want me to pack everyone up and take us back to headquarters?" Sam whispered to Derek as the helitack team pulled up outside the Eagle's Nest, six of them crammed inside the SUV. "They'll get over it."

This was an unscheduled stop. The team had made a trip to Reddington City for personal supplies in two vehicles. A tire had blown on one of them just outside Oak Creek.

Of all the fucking luck.

They could've made it back to camp on the spare, but everyone had damned near lost their minds at the thought of being able to have a couple drinks while this close.

Having the chance to kick back for an evening was definitely more than well deserved after the month they'd had. Things were supposed to have been winding down for the season, but it had been crazy. Late season fires, more rescues than usual, and training new team members.

Derek had welcomed it. The busier he stayed, the better. Kept his mind out of Oak Creek.

Unfortunately, not his body. Not tonight.

"No," he finally responded to Sam. "Everybody needs the break. I'll be fine."

It was a Thursday. Surely not much would be going on inside the Eagle's Nest. And the chances of Becky being here were slim. She wasn't much of a partier.

The team piled in as he stood outside the door. He hadn't been to the Eagle's Nest in over eighteen months. Hadn't been to Oak Creek to see his parents or siblings or…anyone.

Hell, he could probably slip in and out without anyone even knowing he was here. He'd keep a low profile. Nobody would even notice him.

He forced himself to walk through the door. As soon as he did, half a dozen people called his name and rushed over to see him.

So much for not being noticed.

"One beer, that's it," Sam said to the team as they split off. "We're on call."

Various joking mumbles of "Yes, Dad" met him as everyone went their separate ways. Derek could barely hear any of them as friends and neighbors hurried over to hug him and slap him on the back. Everyone wanted to welcome the prodigal asshole home.

He felt Becky before he saw her—his gut had never had a problem knowing when Becky Mackay was around.

His response to her was visceral. It always had been.

It had to do with so much more than her appearance, although everything about her looks appealed to him. That brown hair with streaks of blond running through it, those big brown eyes with flecks of gold in their depths, her trim, athletic build that suited her profession as a veterinarian.

He knew exactly where her head would nestle under his chin if he pulled her into his arms. Knew exactly how their bodies fit together in every possible way. Knew how good it felt.

And knew he'd never feel it again. Not after what had happened.

Shit. He should not have come in here. Should not have taken the chance. He needed to get out before she saw him.

Derek was about to escape—he'd go see his parents or siblings or even wait in the vehicle for the rest of the team to finish here—when her brown eyes turned to him, pinning him where he stood.

It had been eighteen months since they'd last seen each other. Five hundred and fifty-four days, to be exact.

Five hundred and fifty-four days that he'd hated himself.

Still, he took a step toward her. He couldn't stop himself. Freddie Lowell from high school offered to buy Derek a drink in a booming voice, but Derek just shook his head and gave him a half smile. Someone else slapped him on his back. He forced down a cringe—casual touch was something he endured, not enjoyed—and took another step toward Becky, once again not able to stop himself.

And she was taking a step toward him.

That registered much more quickly than the fact that a bitter fire was burning in her brown eyes. She wasn't happy to see him.

Could he blame her?

The crowd in the bar parted as everyone seemed to realize he and Becky were heading toward each other. Sam was back at Derek's side, walking toward Becky also. Derek had no idea why and, honestly, didn't even care.

At this point, there was no stopping himself from going to her.

His eyes were pinned to hers as the distance between them shrank. Even knowing she was pissed as hell couldn't make him get off this collision course he was on with her. He only stopped when they were a few feet from each other.

Close enough to touch her soft skin. Although he didn't.

"What are you doing here?"

Sam and Becky both said it at the same time. Derek finally looked over at his friend and found him staring at the woman beside Becky. Derek immediately recognized the petite brunette as Sam's sister, Eva. Derek hadn't known she was in Oak Creek. Evidently, Sam hadn't either.

Nobody answered the question. Derek's eyes flew back to Becky's. Still fire. Still anger.

But worse—so much worse—*pain*.

He took another step closer to her, the need to drive away that pain consuming him.

"Button…" The endearment slipped out before he could squash it.

The pain was gone from her eyes in an instant. "*No*. You don't get to call me that. Don't you come in here with your helitack uniform and your buddies like this is in any way okay."

He flinched. Nothing about him was okay. He knew that.

He wasn't sure what to do. The bar around them had gotten quiet, everyone waiting to see what was going to happen. Small towns thrived on gossip, and this was going to give them tea for months.

Derek had no idea what to do or say. There was no way to make this better and a thousand ways to make it worse.

Then Becky stepped toward him. If possible, it got even quieter as everyone waited to see what she would do. Slap him? Scream in his face? Kick him hard enough that he'd never be able to father children?

All of those would be acceptable responses.

Instead, she walked right up to him and placed her hands on his shoulders, leaning in so she could whisper in his ear.

"You will meet me in our spot in fifteen minutes, *husband*."

He flinched again, feeling the color draining from his face.

Husband. He couldn't stand that word coming from her lips. Not when he'd made such a mockery of what the word should mean.

Before he could respond—not that he knew what he could possibly say—she'd stepped back and was walking toward the door. All he could do was watch.

"How about a beer, brother?" Theo Lindstrom, Derek's best friend since they were kids, put an arm around his shoulder as he stood there. "I think you could use it."

The crowd dispersed now that the potential drama had passed and there was nothing to keep them entertained. Derek let Theo lead him to the bar.

"You okay?" Theo signaled to the bartender for two beers. "By the way, welcome home, asshole."

Derek let out a grunt of laughter that held no humor to it whatsoever. "Yeah, I fucked this up royally."

"So what's new?" Theo slid the beer toward him with a smile.

"I wouldn't have come tonight if I'd known this was where the team was going. Becky…"

He couldn't get words out about her.

"Maybe keeping secret the fact that you were not only stateside, but basically right in our backyard for the past year wasn't such a good idea." Theo raised an eyebrow. "Also, let's not forget…if Becky ever asks, I had no idea you were here."

"Roger that."

Theo, Derek's brother Bear, and his cousin Lincoln were the only people from Oak Creek who'd known Derek was no longer in the Middle East. Derek hadn't even told his parents.

He had his reasons.

And he hadn't told anyone in the world, even those closest to him, that he and Becky were married. After what had happened, he couldn't believe they were *still* married. Every day in Afghanistan, he'd expected to receive the paperwork announcing their annulment.

It hadn't come. *Why hadn't it come?* Why hadn't Becky ended their farce of a marriage the way she should have?

Suddenly, meeting her at their place like she'd demanded seemed like a good idea. He needed to know why she was still calling him husband at all.

It had nothing to do with every fiber of his being wanting to get closer to her if only for a few moments now that he'd seen her.

"So how's helitack life treating you?" Theo asked, taking a sip of his own beer.

Derek stood up from his stool. "I have to go."

"Ooookay." Theo's eyes narrowed, but he didn't ask for details. "Need backup?"

He scrubbed a hand down his face. "Probably. But I've got to walk into this battle alone. We'll see if I come back out of it in one piece."

"She's got reason to be upset, D."

Derek couldn't hold back his sigh. "More reason than you could possibly know."

"I THOUGHT for a minute you weren't coming." Becky stepped out from the shadows behind the cottonwood tree in the park on the edge of town.

Derek shrugged one shoulder, his eyes drinking in the sight of her again. "Maybe I was waiting for you under the middle school bleachers. Or by Pikes Peak. Or one of our other spots."

At this point, Oak Creek was fairly littered with their *spots*. Under the middle school bleachers was where they'd had their first kiss. Pikes Peak was what the locals called the nearby lake, where the two of them had spent a majority of each summer growing up.

Or it could've been the treehouse they'd basically lived in in middle school. Or Fancy Pants bakery, where they'd gone after school nearly every day to get one of their favorite treats.

But Derek had known exactly where Becky meant when she'd said to meet her at *their spot*. This park—right here under this cottonwood tree—had been where he'd asked her to marry him.

Worst mistake he'd ever made.

And now it was all he could do to keep from touching her. His fingers itched with the need to touch her skin, pull her close.

That would also be a mistake.

"We shouldn't be here, Bu—" He cut himself off before he said Button. "Becky."

"*We* shouldn't be here? How about explaining why you are here at all. Why you just rolled in with the helitack crew. Is that your job now?"

"Yes." He scrubbed a hand down his face. "I'm a pilot for them. I was doubly qualified since I can fly both helicopters and airplanes."

She nodded at that. "When did you start working with them?"

He winced. This was going to hurt, but he couldn't lie to Becky. No matter what they'd been through, he'd never lied to her in his life. "A year ago."

She froze utterly still in the moonlight. "You've been stateside a whole year and are just now coming to town?"

Even through the darkness, he could see the hurt in her brown eyes. It was like being punched in the gut. He had no idea what to say. There was no way to fix this.

No way to fix so much between them.

Becky shook her head slowly when he didn't answer. "And

what about the messages I've been sending for the past eighteen months? Did you get those?"

"Yes," he muttered.

Her face fell. "Well, I guess that tells me everything I need to know about where we stand."

He touched her before he could stop himself. His mind wouldn't allow him to just stand by and do nothing while she was hurting. He couldn't bear it. He kept his fingers loose in case she wanted to pull away, but the soft skin of her wrist felt like heaven.

He honestly hadn't thought he would ever touch her in any way again.

Now both of them were frozen, but at least he had her body under his fingers.

"You know how complicated things are between us," he finally got out. "I thought contacting you would be a mistake."

She shook her head. "Complicated, yes. But until tonight, I thought we were at least on the same team."

They were still touching. He knew he should pull his hand away, but instead, his thumb began to stroke up and down her soft skin. It had been so long since he'd touched her, he was starved for it.

This was what his dreams were made of.

And his nightmares.

"We were always on the same team."

"That can't possibly be true," she whispered. "Because there's no way I could've been in the same place for a *year* and not have been near you. Not have contacted you in some way. There is no way I could've been that close and not seen you. Not needed it as much as I need air to breathe."

Every word was another slice at his heart. "I couldn't."

"Why?"

"You know why." They both did.

"Right," she whispered. "Because one mistake happened, and you just gave up."

Her big, soulful eyes were so full of pain, he almost couldn't breathe. He still held on to her wrist—she wasn't pulling away at all—and he slid his hand down until their fingers were intertwined.

He shouldn't do this. This closeness led to more agony in the long run. But damned if he could let her go right now when she was hurting so much.

"Button…"

He expected anger at the endearment, but she closed her eyes like she was storing the memory for the future. He understood that exact feeling.

Digging into his greatest reserves of strength, Derek stepped back. Lingering was only going to hurt them both more.

He expected her to move back too, but instead, she stepped forward.

The world slowed down to this one moment. Everything in him demanded he move closer too. This was why he'd stayed away all these months.

Because not touching Becky when she was within arm's reach wasn't a battle he knew how to even begin fighting.

So, he stepped forward. As soon as his body was pressed to hers, instinct took over.

There was no awkwardness as their lips met, despite it having been a year and a half since their last kiss. Their bodies knew what to do, and they took over.

Their hands dropped from each other as he gripped her hips, and she slid her arms up and around his neck. Her lips parted, and his tongue immediately took advantage, coaxing hers out to play.

Every warning, every fear, every reasonable thought flew from his mind.

This was Becky in his arms again. Nothing else mattered.

She pulled him closer as he backed her up against the nearby tree, skimming his hands up her sides, across her shoulders to bury them in her thick brown hair. He tilted her head to the side to have better access to her mouth. To *her*.

The sigh she let out was a beautiful sound to his ears. Her melting against him was bliss.

He didn't know if he would ever be able to leave this spot again. Leave her side again.

His phone screeching out an alarm into the darkness had him biting back a curse. Only one call made his phone spit out that sound.

"Ignore it," Becky whispered against his lips.

He shifted just slightly so his forehead rested against hers. "I can't. It's the helitack team. We've been called back. It's an emergency."

"Helitack. Right." She stiffened, dropping her hands from his shoulders. "I guess you better go."

"Button…"

"No. Don't call me that."

"There's still a lot we need to talk about."

She slid out from between him and the tree, wrapping her arms around her trim waist. She'd always been so delicate— her small body belying her inner strength.

The gesture just served as a reminder that her inner strength didn't matter. Not ultimately.

Not when it came to him and the monster he ultimately was.

She saw his expression and dropped her arms to her sides. "Whatever you're thinking about yourself, just stop. This isn't—"

The phone beeped again, reminding him he needed to leave. Good. He couldn't stay here anyway. Touching her had been a mistake. Kissing her... God, he didn't ever deserve the feel of her lips against his.

"I have to go."

"Derek—"

He faded back into the darkness without another word. There was nothing left to say anyway.

The farther he got from her, the safer she would be.

Chapter 5

"Wow. Someone is particularly vicious today. I assume that has to do with a certain Bollinger brother sliding into town last night?"

Becky grunted and spun with a roundhouse kick that would've knocked Lilah to the floor if it had connected. But her friend was a world-class fighter and swept quickly to the side to avoid the hit. There was a reason people came from all over the country to train with and learn from Lilah here at Linear Tactical.

Normally, they wouldn't be sparring this hard after last night's shenanigans, but Becky had called Lilah for an emergency session.

And hell yes, it was because of Derek's reappearance, but Becky didn't respond to Lilah's statement. She didn't trust the other woman not to use the conversation as a "teaching moment." It wouldn't be the first time Lilah had waited for Becky to lose focus and then attacked.

Instead, Becky dropped low in an attempt to sweep Lilah's leg out from under her. She was almost successful, but Lilah jumped back at the last second.

"Good for you," Lilah said, throwing her own double-punch combo, which Becky blocked. "Refusing to get baited. Staying focused. That was more than you had when we first started."

Becky still didn't respond.

All she'd had when she'd come to Lilah for training nearly a year and a half ago was a broken heart and a broken nose and no idea what to do with either.

Everyone in Oak Creek knew something had happened to her, but no one knew exactly what. And she definitely hadn't told anyone it was Derek who'd left her with those bruises. He hated himself enough already for what had happened. He didn't need anyone else giving him grief.

Derek was back.

She was still reeling from the shock of seeing him waltz into the Eagle's Nest like he was coming back from vacation. Definitely not looking as if she hadn't heard a word from him in eighteen months since he'd dropped her off at a hospital.

On their wedding night.

Finding out he'd been so close for nearly a year without contacting her hurt more than her broken nose ever had.

She advanced on Lilah again, using the many skills she'd developed over the past year. Elaborate punch-kick combinations that involved spins and speed.

One of the first things Lilah had taught her was to use her natural advantages. At 5'3" and only a little over a hundred pounds, Becky knew strength was never going to be one of her assets. They'd worked together to improve it as much as possible, but, like for Lilah, strength alone would never make Becky formidable.

So she used her speed, balance, and agility to make up for it. She held nothing back now, going on the offensive where she normally focused on defending herself while Lilah attacked.

Lilah gave a delighted laugh then buckled down, determined to give Becky the fight she was looking for. Their twice-weekly sparring matches didn't tend to be this brutal, but right now, brutal was what Becky wanted.

She wanted to fight the image of Derek out of her mind.

Neither of them was using the dirty tricks Lilah had taught her—since those would result in a trip to the hospital for one or both of them. But they still went at it *hard*. There was no talking from either of them, just the sounds of their labored breathing and grunts as sparring gear made contact with skin.

Becky took more than one hit from her friend—even got knocked to the floor a few times. But she took pride in the fact that Lilah ended up on the floor too.

It didn't take long for Becky to run out of steam. She wasn't in nearly as good of shape endurance-wise as Lilah, but that hadn't ever been the goal of their sparring. Enabling Becky to defend herself long enough to get away from a single attack had always been the goal.

A single attack from the man she'd loved her entire adult life.

"All right, we're done," Lilah finally said, stepping back, both of them breathing heavily. "Form is getting sloppy for both of us."

Becky nodded, and they sat down and pulled off their sparring gloves.

Lilah tossed her a bottle of water then lay back on the bouncy floor of the ring. "You know, when you first came to me after you got mugged, I thought you'd do the normal four or five lessons then start to feel safe again and quit."

"Mugged?"

Lilah raised an eyebrow. "Is that not what happened?"

Becky appreciated that her friend had never asked for details when Becky had requested self-defense lessons. Lilah taught self-defense, situational awareness, and wilderness survival for a living. She made no secret of the fact that she thought everyone should know the basics in all three.

Since Lilah was the daughter of former Navy SEAL, Gabe Collingwood, it was to be expected. Gabe had no doubt taught all three to both Lilah and Scarlett from the day they were born.

"Yeah, I guess," Becky replied. Better to have Lilah think she'd been mugged than to know the truth.

"You came back from that trip to Vegas bruised and scared. You never brought it up, so I didn't think you wanted to talk about it."

Becky hadn't wanted to talk about it. Hadn't known what to do at all.

God, how she wished she had handled the entire situation differently. Wished she hadn't been so scared. Hadn't been so overwhelmed.

Wished she'd been stronger.

But she hadn't. And Derek had walked away because of it. Blaming himself for something he'd been unable to control.

Becky took a sip of her water. "You're right. I didn't want to talk about it."

Lilah shrugged. "You could beat damned near any mugger who made the mistake of coming at you now."

That was true, and they both knew it. "Yeah."

"But it's not a mugger you're afraid of."

Becky stiffened. "I'm not afraid at all."

Lilah stood and grabbed a towel from the table by the sparring ring. "You sure about that? You're definitely...something."

Sad. Tired. Confused. Angry. Lilah could take her pick.

Becky was all of those things. And she'd lied; she was also afraid. Just not of some random mugger.

She wasn't afraid of Derek either, at least not physically, despite what he thought.

But she was terrified that they were really over. Until seeing him again last night, she'd always assumed they'd end up back together. That they would work this out, no matter how difficult it was.

But not anymore.

He'd been back in Wyoming a year and hadn't contacted her once.

"Hey." Lilah tossed her a towel then came to sit next to her in the ring. "You okay? This has to be about Derek and him showing up out of the blue. I'm assuming you didn't know he was part of the helitack team?"

"He failed to mention it." Failed to mention anything at all for the past eighteen months.

Lilah grinned. "You should invite him in here. Kick his ass. That will set him straight."

"If only it were that simple."

"Hey, come on. You two have been a team since you were kids. For a while, I didn't know if it was romantic or not."

Becky shrugged one shoulder. "Neither did we. It only turned that way for sure in high school."

Lilah let out a huge sigh. "Friends to lovers. The greatest romantic trope."

"Maybe. But now, I just don't know. Don't know if we'll be moving forward."

Lilah studied her for a moment then bumped her with her shoulder. "If that's the case, there's plenty of other fish in the sea. Let me know when you're ready to cast the reel, and I'll be right there with you."

Becky smiled at her friend but didn't say anything.

That was the problem. Becky didn't know if she'd ever be ready to move on from Derek. But *not* moving on wasn't an option either.

The only option seemed to be staying miserable.

Chapter 6

Later that afternoon, Becky arrived at the Swanson Valley Ranch, one of the largest in all of Wyoming, for a vet visit. The Swanson family had lived here for generations.

By one of the small planes the Swanson family owned, the ranch was about an hour from Oak Creek. By car, it was about five hours—which, even for native Wyomingites, was a bit of a hike.

Most of the time, Mr. Swanson sent a plane, but today, Becky had welcomed the drive. She told herself it was so she could bring more of her equipment with her in her SUV.

But the truth was, she needed the time in her vehicle to decompress. Not even sweating and bruising it out had been enough to ease her angst about Derek.

The five hours hadn't helped much either, honestly.

"Whatever you're making as the vet for the people in Teton County, we would more than double to have you here full time."

Mr. Swanson was walking her around the main section of his property, showing her their biggest veterinary needs since she'd last been here nearly six months ago.

It wasn't the first time he'd offered her a full-time job.

"It's always tempting, Mr. Swanson."

"More pay, fewer hours. Autonomy here to run things as you wish."

Becky laughed and shook her head. "Why don't you just hire another vet?"

The older man let out a sigh. "Believe me, we've tried. Too remote for some, weather's too harsh for others. Just can't seem to get anyone to stick."

She patted his shoulder as she looked over at the three sheep in the fenced area just outside the barn that'd been showing signs of distress over the past couple weeks—one of the reasons she was here now.

"You know how it is. Wyoming is either in your blood, or it's not. You can't make someone love it."

Mr. Swanson chuckled. "I'd settle for just tolerating it in order to get the paycheck I'm offering."

"You'll find someone."

"I'd rather just have you. You're familiar with the ranch, you're familiar with Wyoming weather. Hell, I'll even fly you in and out of Oak Creek until I can talk you into moving closer."

She let out a snort. They'd had similar conversations before. "Too much for me to do back in Teton County. I'm spread thin as is. Up and leaving isn't an option."

Although, she did have Eva as help now. Beyond becoming a friend, the new vet tech had proven to be highly skilled over the past few weeks. She'd taken over all the duties with the multitude of emotional support animals at Linear Tactical—obviously having caught Theo Lindstrom's attention in the process.

That definitely freed up some of Becky's time. But Oak Creek had always been home. Outside of when she'd gone to college and vet school, she'd never lived anywhere else.

Never wanted to live anywhere else.

Maybe it was time for a change. The weight of how things sat between Derek and her made it nearly impossible to breathe.

"You okay over there?" Mr. Swanson asked, concern crinkling his weathered cheeks further.

She needed to pull it together. "Yeah, I'm okay. Just been a long couple of days."

He gave another gruff chuckle as he led them into the barn. "Sounds like my whole life."

Becky walked toward the stall of the horse she'd been called specifically to check on. "There's my pretty lady. Hey there, Princess."

Mr. Swanson stood next to her as she stroked Princess's nose gently, letting the horse become re-accustomed to her scent. "She rallied for a while after your last visit but has gone back to lethargic in the past few days. I was hoping—"

"Sir, you've got a phone call in your office," one of the ranch hands said from the doorway.

"Okay." Mr. Swanson stepped back. "Everett, can you come help Dr. Mackay and answer any questions she might have."

Becky glanced over at the man in the doorway. He seemed less than thrilled at the babysitting duty, but he didn't argue. "Yes, sir."

"That's not necessary, Mr. Swanson. I know my way around here well enough."

The older man gave her arm an awkward pat. "Everett doesn't mind. Just in case you need anything. I'll be back as soon as I can."

Becky turned back to Princess, rubbing the horse's nose gently again. Everett walked to stand over in the corner of the barn, as far as he could get from her and still be following his boss's orders.

She decided to try to be friendly and raised her hand up in a little wave. "I'm Becky Mackay. I don't think we've met."

"Everett." The man's voice was gruff as he leaned back against the wall, crossing his arms over his chest. He didn't say anything further.

She tried again. "Have you worked here long?"

"A while."

O-kay. Becky turned her attention back to the horse and decided to leave grumpy Everett alone. She started her exam of Princess.

"What's the matter with you, sweet girl?"

Vets always argued that their job was more challenging than being a doctor since animals couldn't communicate where their pain was coming from. That challenge was one of the many reasons Becky loved her profession.

Plus, she just loved animals. Despite their lack of communication skills.

She glanced over at Everett, who was still glaring at her. Maybe she liked animals *because* of their lack of communication skills.

She completed her examination of Princess. Something was definitely wrong with her, but it was going to require more tests to determine exactly what they were dealing with. Becky would do a full blood and fecal work-up to determine what answers she could find.

She grabbed her nanny camera out of her bag. It would be better if she could observe Princess for two or three days in person, but this would be the next best thing.

She needed to put it up high in the corner so she could get a full view of the stall and part of the field. She went into the barn hallway and grabbed the long stepladder.

Everett just watched her struggle to move it into the stall. Didn't offer to help. She ignored him and got the camera situated the way she wanted.

"Really, you can go," she said to the man as she brought the ladder back out where she'd found it after she was done. "I'm not sure exactly what is wrong with Princess."

"Boss said to stay. I'll stay." He muttered something else under his breath, just loudly enough for Becky to make it out.

"I'm sorry, did you just say I have no business being up here?" *Was that really what he'd muttered?*

The man shrugged one shoulder. "Doesn't look like you're doing much good. Certainly not doing much to help Princess. Your fancy high-tech stuff is pretty useless, probably just as much as your fancy schooling."

She blinked and shook her head, trying to make sure she'd heard Everett correctly.

"Are you kidding me right now? Are you calling my vet degree *useless?*" *What in the actual hell?* "Have you got some sort of problem with me, or are you just an asshole in general?"

She took a step toward him, setting down her stethoscope on top of the laptop she'd just recorded the horse's medical details in.

Maybe she was about to spar for the second time today.

She'd never been one to seek out a fight, but today, she might just be willing to. And she definitely wasn't afraid of this jerk, even when he stood up fully and was a good six inches taller and fifty pounds heavier than her.

Today was not the day to mess with her. She'd had her fill of asshole men.

"I'll take over here, Everett," a voice called from the barn doorway. "Go ahead and get back to your work."

Becky glanced to see who'd come in without taking her attention off Everett. First thing Lilah had taught her was to always keep an eye on your opponent.

Everett didn't say anything, just narrowed his eyes at her as he re-situated his hat then walked toward the barn entrance.

He didn't say anything to the man at the door either. Merely left.

What a jerk.

"Sorry about that." The man walked in farther, and she recognized him. Cooper something. He'd been working here for a while and seconded as a pilot when needed. He'd flown Becky from Oak Creek once for an emergency.

"Hi, Cooper. Sorry, I don't think Everett likes me very much."

Cooper shot her a smile. "Everett doesn't like much of anyone. He's been here about four years and still hasn't made any friends. Sorry you got stuck with him."

Why couldn't Cooper have been in here helping for the past half hour? Would've made things a lot easier. Or at least would've made her feel less like she was a trespasser.

"I'm almost through in here. I'm going to need to run Princess's blood work to rule some things out."

Cooper came over and patted the horse's neck. "Yeah, she's been struggling. I hope you can figure out how to help her."

"Oh, I will." She stepped closer to scratch the horse's head again but stepped back again when she realized how close it would bring her to Cooper.

No matter how charming he was, there wasn't anyone she wanted to be close to except Derek.

She froze.

The thought that he no longer wanted that—that he'd truly gone a *year* being so nearby without seeing her—once again sent a bolt of pain through her chest. She rubbed at her breastbone.

"Hey, you okay?" Cooper asked.

He reached out to her, but she stepped toward her equipment bag before he could make contact. "Yeah, just worried about Princess. I've known her since she was in her mama's belly."

"She's tough. She's going to be just fine, I'll bet you."

She looked up and realized he wasn't talking about the horse. Cooper was talking about her.

She nodded. "She is tough."

Cooper showed her the other animals that needed treatment—most of that was routine. Mr. Swanson did run a nice place, Everett notwithstanding. Some of the ranches across the state tended to cut corners when it came to their animals' health—a mistake long-term, but a way to save money immediately. But never Mr. Swanson.

Cooper was good company, helping as needed, patient with all Becky's questions. When she got to the sheep, she sent him on his way. She really didn't need a babysitter.

She checked on Princess one more time, and it was getting dark by the time she made it back to the main house to report in to Mr. Swanson. As usual, she was going to need to spend the night so she could finish up tomorrow. The older man always made the ranch's guesthouse available to her.

No doubt to entice her with the beautiful place she could live rent-free if she wanted to work here.

And some piece of her was actually considering it. What was the point of continuing to defend a home if what had always made it *home* wasn't even there anymore.

She took a deep breath to try to keep herself out of a funk and knocked on the door. Cooper answered, obviously on his way out.

"Mr. Swanson is waiting for you." He offered her that charming smile again.

"Okay, thanks."

"If you're staying overnight, you're welcome to join us in the bunkhouse for our card game. We'll stuff Everett in a closet or something."

"Thanks for the offer, but—"

"The cook's wife joins us, and we have a couple female ranch hands in case you're feeling you might be out of place."

She offered him a smile. "I think I'm just going to check on Princess one more time and then have an early night of it. I'm going to finish everything tomorrow morning then make the drive back to Oak Creek."

Cooper took off his cowboy hat and ran his hand through his hair. It was difficult not to notice how handsome he was. He looked more like he belonged on the cover of a magazine than on a ranch.

"I could fly you back tomorrow, to give you more time. I'm sure Mr. Swanson would authorize it. Then we could get one of the ranch hands to drive your vehicle back tomorrow or the next day—someone is always on their way to Reddington City." He ran his fingers through his hair again. "It would give you a little more free time here."

"Thanks, Cooper, but I can't. I'm—"

She cut herself off before she said the word *married*. She didn't even know if that was true. She was technically and legally married, but in any other way, she hadn't had a husband since a few hours after they'd said *I do*.

"Thanks for the offer, Cooper," she restarted. "But not tonight. Enjoy your game."

"No problem. If you change your mind, just give me a holler." He winked at her, then put his hat back on.

She stepped around him and walked inside the house.

Something was going to have to give in her life. She couldn't move forward, and she couldn't stay where she was.

She felt like she had no options at all.

Chapter 7

Derek stood in front of his cousin's door and watched it open before he could even knock.

Derek knew he shouldn't be surprised. Lincoln Bollinger would know someone was approaching his house almost before they knew it themselves. It wasn't that Lincoln was paranoid about safety as much as the fact that his brain desired to know everything about *everything* all the time.

Prodigious savant was the term thrown around about Linc when it came to his ability at computer coding. And his complete and utter *lack* of ability with people and social situations.

The fact that Lincoln wouldn't want to talk about any emotional stuff or pry into Derek's business was the reason Derek was here. Plus, he needed help only Linc could provide.

He walked inside and set his duffel bag on the floor in the hallway.

Lincoln was leaning against the doorframe to the kitchen, chewing on an apple. "Hey, cuz. You look like shit."

Yep, didn't have to worry about Lincoln wanting to bond emotionally. "Good to see you too, cuz."

Derek was well aware he looked like roadkill peeled off the side of a Wyoming highway. He hadn't slept much in the three days since seeing Becky, partially because of the fire that had brought the crew back from Oak Creek that night.

And partially because every time he closed his eyes, he saw Becky's face—and the hurt in her eyes.

He had the next two weeks off. Helitack rotation wasn't a regular nine-to-five job. It was multiple days on then extended time off. Most of the crew loved that about the job, but not Derek.

Especially not right now. It left him with too much time to think. Something he wanted to avoid at all costs.

He was already conflicted enough since word had gotten out that he was back in Wyoming.

Cue his phone ringing and a stern talking-to yesterday from his parents about not letting them know he was back in Wyoming. Then completely forgiving him in the next moment with an invitation to come over soon.

All his mom wanted was for him to come by so she could make him all his favorite foods and his baby sister River could talk to him about what was happening in high school.

He promised he would, thankful Finn and Charlie Bollinger did not hold grudges.

But his lack of communication had hurt them. He knew it.

And that was his problem, wasn't it? He fucking hurt everyone. Not meaning to wasn't an excuse.

Just like he had no excuse for kissing Becky.

Derek closed his eyes. He'd never thought he'd have the chance to taste her lips again. Feel her body pressed against his. And no matter the temptation or the relief he'd felt when she melted against him, he needed to make sure it didn't happen again.

Ever.

Thus, why he was here.

Lincoln, true to form, was completely unaware of Derek's existential crisis. His cousin just took another bite of his apple and walked toward his office. Derek followed.

"So, what are you doing here?" Lincoln's question held no heat or displeasure, just the curiosity that came with someone showing up unannounced.

Especially when Lincoln was one of the few people who knew Derek had been doing whatever he could for the past year to avoid entanglements in Oak Creek.

The massive command center in Lincoln's office made Derek more jittery than he already was. The room was fairly littered with screens all broadcasting different types of information—a couple of television stations, multiple internet browsers, and a few screens of code Derek couldn't even begin to understand.

"Coming off a long shift," Derek mumbled.

Forty-eight long hours, with little sleep. He was used to it and he liked his job, but it came at a price. If he wasn't careful, lack of sleep could send his mind back to that prison camp where he'd been held for five weeks in which he wasn't allowed to sleep. It was one of the ways the fuckers had tortured him while he was held captive.

He understood why they did it, too. It was incredibly effective.

Would he ever have a long night without feeling like someone was about to jump out of the shadows and throw a hood over his head? Force bright, flashing lights into his eyes and beat him within an inch of his life?

Derek shook his head and looked away from the massive array of screens, the stimulation more than his mind could handle right at that moment.

"But I assume you're here to see me for a specific reason."

That was correct. Linc, with all his many screens and giant brain, was the only one who could help Derek undo what he had done. Help him make the cut he needed. The one Becky needed too.

Lincoln typed away, waiting for Derek to get his thoughts together. At the very least, Derek appreciated that about his cousin and friend. Lincoln never pressured Derek to answer something before he was ready.

Or, more likely, Lincoln was just caught up in his own world and didn't even realize Derek was struggling with anything. He was typing faster than Derek would be able to strike a keyboard even if he were pressing the same letter over and over.

"Are you working on something?" Derek asked.

"Always."

Derek didn't doubt that was true. "I need help making something disappear."

Lincoln stopped typing and looked over his shoulder. "Is it a person?"

Derek raised an eyebrow. "And if it is?"

Lincoln took a deep breath. "Well, first thing we need to do is make sure it's not tied back to us in any way. Let me know who we're going to off, and I can see if they have some sort of medical condition that could be blamed—"

Lincoln would have the whole crime planned out in a couple minutes if Derek didn't stop him. "Jesus, Linc. No, we're not going to kill anyone. But thanks for having my back."

Lincoln sat back in his chair, looking a little disappointed. "Oh, okay. What are we talking about, then?"

"Is it possible to annul a marriage? It would have been eighteen months ago in Las Vegas. I need it to disappear entirely. No trace of it ever existing again."

His chest felt like it was cracking in two as he said the words.

Lincoln started typing again. "It's definitely doable. I could make it so there's no electronic record of it anywhere. But the couple would probably still have papers, and you'd have to destroy those if you truly wanted no proof at all."

"But if there were no papers, then there would be no record of it?"

"Wow. You're trying to erase the record of someone's marriage? Why? Like, revenge? That's a pretty twisted form of revenge to take on someone. But honestly, they would probably just get married again, so I'm not sure if it's worth the effort."

"It's not revenge."

"A prank?" Lincoln still didn't stop typing. "Is it someone local? What chapel were they married in? That will help me figure out—"

Hanging his head, Derek turned to look out the window. "It's me, Linc. It's *my* marriage I need you to make disappear."

The typing stopped. Derek turned back to face his cousin.

Lincoln looked almost afraid. Derek knew he was running scenarios in that huge brain of his to try to figure out what was an appropriate response. "Oh. Uh...congratulations?"

"Can you do it or not?"

Lincoln sucked in a breath. "What the hell kind of alcohol do they give you guys in the military that would make you get drunk and marry someone? Becky's going to kill you. Granted, it sounded like she was already about to kill you the other night at the Eagle's Nest, from what I understand. But if she finds out you got *married*? She'll kill you for whatever you did, resurrect you, and kill you all over again just to say she could."

Derek blew out a breath. "It's Becky."

"What's Becky?" Lincoln asked.

"The person I married," Derek finally admitted. "It's Becky. She and I eloped eighteen months ago in Vegas."

His cousin turned his chair fully around and looked at him, pressing his hands together. "You married Becky Mackay?"

"Yes."

"In Vegas."

"Yes."

"You're married to Becky?"

Derek scrubbed a hand down his face. "Yeah, Linc. It's not complicated. I'm sure your brain can handle the info."

"Not complicated? You've been hiding out for the last year, not telling anyone except for a very select few that you were in Wyoming working at helitack. Hiding it from your *wife*? Definitely not simple."

"Okay, yeah, maybe it's a little complicated."

Lincoln continued to stare at him. Derek didn't know what to say. He should probably tell the full truth, but he couldn't force the words out.

"Listen, Derek, I know I'm not...*good* with emotional stuff," Lincoln finally said. "Hell, I'm probably the worst person to be talking to about this. But why would you want to make a marriage to Becky go away? It doesn't take much to see how in love with each other you are, no matter how long you've spent apart. Or even why you didn't tell her you were back."

Memories of that day flooded his mind.

Becky looking up at him with those gorgeous brown eyes as she said *I do*. Her moaning his name later when he kissed his way down her neck and peeled her out of the silky wedding dress she'd chosen. Making love to her. Falling asleep with her in his arms.

And then waking up to find her sobbing and—

He jerked himself out of the memories. He couldn't let himself drown in them. "I just need you to do it, Linc."

Lincoln stood up. "But why? Explain it to me, cuz. I want to understand."

Derek looked down at his hands that had balled into fists without his even realizing it.

Blood. All he could see was *her* blood on them. All he could hear was Becky crying. It mixed in his mind until it spun together with the screams inside the prison camp—his, his friends…a blur of terror and pain.

He couldn't breathe. There was too much pressure inside him, turning him into a bomb.

"I'm a fucking monster, that's why!" The words exploded out of him. "Is that what you want to know? I'm a monster, and that's why I need the marriage annulled."

His fist was through Lincoln's wall before Derek fully processed the movement. The skin of his knuckles split, and the real, abrupt physical pain pulled him out of the mental anguish. At least a little bit.

Derek stared at the wall, drawing in shaky breaths.

"I'm sorry," he finally said into the silence permeating the office. "I'll get it fixed."

He looked over at Lincoln. His cousin was very still, watching him, obviously unsure of what to do.

"I'm not good with emotions," Lincoln said again. "I made a mistake, didn't I? Said something inappropriate that made you punch the wall. I apologize. I shouldn't have pushed."

Derek let out a sigh, feeling like shit. Dealing with emotions was Lincoln's kryptonite, but this hadn't been his fault. "You didn't push, cuz. This was a *me* problem, not anything you did."

Lincoln looked a little relieved that he hadn't read an emotional situation wrong. How many times had Derek and his brothers had to help Lincoln navigate social situations as they were growing up? How many people had called him a robot? How many fights had the Bollinger boys gotten into because their cousin's big brain had pissed off someone with big muscles?

It had taken Lincoln a lot of years of working with communication and behavioral specialists to be able to socially interact in any meaningful way. It still wasn't easy for him, and he tended to doubt himself.

And now Derek had made him doubt himself once again.

Derek pressed the heels of his hands into his eyes. "I'm sorry, Linc. Really, it wasn't you. It's me. It's all me. You asked what anyone would have asked. I just—"

He faded off, not even sure what he wanted to say. He dropped his hands down in front of him, his own blood on them this time.

He would take a gallon of his own blood a thousand times over a drop of Becky's.

How did he do this? How did he fight off the demons and stop hurting the people he cared about the most?

He had no idea.

"Yes," his cousin finally said in an even voice. "I can make the marriage go away. I can destroy every record of it ever happening. It can be like it never existed, if that's what you really want."

Derek couldn't make himself say the words. It was the last thing he fucking wanted. But nothing changed the fact that it was something he needed. For Becky. He owed her so much more than that, but he could give her this. A clean slate.

"Go take a shower," Lincoln continued. "Use the kitchen. Make something to eat. After, we can talk about it. Make sure it's what you really want."

"Okay."

Lincoln wasn't saying no. That was all that mattered. Not that Derek had thought he ever would.

Derek was to the door when Lincoln spoke again. "Derek, we both know I'm the last one who should try to help out with relationship advice, and I don't know the circumstances around your marriage. But Becky agreed to marry you."

"She shouldn't have."

"So you say. But she did. Even I can see that if you make this marriage disappear, going about it this way, behind Becky's back, she'll never forgive you."

Derek didn't even turn around. "I don't need her to forgive me. I just need to know she's safe and able to move on with her life."

And besides, it didn't matter if Becky forgave him for past sins or not.

He was never going to be able to forgive himself.

Chapter 8

The shower did make Derek feel better. Marginally.

He wasn't going to punch any more walls, but he was still feeling unsettled. Everything simmered too close to the surface, and he didn't know how to calm it down.

Well, he did, but he wanted to get Lincoln on the making the marriage disappear task first. Waiting was a mistake. After he knew Lincoln was on it—which meant it was as good as done—Derek could head to the tiny house he'd rented at the edge of town that no one knew about.

He'd made it to the kitchen when he heard voices from the direction of Lincoln's office. Theo Lindstrom was there and looked surprised to see Derek. They hadn't talked since Derek had left the Eagle's Nest to go after Becky the other night.

Theo shot him a tight smile. "Hey."

Derek took Theo's outstretched hand and didn't protest when his friend pulled him into a hug and pounded on his back a couple of times. Theo let go immediately, knowing Derek's PTSD sometimes made touching hard. Derek wasn't about to own up to the fact that at the moment he was way beyond touch being a trigger.

Everything was a fucking trigger.

"What are you doing here?" Theo asked.

"Long story," he muttered under his breath as he moved over to the couch.

Lincoln was back typing on his keyboard. "But one very worth telling."

Derek gritted his teeth. This was a prime example of Lincoln being unable to read the emotional temperature of the room. Derek definitely didn't want to talk about his marriage with anyone else, even one of his closest friends.

"Another time, Linc. It sounds like Theo has more pressing matters than my shithole of a life."

"Shithole of a love life," Lincoln corrected. "Your life isn't so bad. Your love life, on the other hand…"

Derek met eyes with Theo—at least *he* could tell Derek didn't want to talk about the situation, even if Lincoln couldn't.

Theo raised an eyebrow. "You needed advice on romance, and you came to Lincoln?"

Derek shrugged. "He's my emotional support honey badger."

Theo cracked a hint of a smile. "I'll see if the therapists at Linear want to look into adding that to their repertoire."

His smile fell away, and Derek sat up straighter on the couch as Theo explained that this wasn't a social visit. He was afraid the woman he loved, Eva Dempsey, had been kidnapped by her asshole of an ex-boyfriend, Gareth Metter.

Evidently, the man had been making Eva's life a living hell for years, gaslighting and emotionally abusing her until it was difficult for her to know which reality was correct: what she knew versus the lies he told.

Lincoln did his computer magic, tracking a phone Theo had strategically placed in Metter's car. Once they discovered the man was heading toward the wilderness of the Wyoming mountains, not toward the airport as he'd indicated, Theo stood, ready to go.

"It may be innocent, but I'm not taking that chance. I'm going after them."

Derek and Lincoln stood also. Theo shook his head. "Look, I don't expect you guys to come. We don't know if Metter even has Eva. And he's the type to file a bunch of lawsuits against us if we're wrong. All we've got is my gut instinct that he plans to hurt Eva."

"I've said it once, and I'll say it again—I'll take your gut instinct over hard data any day," Lincoln said.

Derek tilted his head and looked at Theo with one eyebrow raised. Lincoln's words were the highest compliment the other man could give. The guy *loved* hard data.

"I'm with super-brain on this. You've been my best friend since that summer you wandered into Oak Creek. If the woman you love is even *maybe* in trouble, I'm coming to help. You'd do the same for me if it were—"

He cut himself off. He couldn't afford to even mention Becky's name right now. Although he knew without a shadow of a doubt that Becky would want Derek to help Theo get Eva to safety. She was Becky's friend. Hell, Becky would be the first in line to help if she were here.

Theo's eyes narrowed at him. "You sure this is good for you? If things do get ugly with Metter—"

"I'm sure." Derek didn't even hesitate with the lie.

He was in no state to go on a mission right now. He knew that, but like hell was he going to turn his back on his best friend when he needed help. Time to shove it down and bottle it up.

The therapist he'd been working with would be horrified at that thought. They'd been working on Derek *not* bottling for the last year.

But this was real life, and things weren't ideal. It didn't

matter how shaky his emotions were or how close to breaking he might be.

His friend needed help, so he was going to help. He could pay the price for it later.

~

DEREK AND LINCOLN weren't the only ones who were not letting Theo go into this situation alone.

Derek was on the phone to his brother Bear and Lincoln was calling Lilah Collingwood as they ran out the door. There wasn't anybody that Derek trusted at his back more than these people.

Lilah and Bear met them at Linear Tactical, already gathering the weapons they wanted—both of them grabbing enough to go into war.

Bear tossed an AR-15 rifle to Lincoln, who caught it in midair. Their cousin might not be good with people, but weapons, he had no problem with.

Theo grabbed a crossbow, which would seem an odd choice to anyone who didn't know that his mother Ray was damned near brilliant with it. She'd made sure her children were too.

Derek knew he should choose his weapon, prepare for the possible battle ahead. But all he could do was stand there trying to force breath in and out of lungs that seemed to be made of lead.

Theo looked over and must've recognized the panic in his eyes. Derek waited for his friend to suggest he sit this one out.

One more person Derek had let down. Add it to the fucking list.

But Theo grabbed the rifle from Lincoln and handed it to Derek. "Can I ask you to be my eyes in the sky?"

Sniper.

Knowing he wouldn't have to be up close and personal with anyone eased the tightness in his chest enough that Derek could move. "Yeah. Wherever you need me."

Theo nodded, lips tight. "Let's hope it doesn't come to needing all the weapons G.I. Joe and Jane here are prepping for us. But knowing you're in position will take a load off my mind."

"I won't let you down." And goddamn it, he wouldn't. No matter what. He wouldn't screw this up.

Theo clapped him on the shoulder. "It never crossed my mind that you would."

It probably should have.

"Let's move out," Theo said.

None of them spoke as they drove to the location Metter had been tracked to. It was easier that way. There wasn't much call for small talk when getting ready to rescue someone from a psychotic abuser.

Besides, everyone had their own mental rituals for going into battle. Hopefully there wouldn't be a battle, but they would be prepared for anything.

Derek disappeared inside himself on the ride. His thoughts floated down familiar paths, and he pulled them back before they went too far.

How would he feel if this were Becky? He would be feral and so far gone, even riding in the car would have him climbing the walls. That Theo was pulled together enough to drive—despite his knuckles being white on the wheel—impressed Derek.

"We're coming up on it," Lincoln finally said, following a signal on a tablet. "This cabin is the only thing for miles in any direction. Whatever Metter is doing here, he wanted to make sure no one would be around."

Theo's fingers tightened further on the wheel.

"Inside voice, Linc," Bear and Derek said at the same time. It had been their code growing up to let him know he wasn't picking up on the emotional cues going on around him.

"Sorry," Lincoln murmured.

Lilah passed out earpieces, and they put them in.

"We'll park half a mile out and come at the house from multiple angles," Theo said, slowing the vehicle now that they were on a dirt road. "We don't know what we're walking into, and I want us to be prepared for anything. Derek will stay back on sniper duty."

"I'd stop here," Lincoln said. "Any closer and you run the risk of him seeing our dust trail."

Theo pulled the car to the side, and they all got out.

"Bear, Lilah, you guys come around from the north and east. Linc, west. Derek and I will head for the front door."

Everyone tested their comms units then the other three disappeared into the deepening shadows.

Theo looked over at Derek. "Still okay?"

How much truth did his friend want? "I'm a bit shaky, but I'll handle it."

"Good thing I know you don't mean your trigger finger."

"I'll be ready if I'm needed."

"I know you will."

Derek's father Finn had been a sniper in the Special Forces, and Derek had inherited a lot of his skills. He didn't use them very often—hadn't even when he'd been an Air Force Combat Controller—but the skills were still there.

Theo clapped him on the shoulder. "Thank you."

"You never have to say that with me."

"But I'm going to anyway. You're paying a price to be here."

"Let's just get your woman back."

Theo nodded, and they both took off toward the cabin at full speed.

"We're in position," Lilah said in their ears.

"Good. We're about to—"

A scream came from somewhere in the distance, away from the cabin.

"That's Eva," Theo hissed into the comms, as he and Derek both pivoted toward the sound. "Everyone reposition."

"It came from near the river," Lincoln said, breathing heavily, obviously sprinting.

Theo and Derek were running as fast as they could in that direction when another scream broke through the silence before being cut off abruptly.

The sound threw Derek's mind back to that hellhole of a prison camp.

Heat. Sand. The grit between his teeth as his teammates died screaming, like the sound they'd just heard. His heart hurled itself against his ribs.

They weren't going to take him. They weren't going to—

"Go to hell!"

The female voice, now much closer, ripped Derek back from the memories. He blinked, still running, his mind finally remembering where he was.

The wilderness. Rescuing Eva.

He could hear two people talking not far off.

"I've got eyes on them," Bear said into the comms unit. "She's alive, Theo. That's what counts. But Metter has a gun, so play this smart."

Theo slowed slightly as Bear's words got through to him.

Derek reached a tree that would give him an excellent vantage point. "I'm going up. I'll take him out. Just give me the word."

It would cost a piece of his soul, even if it was a righteous kill, but he would do it.

It didn't take long until Metter was in his sights. The branch he chose didn't move under his weight. Swinging the rifle around, he fit it to his shoulder and looked through the scope, slowing his breathing. Pushing everything else out of his mind.

Focus.

He wouldn't be able to do it for too long. He had too much agitation running through his system—trigger after trigger that he'd been holding back all day.

He wasn't going to have the choice to hold it back much longer.

Another breath in through his nose, out through his mouth as Theo took on Metter.

They were talking about something—*so many fucking words* —but Derek couldn't focus on any of them. He just kept breathing, keeping his mental disquiet pushed down. His finger remained light on the side of the trigger, ready to do what needed to be done.

"You got them, cuz?" Lincoln asked in his ear, overriding whatever Metter was saying to Theo.

"I've got them." The crosshairs of his scope centered over Metter's head. Too close to Eva for his liking, but he wouldn't miss if he had to take the shot.

Theo's voice crystallized in his mind. "I found you, and I'll stop you because you made the most basic mistake, Metter."

"Oh yeah, what's that?" Metter's voice dripped with condescension and sarcasm.

"Eva's not alone in this."

Damn right she wasn't. Once you were a part of the Oak Creek family, you were protected.

Metter jerked, and Derek followed him with the scope.

"You're not going to be enough to save her," Metter scoffed at Theo.

"I'm not alone in this either."

Metter went stiff as Theo called out Lincoln then Lilah then Bear, each of them requesting to be the one to take the bastard out.

The man moved, realizing the game had changed. They all froze as Metter lowered the gun from pointing at Theo and pressed it to Eva's head instead, wrapping his arm around her neck. The motion pushed them so close together, Derek briefly lost his shot.

"One of you may get a shot off, but she'll die with me if you do," Metter said.

Derek heard the desperation in the man's voice. Things had just turned ugly.

It looked like Derek was going to have to take the kill shot after all. He breathed in another steadying breath, shoving down the knowledge that this was going to push him over some edge he might never come back from.

"We don't want to kill you, Metter. But there's no way you walk out of this unless you put the gun down now." Theo's voice was tight but even. "Believe me, the most dangerous of us all—a crack shot with a rifle like his father before him—hasn't even made himself known yet. Derek, do me a favor and hold your fire, please."

Derek raised his voice and projected through the trees. "My PTSD is giving me a pretty itchy finger, but I'll try. For the moment."

He understood what Theo was doing—giving Metter one more chance to end this without anyone dying. Sweat trickled down Derek's temple as he waited to see what would happen.

The man had no idea he held more than just his own life in the balance.

The seconds ticked by way too slowly before Metter finally let Eva go and pushed her away. He was disarmed by Theo a second later.

Metter was still talking—making random useless threats

about lawsuits and ruining reputations. Even though the man wasn't a physical danger to anyone anymore, Derek's finger trembled on the trigger. He didn't lower his sights, even when Sheriff Webb showed up and announced he'd followed them.

Derek could take Metter out and rid the world of one more asshole. Do it right now, and he'd never bother anyone again.

The quietest part of his mind told him he should do it. That if he did, he would never have to worry about coming near Becky again. Wouldn't even have to worry about Lincoln making their marriage disappear.

Because he'd be spending the rest of his life in prison.

"Hand me the rifle, little brother."

Bear's voice was quiet but didn't come through the comms unit. Derek had been so focused on Metter, Bear had climbed into the tree next to him without him realizing.

"It's over, Derek. You did your part. You can stand down."

More sweat dripped down his temple. "I—I—"

Bear's hand dropped gently on his shoulder. "I know. Taking him out would be easy, maybe too easy. But that's not who you are."

"I want to kill him."

Bear squeezed his shoulder lightly. "It's okay to want to kill him. But you're not going to do it. Hand me the rifle."

For a second, Derek didn't know if he could do it. One pull of the trigger could end his problems. End Becky's problems. Maybe that was the best way.

"If you can't do it for you, do it for me, D."

Derek's chest caved. This was *Bear*. He'd gotten the ridiculous nickname from Derek when they were both kids and used to track animals, convinced every set of prints they saw belonged to the massive creatures.

For Bear, Derek found the strength to ease his finger back from the trigger. He handed the rifle over to his brother as

Sheriff Webb arrested Metter and marched him back toward the cabin.

"That was the right choice." Bear squeezed his shoulder once more then headed down the tree.

Derek wasn't so sure.

Chapter 9

Becky had been coming to the Frontier Diner most of her life. It was a staple in Oak Creek—the place everyone went for good food and if they wanted to catch up on the town gossip.

But when she stopped in for dinner after the drive back from the Swanson ranch, the buzz inside went well beyond gossip. It was more like a freaking newscast—to the point where Becky hadn't even been able to get a table since everybody was flitting around talking about *the drama*.

Eva Dempsey had been kidnapped.

Eva had been rescued by Theo and some of his Oak Creek friends.

Eva's ex-boyfriend was a gaslighting asshole and going to jail for a lot of things.

Eva was okay, had been checked out at the hospital, and was now resting with Theo.

Becky was still trying to wrap her head around it all, trying to explain to everyone that she didn't have any details about anything, despite being Eva's boss.

And evidently, Eva had been at Becky's house when she'd gotten kidnapped—something Becky had no idea about. Not that Becky minded the other woman staying at her house…but *what in the world was going on*?

She left for two days, and everything went batshit crazy in town.

Becky finally just took her order to go since she couldn't find a table anyway and was frustrated that she couldn't answer anybody's questions about the whole brouhaha.

Already munching on her to-go fries, she called Eva to get the details of what had happened. The call went straight to voice mail, which didn't surprise her. She left a message to call back when Eva was feeling up to it.

But that could take days. She called Lilah next. If Theo had gone on a rescue mission, no doubt he'd wanted Lilah at his back. But there was no answer there either.

Theo had probably taken Lincoln also, but talking to him would be like hearing it from a robot, so Becky didn't bother contacting him.

Finally, she called the main line at Linear Tactical, hoping somebody there could give her an answer. She practically growled when it ended with their friendly recorded greeting.

She unwrapped the rest of her order and took a bite of her burger as she started her car. If no one was answering their phone, then she would go to the Linear property herself and find someone. She wanted the story from a primary source.

By the time she arrived, her burger and fries were done. She tossed the trash back in the bag as she looked around. The Linear Tactical campus seemed strangely empty. Usually there was at least someone around. With a full roster of defense classes and other training, it was rare for Linear to feel like a ghost town. But today, it did.

No one was in the office, nor the barns. She did a quick check on the therapy animals Linear housed—they all looked fine and had everything they needed. That was at least a sign that someone had been around. No one would let the animals suffer, no matter what crazy rescues might be afoot.

She decided to check the gym in a last-ditch effort to find someone who could give her info.

As she approached the door, she heard something. Not just *something*—it sounded like a battle was going on inside. Becky was well familiar with the sounds of sparring, but this went way beyond merely that. Whoever was working out inside was dealing with some real aggression.

She pushed the door open and froze.

Derek.

He was the one in the heart of the battle. And it was a battle against himself. No one else was around.

He was surrounded by a ring of training dummies, fighting them with deadly fury. He knocked one over with a flying kick so hard the dummy lifted off the floor.

The fire in Derek—the strength and ferocious rage with which he fought—was nothing like she'd ever seen. His hands were bloody, the air in the gym saturated with violence. The sweat streaming down his face attested that he'd been at this for a while.

Becky took a deep breath in and out.

This should scare her, right? After what had happened on their wedding night, seeing Derek like this should send her screaming for the hills.

Before she'd started training with Lilah, maybe this sight would have scared her. She would have only seen the terrifying violence in the deadly way he was attacking the dummies and how the blood dripped down his hands.

Becky wouldn't have been able to recognize the truth behind what was happening here.

This wasn't Derek out of control.

This was Derek fighting his demons to stay *in* control.

The deadly dance entranced her. Knowing what she did

now about fighting, she realized how much balance, coordination, strength, and endurance it took to do what he was doing at such a speed and full force.

His shirtless body moved in a choreography that spoke of primal dichotomies: power and restraint, strength and surrender, violence and control.

Becky didn't want to disturb him. Derek obviously needed this for whatever reason, and she wasn't going to interfere. They still had a lot to talk about, and everything in her wanted to go to him.

But she would never stand in the way of him trying to find control or heal. That was always most important.

As if he'd heard her thoughts out loud, Derek froze, his gaze snapping up to hers. He stood there, chest heaving, staring at her—the two of them suspended in time, neither moving.

She couldn't stop herself; she finally took a step forward, the need to be closer to him driving her the way it always had.

It broke whatever spell they were under. Derek blinked twice, then turned and strode away, grabbing his T-shirt off the floor and putting it on as he headed straight for the gym's other door.

No. Not again.

She charged after him. "You're just going to run away?"

He didn't answer her. He was out the door and moving quickly across the open field by the time she made it out of the gym. He was going straight toward the big house—the sprawling building with a dozen rooms so visiting teams and guests could stay when they came to train.

Was Derek staying there? Why? Why was he here at all? Why wasn't he at the helitack base?

She ran across the field after him, slowing as a thought burned through her mind.

Damn it, had he been part of Eva's rescue? That could've triggered whatever violence she'd just seen.

And damn his long legs taking him across the field so quickly. She started to jog again. "Derek."

He didn't respond, climbing the steps of the big house.

"Is this how it's going to be?" she called. "We've gone from you hiding and not letting me know you're anywhere around, to you just ignoring me if I show up?"

The door slammed behind him, and, muttering a curse, she followed. When she stepped inside, she stopped. He was going from door to door, looking through the kitchen, the large dining area, and even glancing out onto the back porch.

It hit her. He was looking for someone. *Anyone.* She caught sight of his face, and the panic on it was undeniable. He was afraid to be alone with her.

Some of her anger fled.

"Derek, stop," she said gently.

He charged down the hallway to one of the bedrooms, failing to close the door before she got there.

"Derek…"

He shook his head, stepping backward as she stepped forward. "You need to leave, Becky. You shouldn't be around me."

He walked the rest of the way through the room to the attached bathroom and shut the door behind him.

Becky stood there for one second before walking forward and pushing the door open.

He was shirtless again. It had been eighteen months since she'd been close to him like this—close enough to touch the firm muscles of his chest—and she had to swallow down both grief and desire.

"You shouldn't be in here," he said, the words nearly a growl.

"Have you forgotten how many times I've seen you naked?"

"I don't fucking care about my body, Becky. I'm not in control. I have triggers, and all the stress has me ready to snap. I can't be near you. Not right now."

The impossible heartbreak in his voice shattered her. Any remaining anger she'd had disappeared.

Or at least the anger toward *him*. "You helped rescue Eva, didn't you?"

When he didn't deny it immediately, she knew it was true.

"Theo shouldn't have asked for your help. He knows about your past better than anyone." More even than her. "Knows your triggers."

"He didn't ask. I volunteered. There was no way I was letting him go without backup."

Of course not. Derek would literally rather die than leave a friend in need. It was how he'd ended up in that enemy prison camp. Becky didn't know all the details, but she knew that much.

"You did it, even knowing how much it would cost you?"

He turned and gripped the sink counter. "He needed me."

I need you!

She wanted to scream the words, but that wasn't what was needed right now.

Although honestly, she wasn't sure what was needed, beyond clearing some of those demons from his eyes. She took a step closer and touched his bicep.

"I'm glad you were able to help rescue Eva." This definitely wasn't the time to press for details, even though he was one of the primary sources she'd been looking for.

He didn't pull away, but in the mirror, he was staring at where her fingers rested against his skin.

"I'm not afraid of you," she finally said when he didn't say anything.

"I remember when you were." His face scarred over in the cruelest pain. "I see it every fucking time I close my eyes. You in pain, afraid of who I am."

Frustration built in her chest again. "Yes."

His eyes flashed to hers, the hurt there real and palpable like a dagger to the heart.

"Yes, in those moments, I was afraid. I was confused. What happened was fast and scary and painful." Her voice broke a little, and she hated it. "It's not fair to hold that against me."

He shook his head. "I don't. I don't hold any of it against you."

He held it against himself. He didn't have to say the words. She knew it was true.

"I'm not afraid of you right now. I'm not even afraid of the demons in your mind."

His eyes dropped from hers in the mirror, like he couldn't even hope that what she was saying was true.

She took the risk and stepped closer, reaching for his hand. He didn't pull away, and relief flooded her.

"I'm not in control," he muttered.

"If you're in control enough to worry about being in control, then you're in more control than most people on any given day."

Pulling him closer, she turned on the water in the sink and waited for it to warm. A washcloth sat folded on the counter, and she picked it up, gently soaking the cloth before cleaning his bloody hands and knuckles.

As she washed his skin, Derek's breathing eased. When she reached for his other hand, he stepped closer to give it to her. So close, she could feel the heat of him.

It was impossible not to think about the other night at their tree. Everything about him called to her, and she couldn't pretend that kiss, and his hands on her, hadn't been the best thing she'd felt in forever.

She almost dreaded the blood disappearing from his hands, because it meant she would have to let him go.

Finally, his hands were clean. He stood so close, she breathed him in, not ready to step away.

She wanted more.

But she would always want more with this man.

She cleared her throat. "You're going to need bandages for these."

"Button," he breathed the nickname against her forehead, barely a whisper. She felt that whisper all the way down to her toes.

She had no idea who moved first—gravity pulled them together.

Derek's mouth came down on hers, hot and hard, his strong arms circling her like she was the only thing connecting him to the earth.

She knew immediately a kiss wasn't going to be enough. Not like the other night. She needed more than this.

"Shower," she said when his lips moved along her jaw. She gasped for breath. "Get in the shower with me."

"No."

Her heart fell, but Derek didn't pull away. He lifted her onto the countertop, only stopping to pull down her pants and shove them onto the floor. She was entirely exposed to him, and she didn't care.

It was Derek. *Derek*.

The man she'd loved since she was a teenager.

Her husband.

It was Derek whose mouth pushed between her legs and consumed her. Derek who made a sound like a starving man, pulling her hips to the edge and spreading her legs wide so he could taste more of her at once.

Becky fell back against the mirror, all the strength gone out of her under the power of his mouth. In their time apart, he hadn't forgotten what sent her over the edge. And he was using it all to his advantage—and hers—now.

"Derek," she managed to say his name, and it was all she had.

The sound of it seemed to drive him deeper. His tongue dipped down inside her as he looked up and locked eyes with her.

After this long without him, she knew it would take almost nothing to send her over the edge. She was already close, her breath hitching just at the sight of those gorgeous blue eyes filled with heat.

Heat because he was devouring *her*.

Derek didn't deviate. He held the pressure and movements of his mouth steady, exactly how he knew she liked them. She was powerless to stop the pleasure from building and spilling over.

Her whole body shook, writhing and grinding against his mouth in the relentless pursuit of that bliss. One hand ended up in his hair, and his name hissed out of her mouth.

When she came down from her orgasm, his tongue was still on her, dragging out aftershocks. She tightened her hand in his hair, pulling him up and closer to her face.

"Now take a shower with me." Her voice was breathy, but she didn't care. She smoothed her hands over his shoulders, enjoying the luxury of his skin all over again. "I need you, Derek."

His eyes dropped to her lips, and he lowered his head toward hers. "I…"

He trailed off, a look of self-loathing on his face, but took her hand. All Becky could feel was relief that he wasn't going to say no. They would sort the rest out later.

A sharp knock had them jerking apart.

"Hey, Derek?" It was Lilah's voice on the other side of the

door. "Sorry to bother you, but Sheriff Webb is here. He wants to talk to you about the rescue."

The silence lasted an eternity, and for the second time today, Becky took a risk. She cleared her throat so she could get words out clearly. "Now isn't a good time, Lilah."

"Oh. Becky. Hey. Umm... Okay. Yeah, I, um—"

"No, I'll be right there." Derek cut off Lilah's awkward word vomit.

Becky's gaze snapped back to him.

She was still spread open on top of the sink. His mouth still shone with the remnants of her orgasm, and he was going to *talk to the sheriff?* Callum Webb could damn well ask Derek whatever questions he had over the phone.

Later.

Long after she took her husband into the shower and let him fuck her against the wall like she'd been dreaming about for months.

But he was pulling away.

"Derek," she whispered. "Don't do this."

His eyes were so much clearer than when she'd stormed into the bathroom after him—the demons back at bay. So why did it feel like the invisible wall between them was thickening? Like he was building it more solidly than ever?

Picking up his discarded T-shirt, he slipped it on and went to the door. He paused, and she prayed, begged the universe that he would turn back to her.

Please.

He scrubbed a hand down his face but didn't turn back to her. "I have to go. Believe me, it's better this way."

He opened the door and left, closing it gently behind him.

Becky's eyes blurred with tears, and she blinked them back. The effort made them burn. She slid off the counter and found her jeans and underwear, pulling them back into place.

Before she left the bathroom, she made sure she looked

acceptable. Her hair wasn't out of place, and it didn't look like she'd just been eaten out on a bathroom counter.

Hell, nobody would even notice the fact that her eyes were red if they weren't looking for it.

She pushed out of the bathroom and slipped down the hall, grateful that Lilah hadn't waited around and that Linear Tactical as a whole was so empty today. Normally, there were half a dozen people she'd be happy to see here, because she loved her friends. But she didn't want anyone to see her like this.

Sad. Broken.

And alone.

Chapter 10

Becky's body was still a mess of sensation and friction as she arrived at the street leading to her house half an hour later. Utterly satisfied from the best orgasm she'd had since her wedding night, but beneath that, frustration and restlessness. She wanted to go back to Linear, take the gym Derek had been using, and beat the shit out of those same fighting dummies.

For one brief, hopeful moment, she'd thought she and Derek were going to make progress. Now she felt like they were further apart than ever, despite the brief connection. It made her tired and sad. And the fact that there was nothing to do with those feelings made it even worse.

Lilah had caught Becky on her way out of the big house and—without mentioning or asking what had happened between Becky and Derek in that bathroom—had explained what had happened. Eva had, indeed, been kidnapped, although Lilah didn't know why she'd been staying at Becky's house to begin with. Theo had been the only one to realize there was a problem and, true to form, had acted on it. Derek and the rest of the gang had stepped up to help.

Derek helping despite the fact that he would pay a high mental and emotional cost.

She hit the brakes as she saw two police vehicles parked outside of her home. She groaned. So much for curling up on her couch and digging into the emergency cookies and ice cream she kept in the freezer.

She should have expected this, though.

Getting out of the car, she approached Sheriff Webb where he stood near his vehicle, typing out something on his cell. "Hey, Callum. Can I go in?"

He looked up, a tight smile on his face. "I'm sorry about this. It's a crime scene. This is where Metter took Eva from. Evidently, your mom had offered your house for Eva to stay at."

Becky nodded. Since Lilah had explained, she knew the basics. But at the same time, knowing something happened and seeing the consequences were two very different things. "Yeah."

"I know it's a pain in the ass," the older man said. "But don't worry, we're being careful. It will be a few more hours. I'd like to be thorough now so we can nail this asshole, and also so we don't have to inconvenience you more later."

Becky swallowed. "Yeah, okay. I'll...I'll be back later, then."

"I'll let you know when it's clear."

"Thanks."

She wasn't even fully thinking as she got in the car and started driving, planning to go to her parents' house. But as much as she loved them, she didn't want to talk to them right now. Didn't want to answer hard questions about Derek being back in Wyoming and how she felt about that.

She couldn't even figure it out herself, much less articulate it for her parents.

She ended up at Ella's house. Her friend didn't live far, and a few minutes later, Becky was pulling up in front of her quiet and cozy place.

It always surprised Becky that Ella chose to live so simply. Her father—Cade Conner—had been one of the most popular country musicians of all time, so Ella certainly could afford something much bigger. Hell, she didn't even have to work at Fancy Pants bakery, but she did so anyway.

Ella was one of the most genuine people Becky knew. She wouldn't even blink at Becky arriving unannounced. She pulled up into the drive.

Sure enough, Ella opened the door before Becky could even knock. "Hey, stranger."

"Hey." Becky's voice was raspy. "Callum and the crime scene people are crawling all over my house right now, so I—"

Ella shoved the door open farther. "Are you kidding? Come in."

"Thanks."

"I heard something about Eva earlier today at Fancy Pants, but I couldn't put it together. What the hell happened?"

Becky filled her in on the parts she knew. Ella made them both tea while she spoke.

"That's wild. I'm glad she's okay."

"Me too."

Becky glanced at Ella's computer sitting on the small kitchen island. The screen happened to be open to a video of Colton Harrison. It was frozen on his smiling face, clearly him giving an interview after some crazy stunt. Because like his father before him—Riley Harrison, aka *Phoenix*—all of Colton's stunts were crazy. Didn't matter if it was on skis, a motorcycle, or something with a parachute. Extreme sports were Colton's life.

Becky grinned at Ella. "Dreaming about someone?"

"No." Ella shut the laptop way too quickly. "That interview just came up on my feed, and it was impressive."

"Have you talked to Colton lately?"

Ella's face heated. "We chat via text every once in a while."

Becky took another sip of tea. "The next time he's in town, you should ask him out. Take him somewhere other than the Eagle's Nest and get cozy."

Ella leaned over and reopened the laptop then tapped the space bar to resume playing the video. The sound wasn't on, but Colton looked alive and vibrant.

There was snow where he was, his cheeks red from the cold. He was laughing, and the camera panned over to the woman interviewing him. A gorgeous blonde who looked like she'd walked off a runway.

"I'm pretty sure that's the type of person Colton Harrison is used to going home with." Ella closed the screen again. "I'm not exactly his type."

"You don't know that. Just because he's smiling at that reporter doesn't mean she's his type. You might be exactly what he wants."

Ella rolled her eyes. "Yeah, plump and plain. Exactly what every gorgeous extreme sport athlete is famous for wanting."

"You better be quiet, or I'm going to call Lilah to come fight you."

"Listen, I know what I bring to the table. Literally and figuratively." Ella gave a soft laugh. "But I'm never going to be Colton's type."

"You don't know that unless you let him know you're interested."

Ella took a sip of her tea. "So, Derek's back." It was clearly a deflection away from talk about her and Colton, but Becky decided to let her get away with it. "How's that going?"

Becky ran her hands over her face. How much did she tell Ella? For so long, she'd been keeping everything about Derek's and her relationship a secret. But now that he was back and she was so confused, it was bubbling up like a shaken soda. If she didn't tell someone, it would come exploding out of her at the worst time. Better Ella than someone else. "Honestly?"

"Always."

Becky sighed. "I have no idea what's going on. Had no idea he's been part of the helitack team. He's been here for a *year*, El, and never told me."

Her friend looked at her before standing up and going to retrieve a plate of cookies Becky hadn't even seen. Ella put them down in front of her, and Becky snatched one up, barely stopping a moan.

The cookie wouldn't fix her relationship, but Becky didn't care.

"It will work out," Ella said quietly. "You and Derek are connected. Deeper than anyone realizes. Even the two of you. And you always will be, despite whatever happened between the two of you on that trip to Vegas."

Becky froze, second cookie halfway to her mouth. "I'm not sure what you mean."

Ella said nothing, but she raised a single eyebrow. The other woman was an observer. She saw things about people they didn't want her to see. Quiet and astute, she'd probably figured out the truth—or close enough to it—long before now.

"I don't even know how to say it," Becky admitted.

"Take your time. We've got cookies and we've got tea, and I'm not going anywhere. So, spill. You've been holding this in for a long damn time."

Becky took a slow sip of her tea and another bite of cookie to fortify herself. Even so, her breath was shaky. "We got married."

Ella didn't look surprised. She just nodded.

"We were planning on having a big wedding later, for everyone. But neither of us wanted to wait. We thought it would be a good idea."

The familiar spiral of dread and sadness spun through

Becky, followed by the longing and frustration now that Derek was so close.

"What happened?" Ella asked. "You don't have to tell me, of course. But if it would help you, then this is a safe space. No judgment, no matter what."

Becky closed her eyes. "The wedding was great. Small and plain, classic Vegas wedding, but it was what we wanted. Just us."

She still remembered the way Derek had looked at her that day in the chapel. Like she was the only thing in his world.

He still looked at her like that, but now it was laced with pain neither of them wanted to be there.

"We had some champagne, went back to our suite. It was incredible."

She wouldn't give Ella details of how Derek had made love to her like they had forever. It had been the most amazing night of her life.

The first part of it, at least.

"We fell asleep. I don't know how much later I woke up to him choking me. A PTSD episode he was caught in the middle of." The words were stiff on her tongue. She had to force them out. "I tried to get out of the bed, and he punched me twice. Broke my nose."

Now Ella was surprised. "Becky—"

Becky forged onward, fully aware that if she stopped speaking, she'd never be able to get it all out.

"He snapped out of it pretty quickly. Realized what he'd done." Becky couldn't stop the tears flowing down her cheeks. Not for what she'd gone through but for the anguish that had ravaged Derek's face when he'd become aware of what had happened. She rubbed the heels of her hands over her eyes in an effort to erase the images. It didn't work.

"My pain was nothing in comparison, Ella. I'd never seen anyone so...destroyed. He wanted to call nine-one-one and turn himself in. I told him not to. Begged him not to. Instead, I had him drive me to the hospital. While I was being examined, he called my parents. I didn't know he'd done that, but they got there a few hours later, and then he just…left."

The tears were well and truly flowing now. Becky pressed a hand to her chest, trying to ease some of the torment that had never been far below the surface the last year and a half. "That was the last time I saw him until a few days ago."

"Oh, Becky." Ella reached across the table and took her hand.

"The doctors asked if I wanted to press charges, and of course, I said no. Derek was gutted by what happened. Those actions weren't him. It was a PTSD episode that got the better of his mind, and as soon as he was clear, he stopped."

"Of course he did. We've both known Derek our whole lives. He would never hurt you willingly."

"I know his PTSD is from when he was held in that prison camp three years ago. He never talks about what happened, but I know Derek was tortured, and he was the only one who made it out alive. His teammates died."

Ella was quiet for a long moment, and Becky wiped her eyes then polished off what was left of the cookie, grateful for the solace of chocolate.

"Do you want a divorce?"

That was the question, wasn't it?

"Honestly? I don't know. If you had asked me six months ago, I would've said no. Hell, if you'd asked me before Derek walked into the Eagle's Nest a few days ago, I would've said no."

"But now?"

"Until this week, I hadn't talked to Derek once since our wedding night. I thought he was overseas. I wanted to give him space to sort things through in his mind. I thought we would figure out a plan once he got back."

Becky rubbed her hands up and down her arms. He'd been here the whole time.

"Finding out he's been so close for so long?" Becky's voice broke. "He was just a couple hours away for a *year*, Ella. That kills me. He's been so close, and he didn't even tell me."

"I know, sweetie."

"It's so much harder to forgive that. I would never blame him for the trauma of our wedding night. But he chose to be here without telling me he came back. Maybe he already decided for us. Maybe he just doesn't want me anymore."

It hadn't felt like that a couple of hours ago when his head had been between her thighs, but at the same time, she'd had to chase him down. She'd basically forced him to touch her.

Maybe he hadn't wanted that. Maybe he'd been trying to get her to leave him alone.

The thought broke her.

"I don't buy that for a single second," Ella said. "Derek Bollinger has been in love with you for as long as he's known what love was. If anything, he's trying to protect you. Because that's who he is. And if you still want to be with him, I'm with you one hundred percent."

"You are?"

"Absolutely. Or, if this is too much—and you need to cut your losses and move on? Then I support that too. Either way, you're not alone."

"Thank you."

Ella reached over and hugged her. "Never alone. You got that?"

"Yes, ma'am."

"I have to get over to Fancy Pants to help close. Want to come with?"

Becky appreciated the quick change of subject. Ella was a good listener and also knew when to let a subject die.

Becky glanced at her phone. No word from Callum, so her home was probably still invaded. "Sure."

"Okay. Hang tight for a second while I change."

She disappeared, and Becky pulled up the app on her phone that gave her access to the camera set up in Princess's stall at the Swanson Valley Ranch.

"Goddamn it." This day just kept getting worse. The camera must have gotten hit by something because it wasn't pointing where she'd left it. Instead of pointing into the stall where she could observe Princess, it now pointed toward the door of the barn. Not exactly helpful.

Driving all the way back up there to fix the camera herself wasn't going to happen. She'd have to call and get someone to reposition it.

"All ready," Ella said. "Want to drive with me?"

"That's okay. Hopefully Callum and the crime squad will be done soon and I can go straight home from the bakery."

It didn't take long for them to get into town. Ella swept into the bakery in all her glory, and Becky hung back to make her call, fully planning on helping her friend clean when it was done.

"Swanson Valley Ranch." A male voice answered, but not Mr. Swanson's.

"Can I speak to Mr. Swanson?"

"He's not here."

Becky barely kept her annoyance in check when nothing else was said. "Who am I speaking to now?"

"Everett."

The asshole. Great. "Everett, this is Becky Mackay."

She thought she heard him sigh before he spoke. "I'll tell Swanson you called."

"Wait," she said. "You don't have to bother him. I just need someone to reposition the camera in Princess's stall—

focus it back on her. It got spun, so it's pointing to the back of the barn. Can you move it for me?"

"I'll tell him you called," Everett said again a second before the line went dead.

"So that's a no, then?" Becky asked the empty air. Hopefully Everett would at least tell Mr. Swanson she'd called so he'd call back.

She helped Ella and the others clean, and they left her to her thoughts, which she appreciated. By the time they finished cleaning the bakery, she had a text on her phone telling her she was free to go home.

At least one thing was good after this day.

Chapter 11

Derek stumbled into the small house he'd rented a few months ago on the far east edge of Oak Creek. It was back behind some other buildings and barely noticeable at all from the main road.

There was no one to see him here. No one to wonder what he was doing. That was why he'd gotten this place. He could be alone yet…still be somewhat close to Becky.

Would she be more or less mad if she knew he'd been even closer than she'd known a lot of the past year? Every period he'd had time off from helitack, he'd come here.

She thought he hadn't felt the need to be near her? Nothing could've been further from the truth. The need had burned under his skin every single day.

This place had been the closest he would allow himself.

Shit. At least until a couple of days ago and definitely today.

He could still hear Becky's moans as he'd tasted her. Nothing was more beautiful than that sound. His fingers flexed as if they wanted to reach for her hips once again and pull her closer.

Instead, he unlocked the door and walked inside the house.

The sight of the place eased something inside him, despite the fact that it was only two bedrooms with the barest furniture inside. A table and couch. A mattress on the floor.

This place wasn't meant to be a home. It was a place he could be entirely alone and find solitude. Enough for him to piece himself back together when he was falling apart at the seams.

It gave him what he needed.

Despite the exhaustion that pulled at him, he walked straight past the bedroom with the mattress into the second bedroom. That room held what he needed.

Canvases stacked up against all the walls—some blank, some painted. The multiple shelves were covered in paints and brushes. A number of easels stood around the room. This was Derek's safe space.

A place only one person in the world would truly understand besides him—his Aunt Wavy.

She hadn't been captured, held, and tortured in an Afghan prison camp, but she had her own tragedy. The psychopath who'd kidnapped her had left emotional scars that still affected her.

Wavy had been the one who'd introduced him to painting as a form of dealing with trauma. A way to help get out of his head and cope, just like she had.

Wavy was now world-famous for her art. There was no way he would ever have that sort of talent. But he didn't need to. He didn't paint for fame; it was to quiet the roaring in his head.

Yes, this was definitely what he needed. Between Eva's rescue and the showdown with Becky, it felt like the pressure inside him was about to erupt.

He put a blank canvas on the easel and sat on the stool in front of it. He prepared a palette with primary colors, more than eager to get started, but when he turned back to the white canvas in front of him, he found himself frozen.

He couldn't figure out what to do. His hand couldn't remember how to move or apply the paint.

He stared at the blank canvas for a long moment, willing his body to move. But nothing happened.

Finally, he pulled out his phone and set it on the nearby windowsill, dialing Wavy on speaker. She answered after a couple rings. "Hey, bud. Rough day?"

Shame washed over him. He needed to call her more. But somehow, the only times he did were when he was in the middle of a crisis. She deserved better than that. "I'm sorry, Aunt Wavy. I shouldn't only call you—"

"It's not an issue, Derek. Trust me." She'd cut him off, but it wasn't a slap. It was a firm, intentional move meant to calm. "It means more to me that you'll call when you need me and you're struggling, than to call and make small talk."

Taking a shaky breath, Derek shoved his hands through his hair. There was no way he could tell her everything about today. And in the end, it didn't matter anyway. That was what the painting was for—when he couldn't get words or thoughts out.

"I'm shaky," he finally admitted. "I'm sitting in front of the canvas, and I can't start."

It wasn't the first time he'd had this problem, sitting in front of something empty without a way inside it. Like looking through a window to a peaceful landscape, but the window was locked and the glass unbreakable.

"What do you have?" she asked.

"Canvas. Primary colors."

"Do you have a brush?"

He didn't. It was the one thing he forgot. Quickly, he grabbed the cup full of them and set them on the windowsill by the phone. "Now I do."

"Pick a color."

Blue.

When he looked down at the palette, everything in him viscerally shied away from red. Once there were other colors, maybe. But the thought of red alone on a canvas was unfathomable right now.

"Make a mark on the canvas," Wavy said. "It doesn't matter how, why, or where. What matters is that the canvas isn't pristine anymore."

Derek dipped his brush in the blue paint and intentionally didn't look at the canvas as he swiped the paint across it. No thoughts. "Okay."

"Keep going," she says gently. "The strokes don't matter. The colors don't matter. The plan doesn't matter and isn't necessary. Plans can get in the way of things."

He looked up at the canvas, the stark streak of blue marring the once-perfect white. Something released in his chest. It was the horror of perfection that often stopped him from starting this. From ruining it like he ruined everything else.

Shaking his head, he added another line to the first, moving on pure instinct. The lines felt right, even when they shifted from long lines to shorter strokes.

"What color did you pick?" Wavy asked.

"Blue."

"That's nice. What kind of blue?"

Derek swallowed. "Ultramarine."

"Ooh, good choice. Maybe I'll paint too."

Adding some white next to the blue on his palette, Derek started to add variations. The mess in front of him looked like mountains. Or a heartbeat. Or just emotion. It could be anything, and he loved that about the process. He didn't have to explain the turmoil that whirled around in his mind when he was painting. It simply was.

Wavy kept talking, voice easy. Somewhere Derek heard her talking about the canvas she was setting up and what color she was just going to go with. But he wasn't really listening, and he knew Wavy didn't expect him to.

Now that he'd started, the process came more easily. He'd been doing this for over a year now, and if he could take his eyes off the canvas in front of him, he'd be able to see the stacks of them behind the easel already covered in paint from days just like this one.

Every stroke of paint he laid down felt like something loosening in his chest. And it was so fucking welcome, as much as it was exhausting. Being so keyed up and on edge for days at a time drained him.

At some point, Derek realized he was painting in silence. Wavy had ended the call. He knew it wasn't out of anger, but understanding how deeply he was in the process now.

One canvas disappeared under coats of paint and pain, and Derek grabbed another one, diving straight into the blankness without issue. This was the best he'd felt in a while. Since before he'd seen Becky at the Eagle's Nest.

Becky.

His wife was in his thoughts constantly. God, he loved her so much. Which made the choice to stay away from her at once so much easier and so much harder. It was easy to protect her. It hurt to be so far away.

He continued to paint, even as the room grew dark and he had to turn on the lights. He didn't stop.

Sound eventually cracked through the trance he was in, his cell phone ringing where it still sat on the windowsill.

Derek looked around, body suddenly feeling the reality of how long he'd been sitting on the stool in front of the easel. His phone display told him it was almost midnight.

Exhaustion swept over him in a wave. He felt better. Not jittery or on edge. Calm. Calm the way he craved to be always.

The phone went silent, and Derek rubbed his hands over his face, jumping when it rang a third time. He grabbed it.

Lincoln.

"Hey, Linc." Derek's voice scratched from hours of disuse. "I still don't know what I want to do about the marriage thing. Sorry I was—"

"Derek."

The way Lincoln said his name had him sitting up straighter. Instantly, he was back on alert. "What is it?"

He cleared his throat. "Do you remember when we had those break-ins around town a few years ago, and you asked me to put up surveillance measures around Becky's house so somebody could get to her if needed?"

Derek blinked. Honestly, he'd forgotten about that. The break-ins had passed without incident anywhere near Becky.

"Barely," Derek said. "Why?"

"They're still in place."

Derek rubbed his eyes. "I think we can ditch those now." That would be one more thing she'd be pissed at him for. The list was long enough already.

"Yeah, well…one of the sensors just went off, and I called you first. Becky's house is on fire."

Chapter 12

Derek was on his feet before Lincoln even finished the sentence, grabbing his keys and running to his truck. "Call the fire department if they're not already on the way."

Hanging up, he tossed his cell on the seat and slammed the truck into drive. Thank fuck he'd come to this house and gotten his mind under control. Focus fueled him as he drove toward his wife.

His *wife*.

He would have to deal with that later.

Derek wasn't calm, but he wasn't panicked either, and for now, that was good enough.

He skidded into Becky's gravel drive, slamming to a stop. Thankfully, the whole house wasn't engulfed in flames, and he saw Becky standing at the back corner of the house using a fire extinguisher.

For a second, he fought a smile, because Becky's face looked like she was annoyed more than anything else. Sirens rang in the air as he hopped down from the cab and grabbed the extra fire extinguisher from the bed of his truck.

Becky looked at him, taking in him and the extinguisher at

once. She nodded, and they turned back to the flames together. Luckily, it seemed contained to the back of her house —her home office.

Minutes later, the firefighters arrived, and both Derek and Becky stood back and let them finish taking care of it. Becky stared at the house, and Derek stared at her. Now that he had a clear head and she was in proximity, it was impossible for him to keep his hands off her.

Again.

Dropping the fire extinguisher, he turned her to him, running his hands over her arms and shoulders. "Are you okay? What happened?"

She shuddered, looking from the fire to him. The way she stared at him, Derek wasn't sure if she wanted him there, or if she felt like he was some apparition from a dream. She looked at him like she didn't quite believe he was real.

"Button, are you okay?"

She flinched when he called her that, and it tore his heart open. He dropped his hands away from her.

"Yes, I'm okay. I woke up to the smoke detector going off, and I rushed in. I'm not sure exactly what happened. It was in my office, not even the kitchen or something that would make sense. I don't know what could've caught fire in there."

"The important thing is you're not hurt." He couldn't stop himself from looking her over once more just to be sure. She looked fine, although had obviously been sleeping when all this went down—she was barefoot and in her pajamas.

The fact that her pajamas were still one of his old T-shirts and some sweatpants she'd pulled on should not mean anything to him.

But it did.

He yanked his thoughts back from her sleeping clothes. Becky's house wasn't that big, and a fire in it could've been deadly—especially while she'd been asleep. If the smoke detector had failed…

This small fire was nothing compared to the brutal wilderness fires Derek had faced on a regular basis with the helitack team over the past year. But somehow much more terrifying, even standing right here next to Becky and knowing she was okay.

They watched together silently as the firefighters got the fire under control. It wasn't long before Sheriff Webb showed up.

"Heard the call on the radio," Callum said by way of a greeting. "Everybody okay?"

Becky nodded. "You could roast marshmallows over my office, but I'm fine and I think we stopped it before it spread anywhere else."

Callum ran his hand through his hair. "Do you know what caused it?"

"No idea." Becky was still staring at the firefighters while they began to gather their gear now that the flames were completely out. "The kitchen, I could possibly understand, but my office?"

"Might be electrical," Derek said.

"Maybe." Becky turned to Callum. "Do you think it could have anything to do with Eva's kidnapping? This place has already been a crime scene once today."

"I don't ever rule anything out, but it seems highly unlikely. Gareth Metter is still in custody and doesn't have anything to gain by torching this place. We've already processed it for evidence."

Becky rubbed her eyes. "That's good, I guess."

Callum nodded. "Also good that you were able to keep it contained until the fire department got here. I'm surprised there wasn't more damage."

"I hit it with the fire extinguisher immediately, then Derek showed up and helped."

"Let me go talk to the crew," Callum said. "Maybe they'll have an idea of what caused it. If there's anything to report, I'll let you know."

Callum was barely out of earshot before she turned to Derek. "How *did* you get here so fast?" She frowned. "How did you even know about the fire, let alone beat the fire department?"

Derek reached up and wrapped a hand around the back of his neck, wincing. "I…" He cleared his throat. He wasn't going to lie to her, not about this. "When I went overseas, I had Lincoln set up some stuff to monitor you. Before…the wedding."

She stood there looking at him with one eyebrow raised, so he continued. "Not because I didn't trust you or wanted to invade your privacy. Just because I knew your house was sort of away from town, and if there was an emergency…"

Anger flooded Becky's face. "Seriously?"

"I'm sorry," he said. "I just wanted to keep you safe. I forgot I'd even asked him to do that until he called me and told me about the fire. I'll have him disable everything as soon as he can. I promise no one's been watching."

She crossed her arms and sighed. "That's not what I'm angry about, Derek."

He froze, confused. If someone had set up stuff to monitor him without his consent, he would be mad. The anger was expected. But if it wasn't about that…

"What are you angry about?" he asked softly.

Becky huffed out a laugh. "If I listed all the things I'm currently angry about, we'd be here all night. But right now? In this moment? I'm mad at the two fucking sides of you that I can't seem to make match up."

"What—"

"You set up measures to monitor me and the house. You did that so you could make sure I was safe when you were half a world away, but you've been hours away from me for the last year and you haven't bothered to fight for our relationship."

He shook his head. "After what happened—"

"I don't need you to keep me safe, Derek." Becky gestured to the house. "I can take care of myself. I'm grateful you were here, but even if you hadn't been, I was taking care of it. I didn't ask for safety. That's not what I want."

Derek said nothing. What could he say?

"What I need is my husband," she said, voice breaking. "My husband. I know we eloped, but we still took vows, Derek. It wasn't a fling, and it wasn't a whim. I meant the vows I made to you, and I want to keep them. I want a partner. Someone who's there for me all the time and not just when some monitor tells him she's in trouble. If you want to do something? Do that. *Be* that."

She shook her head. "But you can't seem to stop running long enough to be a partner or a husband, and I am done with it, Derek. I'm finished with you and how you've chosen to act. I'm done."

Becky turned and walked toward the back door of the house where Callum and the firefighters were standing, leaving Derek there alone in the dark.

I'm done.

That's what he'd wanted, right? To finally make sure she was free from him? That's why he'd put the wheels in motion with Lincoln to annul the marriage.

I'm finished with you.

It was what he wanted. What was best for Becky and for him.

Then why did it feel like the whole world was crumbling at his feet?

Chapter 13

Ella set down a cup of coffee in front of Becky and smiled, despite the look on Becky's face. She was on the verge of throwing her phone across the bakery. Since her home office was mostly char, she'd come over to Fancy Pants to talk to the insurance company.

They were being incredibly unhelpful.

"Yes," Becky said. "But—"

"Miss Mackay, I've done as much as I can for you right now. I told you we'd get back to you later today, and we will. You'll just need to give us a little bit of time to do our job, please."

The line went dead, and Becky growled in frustration. "Thank you for nothing."

The fire had come from a faulty fuse box just outside her home office. Insurance would cover it, but it was going to take a while.

At this point, Becky was just happy that her whole house hadn't burned down. The problem was that even though the fire had been isolated to the office, the house still wasn't in great shape, thanks to soot and smoke. It wasn't habitable until the specialty cleaners came in and did their job, and they hadn't had any openings until the next week. Which was why she was wanting the insurance company to pay for a hotel.

But she would wait a couple hours before pestering them again. Hopefully in that time, her blood pressure would come down. Not likely, given everything else on her mind. Like Derek.

Derek…

Becky sagged in her chair, letting her head sink onto the table. She'd told him how she felt, hoping that would be enough to galvanize him into action in some way. That telling him she was so tired of him running away would cause him to actually stop running.

But when she'd turned back around to him after talking to Callum and the firefighters, he'd been gone. Again. Almost as if he'd never been there at all. Definitely hadn't stayed around to fight for her.

Hot tears pressed against her eyelids, and she forced them back. All this time, she'd believed—truly believed—that everything would work out between them. That the man she loved was still inside him, and she'd be able to see him again. She still hoped, but it was fading quickly.

That hurt just as much.

Her phone rang on the table, jerking her upright. But it wasn't the insurance company calling her back. It was the Swanson Valley Ranch. "Hello?"

"Hey, Becky, this is Cooper over at Swanson Valley."

"Hi, Cooper." Even through the phone, his voice was smiling and charming. As far as you could get from Everett.

She heard the sound of shuffling papers. "There was a message that you called about something. Everything okay?"

"Oh. Did Everett fix the camera in Princess's stall? That's what I called about. It had gotten hit or something, so it was pointing entirely the wrong direction, which won't help me figure out what Princess's problem is. I asked Everett to fix it, but he didn't seem...particularly inclined, and I haven't had a chance to look yet."

Cooper groaned. "Honestly, I don't know if he did or not. He didn't mention you'd called. I found out since it was scribbled on a Post-it on the desk in the office, with handwriting so bad it might as well be a doctor's writing. Are you able to access the footage?"

"I can, but I haven't had a chance to look at anything yet. There was a fire at my house last night. Small, and everything is mostly okay, but it's taking some time to sort out."

"Well, shit," Cooper said. "I'm sorry about that. I guess that means footage from the camera here was wiped. Don't you worry about it. We've got a camera we can use. I'll replace yours in Princess's stall myself. I'll make sure that camera is pointed properly, so it's there when you're ready for it."

"No, no need to make any effort like that. The fire didn't damage anything with the camera or footage—it's all stored in the cloud. I just need a minute to go through everything."

"Don't worry about it right now. You have enough on your plate. Princess is doing well. We'll let you know if that changes."

"I appreciate that. Please just let Mr. Swanson know I'll go back through the footage I have and see if anything's usable to diagnose Princess, and I'll keep checking it regularly once you get it situated again."

She took a sip of her coffee and noticed there was now a small plate with a chocolate croissant on the table. Ella must have snuck it there when she was flopped over on the table like a sack of beans. It was delicious.

"Sounds like you have a lot going on. Like I said, don't worry about it."

"Yeah. But I still feel bad. I don't want this to slow things down. We want to get Princess back into perfect shape as soon as possible."

Cooper cleared his throat. "Well, if you want to come back out, we have to take one of the planes down to Reddington City tomorrow for some supplies. Easy enough for you to hop aboard and come back with me. Faster, too."

She was quiet, considering. Being at the ranch would help her diagnose Princess more quickly, but she had a lot to do around here.

The words to decline the invitation were on her lips when the bell jingled over the bakery's door. Becky turned to find Derek standing there, eyes locked on her. The look on his face... She didn't know how to describe it. Somewhere between fear and raw longing.

Their eyes locked, neither of them able to look away. He took a step forward as if he couldn't help the movement. Becky found herself standing—gravitating toward him, despite the phone still pressed to her cheek.

Then Derek shook his head, turned, and left the building, not coming inside to do or buy whatever he'd intended.

He was running. *Again.* Rather than coming inside and fighting it out with her.

Her eyes burned.

Fuck this.

"Actually," she finally said to Cooper, "That would be great, thanks. If you'll send the plane, I'll travel up tomorrow and see what I can do. Besides, I need to get away from Oak Creek for a bit."

"Great." She heard the pleasure in Cooper's voice. "I'll text you all the details. In the meantime, don't worry about Princess. She was a little perkier this morning. Take care of whatever you need to with your house, and I'll see you tomorrow."

"Okay. Bye."

She disconnected the call and sat back down. Maybe this wasn't the best of plans, but it was better than staying here.

At least this time, she was the one who was running.

THE NEXT MORNING, Derek stood outside the hangar of the regional airport just outside town. He had all his gear and was heading back to helitack. Sam had approved the overtime since they always needed another pilot around, no matter what team was working.

There was no point in staying in Oak Creek if Becky was done with him. There was too much history here. Everywhere in town was just a source of memories that tore into him like claws each time he walked down the street.

Not to mention seeing her.

When he'd walked into Fancy Pants yesterday, just planning on getting some coffee, and saw her sitting there, all he'd wanted to do was scoop her up off the chair and press her against the wall.

He'd been damned near desperate to feel her. When she'd stood up and he'd started gravitating toward her, he'd forced himself to stop.

I'm finished with you.

What would it do to touch her? All it would do was draw out the painful inevitable. She was finally ready to end things. It was better this way. Derek would have Lincoln annul the marriage, and Becky would be free of him.

It was going to mean his having to leave Oak Creek permanently, but that was the way it was. He would have to find another way to visit his family.

But right now, it was better just to go. So here he was at the regional airport.

His boss had asked Derek if he wanted to make some extra

cash by piloting a delivery run up to the Swanson Valley Ranch. It was their plane, and then helitack would send someone to pick him up. It was good money for an easy flight. Why not?

Loading his bag into the Cessna 408, he was situating everything to make sure the plane was balanced when he heard a throat clear behind him.

He turned, shocked to find Becky. She was just as shocked he was there.

"What are you doing here?"

"I'm waiting for someone to fly me to the Swanson ranch. I was told to come here."

"So you're my cargo."

"Yours?" Becky frowned. "I thought Cooper was going to fly me."

Cooper. Derek fought a grimace. He knew Cooper Ellis. Friendly, charming, handsome. The perfect image of a Wyoming cowboy and, more importantly, everything Derek wasn't.

He shook his head. "Evidently, plans changed. I was hired to fly this plane and its cargo up to Swanson."

"Oh."

Neither of them said anything, the space between them thick with tension. Derek finally managed to find his voice. "I'm almost ready. Let me have that, and I'll finish the inspection. Then we're ready."

Becky handed him her bag, and he settled it right next to his own. Like it should be. He shook his head. He needed to stop thinking that way.

Maybe this trip would be good closure for the both of them.

Derek ducked into the plane after Becky, leaning over her to help her with the harness. He tried not to touch her—the tiny brushes of her against his fingers were torture, when he wanted so much more.

When he pulled away, Becky's eyes were bright, breath shallow. Her cheeks were flushed, and they were so close, he could lean forward and cover her lips with his own.

No.

He'd tasted his wife's lips for the last time. Forcing himself out of the plane, he threw himself into the rest of the inspection to get his mind and his heart in check.

Everything looked fine. The inspection didn't take long, and Derek wished it took longer. Because now he faced climbing into the plane with Becky. They'd be alone for the rest of the flight, and then he would have to watch her walk away into the arms of fucking Cooper Ellis.

Rage stung his eyes, and he breathed in and out slowly, trying to control the immediate reaction. Going alpha male and trying to stake his claim on Becky like a caveman wasn't going to help anything, despite it being the only thing he wanted.

With one final glance at the wing, he swung himself into the plane and sealed it shut. Becky already had her headset on. Derek strapped himself in and donned his headset, steadfastly ignoring the awareness his body had of the woman beside him. "All ready to go," he said. "It'll be a short flight."

"Good."

The clipped word was a knife to his chest.

He let himself fade away into the rhythm of takeoff. This, he could do. Almost with his eyes closed. The simple steps lent him a calm he didn't truly feel, but at the least, he was hanging on.

Once they were in the air and heading north, the silence between them became a living thing once more. If this was the last time he would be able to speak to her, he needed to use it.

The idea of spending the entire flight in silence, only to watch her walk away, was unbearable.

The ascent had taken them up and over the mountains, well on their way to the Swanson Valley Ranch. It was now or never.

Derek cleared his throat. "I'm going back to helitack. I'll be out of Oak Creek permanently."

Becky said nothing.

One glance told him she was looking straight ahead out the plane's windshield, arms crossed over her chest. It didn't appear as though she'd heard him.

"Becky—"

"Is anything about that supposed to surprise me? Once again, running." She gave a sigh that tugged at the deepest parts of him. "You think I'd be used to it by now, but every time, it hurts."

Confusion overtook him. What did she mean? She'd said… He cleared his throat again, checking the instruments out of instinct and habit. "You told me it was over. That you were done." His voice was low in his own ears. "And I don't blame you. I didn't think you'd want me to stick around. So, I'm leaving."

Becky looked at him then. He met her gaze, and it shook him to the core. Her face was filled with such a potent combination of confusion and rage, if there had been room to step backward in this tiny plane, he would have tried.

"*What the hell did you say?*" she whispered. He wouldn't have been able to hear if they hadn't had a comms channel on.

"You said we were over. Basically, to fuck off and disappear."

"I did not say anything of the sort."

"Button—"

She turned as much in her seat as the harness would allow. "Don't you dare *Button* me. I told you I needed my husband. I told you to be a partner instead of monitoring me from afar. I told you I was done with you running. None of that was me telling you to *fuck off and disappear*. I want you to fight for me. To try to make this work. The literal opposite of whatever the hell you think I said."

Shock rolled over him. *That's* what she meant? "Then why did you walk away?"

"Because I wanted you to follow me. The perfect opportunity to show me you weren't running. Fight for me right then and there. But you didn't. You ran. Again. Like you're running now."

He took a breath. Ultimately, it didn't matter if he'd misunderstood her words or not. "Leaving you alone is the best option for you."

"Because of what happened on our wedding night."

"Yes."

"And if I don't want you to leave me alone?"

"Why would you possibly want me anywhere near you?"

Derek didn't look over at her. Because he heard the hitch in her breath and the creak in her voice, and he knew if he looked at her, he would find tears in her eyes. "Because you're my husband. Because, in spite of everything that happened, there's a reason I married you. If you don't want me, I'll survive it." She drew in a ragged breath. "But at the very least, you owe me an explanation."

He opened his mouth to speak, and she cut him off. "I know there are things you can't tell me. Or things you're not ready to tell me. That's fine. But I want to know how you could be so close and say nothing. Do you have any idea how that makes me feel?"

"Because I needed—" An alarm cut off Derek's words. The engines… "What the fuck?"

He turned off the alarm then tore off his headphones to check for himself what the sensors were saying.

Shit. They'd definitely lost one engine.

"Derek?"

"For some reason, one of the engines has burned out."

"What does that mean?"

"Means bad fucking luck."

An engine had flamed out. It just fucking flamed out. What the hell? There's no way that should have happened. They weren't flying in any sort of dangerous way. Their speed and altitude were well within normal limits. Far, far from the limits that would cause an engine to flame and die.

The tension between Becky and him disappeared, their attention now sharp and focused.

"We're still flying," Becky said. "What's going on?"

Her voice was calm, and it soothed something in him. She'd always been good in a crisis. It was one of the things that made her a good veterinarian. Even when things were going wrong, she was able to assess and take action.

"Derek?" she asked. "How much trouble are we in right now? Is there any way I can help?"

Taking a breath in, he kept his grip light on the yoke. "As long as we don't lose the second engine, we'll be okay. There's no way we'll make it to the ranch, but we should be able to make it back to Reddington City. We'll be okay."

This was far from the first time he'd had issues midflight. The very nature of being a helitack pilot meant being able to quickly make decisions and reevaluate, preparing for the worst. Usually while flying over fires that would burn you to a fucking crisp.

"I have to talk to ATC," he said, so she wasn't taken off guard. Flipping over the channels, he addressed air traffic control. "ATC, this is Cessna one-two-six-five-zero en route to Swanson Valley Ranch. We've experienced an engine flameout in one engine. Over."

A crackle sounded in Derek's ear. "Roger, Cessna one-two-six-five-zero. Are you stable? Over."

"Affirmative. Currently changing course to return to Reddington City Regional."

"Roger that, Cessna one-two—"

The air traffic controller was cut off as the entire plane shuddered, a sound somewhere between a roar and a boom echoing through both Derek's body and the plane.

The second engine was gone.

Chapter 14

Fuck.

Now they had a problem. The plane was basically now a giant glider. Derek was going to have to try to find a smooth place to land, and the only things in view were mountains.

There was no way this should've happened. Ever.

"Cessna—"

"ATC, our other engine has gone out." The nose of the plane tipped down toward the earth at the same time Becky looked over at him. He met her eyes briefly, seeing the fear there, though she was still calm. "We won't make it back to the airport. We'll try to find a place to land."

Derek's muscles screamed as he fought with the yoke, trying to get a vessel of metal to ignore gravity with no power other than will.

"Cessna, give me your coordinates. We'll dispatch emergency services to you as soon as possible. Over."

"Coordinates," he said. The GPS was right there, but trying to focus on the screen and keeping the nose as high as possible were two full-time jobs he couldn't complete at the same time.

Reaching, he flicked one more switch, adding Becky to the channel with ATC.

"Cessna, we need those coordinates and a status update. Tell us what's going on."

As soon as Becky heard ATC, she understood. "ATC, our current coordinates are latitude 44.188 and longitude negative 110.577. Heading east."

Somewhere. There had to be somewhere he could land this thing. They weren't too deep in the mountains, and if they were lucky, they could glide over the worst of it, but this was Wyoming. Barely half a million people lived in the state. They were in the middle of nowhere, and this landscape was far from forgiving.

He fought, dragging the plane up a fraction, enough to bring them over the highest mountain they were near, but they weren't high enough. Losing altitude fast.

"What about there?"

Becky pointed to a ravine in the distance. It was narrow but clear of trees and the huge boulders damned near everywhere in this area—deathtraps for their current situation. The ravine might just give them a chance to survive.

At this point, that was the best to hope for.

"Better than nothing," he ground out, angling the yoke to the right.

"Cessna one-two-six-five-zero, report. Over."

"We're about to try for a landing," he said to them. "Send help when you have it. Going dark and trying not to die. Over."

He managed to flip the two of them over to a private channel. There was nothing else air traffic control could do for them right now. It was just him and Becky.

His wife.

"This is going to be rough," he told her. "Even if that's as flat as it looks, I have no way to slow us. Get your harness as tight as possible. If you think it's too tight? Make it tighter."

She moved, and he glanced over at her, panic shearing through him. "Becky. Becky. What are you—" His wife undid her harness entirely, standing. "Sit down. Please."

"I will," she said, coming behind his seat and moving her hands over his own harness. She yanked it tight, hard enough that he groaned. But it was better. He wasn't able to do that himself. Not when he couldn't let go of the yoke without the plane falling into a complete dive.

One by one, the points of his harness tightened until there was no way he would move. Only then did Becky stop. Her hands on his shoulders, she leaned around and brushed her lips to his cheek. "I believe in you," she said softly.

If it were anything other than life and death in that moment, he wasn't sure he could have resisted the temptation to throw on autopilot and haul her into his arms. Showing her exactly how much he wanted her and how much he'd never wanted to walk away.

In order to do that, he had to keep them alive.

Becky got back in her own seat and followed his instructions. In the corner of his eye, he saw her tighten all the points of her harness, and he breathed a little easier when she was entirely secure.

They were losing altitude fast now. Derek did as much as he could, but there was only so much to do when you were in a metal capsule hurtling toward the earth.

The little ravine came into closer view. It wasn't even close to perfect—far rockier than it had looked from above and not smooth. But it was enough. It would have to be enough.

Derek wasn't a praying man, but right now, he did. He prayed to whoever might listen that his wife would be spared this. That she would survive, even if he didn't. She deserved far more than this. Far more than the life he'd chained her to. And if both of them made it out of this alive?

If she walked away afterward? He could live with that.

The trees were so close, his heart was in his throat. He threw down the landing gear. It probably wouldn't help, but maybe it would take off more of their speed.

He pulled the yoke back, desperate to try to slow their speed as much as he could. Screeching sounded through his headset. The absence of the engines made the sound of the trees scraping along the metal hull loud. Everything shook, and his arms ached with the effort of keeping the nose upward.

A losing battle.

The plane hit more trees and flew into the ravine, striking the earth hard. It bounced back into the air and slammed to the ground again. His bones shook, and he resisted the urge to look at Becky to make sure she was okay. He had to believe she was.

Derek jerked the yoke to the left, throwing the plane into a turn in a final effort to slow them the fuck down. Grating metal screamed, and the body of the plane dropped again as the landing gear collapsed under the weight and the speed. Everything felt off-balance. Either one wing was gone, or the side of the plane was collapsing. At the very least, they weren't a ball of flames and smoke.

Small favors.

But they were still going too fast.

"Derek," Becky said.

A rock tossed the plane up again.

The yoke flew out of Derek's hands as the plane lifted into the air and fell again, jarring their bones. There was nothing left to do but hold on and pray the universe would look on them with some kindness.

Another bounce. His teeth rattled. Another.

The end of the ravine was coming at them way too fast. Derek hoped he'd slowed them enough for them not to be splattered into a canyon wall. There was nothing else he could do now.

He reached for Becky's hand, and she slipped hers into his. They wove their fingers together, and Derek felt calmer than he'd imagined he could.

The plane slammed into the tree line, and everything went black.

Chapter 15

Becky came to consciousness in that way someone did when they slept too deeply. When being awake wasn't where the body wanted to be, so darkness and sleep clung longer than normal.

It felt like she was swimming her way to the surface. But something wasn't right. She wasn't in her bed, and wherever the hell she was? Not remotely comfortable.

She cracked her eyes open, and dizziness splintered through her brain. What the hell?

The plane.

Everything surged back to reality. She and Derek had been flying, and then they weren't. They'd hit the trees with the force of a train. Now she was...

She shook her head and stopped. That was a bad idea. She was hanging sideways, the harness Derek had her tighten holding her in.

Check things, Becky.

Wiggling her fingers and toes, she felt relief sweep through her. All of them moving was a good sign, if a small one. No pain jumped out at her, other than a pounding headache and the dizziness from hanging in such an awkward position.

But what was—

Smoke.

Smoke filled the cockpit, and it was getting thicker. That was bad. "Derek?"

She reached up and stripped off the headset, the vast silence and sounds of nature assaulting her ears, suddenly loud. It didn't sound like the plane was on fire, but that didn't mean much. Her heart was pounding in her ears—she didn't fully trust her senses right now. "Derek?"

He didn't say anything. Panic spiked through her veins. "Derek. Say something."

Becky struggled, working her way out of the too-tight harness without falling on her face. She was above him, the plane on its left side. Derek was still in his seat, harness buckling him in. She couldn't tell if he was breathing.

Slowly lowering herself to his side, she almost couldn't bring herself to find out, because if Derek was dead, she didn't know what she'd do.

She swallowed, pressing her fingers to his limp wrist and nearly sobbing in relief when his pulse came back to her. Steady and strong.

Derek shifted, not conscious, but a small sound came from him. Like he was just on the other side of waking up and not quite there yet. Pulling off his headset and letting it drop, she called to him. "Derek?"

The air in the plane was thickening with smoke. They needed to get out.

With this much smoke, she knew there was a fire somewhere, even if she couldn't see it or hear it. And if they'd both survived the crash, like hell was she going to let them die in the plane blowing up after it.

"Derek, we have to get out of the plane," she said. "I need to move you."

Becky tried to undo his harness, but like hers, it was too tight. Unlike hers, it was holding her much-larger husband, and it wasn't about to let him go. Shit.

Without his being awake, Becky had no way to know if he was injured. Moving him would be bad if the crash had injured something vital, like his spine. But getting blown up would definitely kill him, so she didn't have a choice.

A thought sprang into her head. Derek's backpack. He always carried things to survive. Like a knife.

Taking a breath of the air in the cockpit—clearer than the air in the back, she ducked to where she'd seen him stow his bag and found the familiar hilt stuck through a loop in the side.

She took sipping breaths, trying not to panic. She didn't tend to lose her head when bad things happened, but this was unlike anything else she'd ever been through. Derek was unconscious, and they were in the middle of nowhere—nobody was coming to help. It was up to her to get him out. Choking back her fear, she returned to the front of the plane.

The blade sliced through the harness relatively easily, but there was nothing she could do to keep him from crashing painfully into the yoke, instruments, and the side of the plane once the harness released its hold.

"Becky?" Derek's voice was a balm of pure relief. "Becky."

He was clearly groggy, but groggy was better than out cold. "Hey, you. We crashed. We made it. But we have to get out of the plane, okay? There's smoke. I don't know where it's coming from, but we have to go, and I'm going to help you."

"Becky," he whispered again, and her heart jumped into her throat. Blood stained his shirt that she hadn't seen before. He might be more injured than she'd thought.

"I need you to focus for me, Derek. Put your arm around

my shoulders. I'm not strong enough to lift you, but if you help me, we can get out of here."

He obeyed as she moved him, twisting and putting his arm around her shoulder exactly like she'd asked him to. His other arm didn't look quite right, but she couldn't worry about it now.

"Okay, here we go," she told him. "Use your legs."

Together, they stumbled and crouched to the center of the tiny craft, slipping at the angle of the floor.

Becky ducked out from beneath Derek's arm, trying to get the door open on the side of the plane that was upright. It unlocked but didn't budge. An inch, maybe, but—

"Help me," she begged. "Come on, Derek. We can do this."

A certain clearness came to his eyes. He wasn't fully back, but he was back enough. Leaning against her, he shoved himself against the back of the pilot's chair and braced himself. "Let's kick."

Right. They could kick it.

Becky counted them down, and they kicked the door together. It moved, but not enough. "Again."

They kicked it again and a third time, the door finally breaking free of the hull's crumpled metal to swing open.

"Yes," she gasped the word, grabbing Derek and not letting him rest. It wasn't on her own strength that she got him out of the plane. This was pure adrenaline. She had to get him out and away.

The smoke in the cabin poured into the sky, fresh air clearing her lungs as they got out, nearly stumbling. The distance to the ground was a touch too far, but it didn't matter. She pushed and dragged Derek away from the plane and into the trees. A little alcove of rocks snagged her gaze, and she guided him there, getting him to sit.

"Stay here." She wheezed the word out.

"Where are you going?"

"Getting your backpack."

Given who he was and doing what he did, she knew he'd have emergency supplies in his backpack. They were going to need it. Air traffic control had their last coordinates, but it could still be hours until help came.

She sprinted back toward the plane, gaping at the flames coming out of the tail. Fuck. It was definitely, definitely on fire.

But the backpack was all she needed. Leaning into the adrenaline, she launched herself back up into the plane's cabin, coughing on the thick, roiling smoke filling the space. She was blind with it, fumbling to feel for the bag and cursing herself for not just grabbing it when she'd taken the knife.

There. Finally, she felt it under her fingers.

She grabbed it and slithered backward, falling to the ground and getting the hell away from the plane, only to run into Derek. He looked almost delirious, walking slowly back to the site of the crash.

"What are you doing?" she gasped.

He shook his head. "Saw the smoke. I didn't know where you were. Thought you were in trouble."

Her heart stuttered. "We needed your backpack. I…"

"Becky." Derek's voice was entirely lucid. "The smoke. It's almost pure black. That means—"

He didn't finish the sentence. Heat and sound rocked behind her, throwing her into him. One arm came around her, and he helped her find her footing as they turned to look at the place where the plane had just been. Now it was just a huge column of smoke.

Becky swallowed. That was closer than she'd thought. Even a minute slower, and she wouldn't have made it out of that plane.

Derek stumbled a little, holding his arm strangely. There

was still blood on his shirt too. "Are you okay? What's wrong with your arm?"

He grimaced. "I think my shoulder is dislocated."

"Shit," she muttered under her breath. "Come on."

He didn't fight her as she led him back to the little rock alcove where she'd first stashed him. That gave them a good view of the surrounding area and provided a little shelter.

"We need to get that shoulder back in its socket," she said. The thought of causing Derek pain made her stomach twist with nausea, but his shoulder was already hurting him and would only get worse until it was reset. Plus, she would need his help—with *two* functional arms—before this was over.

She was a vet, not a doctor, but she knew enough about the human body to get a shoulder back in the socket. And she knew it was going to hurt.

"I'm so sorry," she whispered, helping him over against the rock outcropping.

"It's fine." He gritted the words through his teeth. "Has to be done."

He had enough field medic training to know how to make the first move. He turned and slid until he was lying flat on the ground so she had access to his arm.

"Are you sure?" God, she didn't want to do this.

"Do it, Button."

She didn't even reprimand him about the nickname—at least nicknames meant he was coherent enough to use them.

Carefully, she moved his arm up, slowly aligning it with his shoulder. She knew it was agonizing, but the only sign of pain that escaped him was a tightening in his jaw and his hand curling into a fist.

She didn't provide him a countdown, knowing that would cause him to tense up and make things worse. Applying pressure to the joint, she moved it back into place, the popping noise making her shudder.

He didn't make a sound the whole time. She forced away the thought that he'd been through much, much worse than this. She couldn't bear the thought of it.

"Okay," she said. "It's in. I grabbed your bag because I thought you might have some emergency stuff."

"Yeah." Derek's voice was rough. "Good."

"You have painkillers? Anti-inflammatories?" Keeping the swelling down would be just as important as managing the pain.

"Should be some."

Becky dug in the bag and found what she was looking for —a first aid kit that included painkillers, along with a water bottle. "Here."

He swallowed the pills, and she examined the kit. She saw a needle and thread inside, though she hoped she wouldn't need to use them. Elastic bandages too, and she grabbed those. "Let me see where you're bleeding."

Derek watched her carefully and didn't fight her when she lifted his shirt over his head, careful of his shoulder. Despite their surroundings, she was immediately reminded of their encounter in the bathroom. Derek was here. Alive. Breathing.

And at the moment, nothing seemed important in comparison to that.

On Derek's left side was a nasty gash across his ribs. Damn it, this was going to hurt too. "You need stitches."

"That's fine."

"I don't want to hurt you more," she said quietly, using an elastic bandage to form a makeshift sling for Derek's arm. She would redo it when he had to put his shirt back on. For now, his arm needed to rest as comfortably as possible.

Derek laughed softly. "I've had worse, Button. Do it."

"Worse? You mean when you were held prisoner." She forced herself to open the first aid kit and grab the alcohol wipes.

When the alcohol touched the wound, he stiffened, but he started to speak. "Yes, when I was held, but also from my SERE training."

"SERE training?" She should know what that meant, but her brain couldn't wrap itself around the details right now as she grabbed the needle and thread she'd need for the sutures. "What is that?"

She blew a breath in and out, trying to steady her hand that was shaking. What the hell was her problem? Derek was the one who was going to be suffering.

He placed his free hand over hers and squeezed, stopping the shaking. "SERE is a type of training all combat pilots do in the Air Force. Stands for survival, evasion, resistance, and escape," he said quietly.

"Right." His hand on hers was helping her settle. "I remember overhearing you talk about it with Bear and Lincoln once."

He moved his hand so she could continue. "It's nearly a three-week course. They wanted us to be as prepared as possible if we went down behind enemy lines."

"Yeah?" Becky took a deep breath and began to close the wound.

Derek kept talking. "They teach you how to escape from a vehicle that's trapped underwater—that was my personal favorite. How to treat cold injuries. Hot injuries. Every type of injury."

She poked through his skin, forcing herself to think of it as an animal she was stitching—one who'd already had local anesthesia and wasn't feeling any pain. She glanced up and found Derek's blue eyes steady on hers.

"It wasn't fun, but it was definitely useful. And I know I can make it out of both a car and plane that are underwater. Too bad we didn't find a lake to crash into. I would've been a lot more helpful."

She couldn't stop her small smile. She'd thought he was talking to keep his mind off the pain or what she was doing, but he was talking to calm *her* down.

"I know what you're doing," she whispered. "Thank you."

He gave her a small nod. "Get it done, Button. I'm okay."

She worked as quickly as she could. They fell into silence, but now that her hand was steady, she didn't waste time. And just like with his shoulder, he did very little to give away that she was hurting him at all.

"There," she said, placing the medical gear back in the box after placing a bandage over the stitches. "It's not perfect, but at least it's closed."

"Thank you."

Now, she nodded. Together, they worked to get his shirt back on and the sling back in place. By the time they finished, the adrenaline in Becky's veins was dying, and all she wanted to do was sit and not move for ten or twelve hours.

"Let's rest for a bit," Derek said. "Then we'll figure out our next move, all right?"

"Yeah."

Becky sat down next to him and leaned against the rock. She closed her eyes.

They were alive. That was the only thing that mattered.

Chapter 16

Derek dragged his eyes open and looked around. The angle of the sun had changed. It was afternoon now, the bright sweetness of the morning long gone.

And fuck, if everything in his damned body didn't hurt.

His shoulder throbbed, and the wound in his side ached. He held himself as still as possible, knowing movement was just going to cause further pain, but that was inevitable.

And he'd lived through a lot worse than this. Survival was always the most important thing. The good thing about pain was that it let you know you were still alive.

He looked back toward where the plane had gone down, his mind much clearer now that his body had been able to rest and his Becky had patched up the worst of him.

He stared toward the wreckage. He needed to look at whatever was left of the plane so he could figure out what the hell went wrong. There was no way on a plane like that, with the way they'd been flying, that he should've lost both engines.

It was statistically possible, but the chances were so astronomical he couldn't wrap his head around it.

His eyes shifted up to the sky. Sun positioning put them at

late afternoon, probably around three p.m. Four hours since the crash. Clearly, air traffic control knew they'd gone down, but they wouldn't have been fast enough for anyone to see the smoke from the explosion. And judging by the clearness of the air, said explosion hadn't caught the surrounding forest on fire.

Derek needed to go take a closer look at the wreckage and see how to best prep them for when help arrived. He was a little surprised there'd been no sign of anyone yet.

He turned his body the other direction toward Becky. She slept, leaning against the rock, her face still slightly distressed despite her being unconscious. Surviving a plane crash would do that to a person. But he knew it was just as much the fact that she'd had to fix him up.

Despite everything, she couldn't stand the thought of causing him pain. It had been clear in every touch as she'd slipped his arm back in the socket and stitched his wound. If she could've taken the pain on herself, she would've.

The woman's soul was damned near as beautiful as her face, and that was saying something since Derek considered her the most gorgeous person on the planet.

It didn't surprise him in the slightest that Becky had chosen to be a vet. She wasn't shy like her mom, but she was gentle like Dr. Annie. Both women hated seeing pain in anyone. For Becky, especially animals.

Watching her lie there so vulnerable reminded him why he needed to keep his distance from this beautiful creature. Monsters and angels couldn't live together and survive unscathed. The monster would taint the angel. Bring her down with him and tarnish her forever.

His chest ached, heart hurting in an entirely different way from the rest of his body as he looked at Becky.

I want you to fight for me. To try to make this work.

She wanted him to stay.

In that moment, given that they were both sitting there

alive and relatively unharmed, he couldn't lie to himself and say that Becky hadn't given him a spark of hope in their argument.

She wanted to stay married to him.

But how could he stay after what he'd done? How could he make sure it didn't ever happen again?

Until he had the answer to that, nothing had changed.

He needed to check on the wreckage. Shifting slowly, he tried to move silently, but his shoulder threw him slightly off-balance. He slipped, and Becky's eyes opened. She startled, looking around like she didn't know where she was before her eyes settled on him once more, memories returning.

"How are you feeling? Are you okay? What are you doing?"

"I want to go see what is left. Was going to try not to wake you. You can rest."

She shook her head, getting up. "No, I'll come with you."

Together, they walked the distance to the plane and observed the wreckage. A few pieces were strewn here and there, but on the whole, the hull was still intact, if charred from the flames and the explosion. Heat still rose, and a few stray, weak flames dotted the ground.

But there wasn't nearly enough for Derek to determine what had gone wrong. Not unless he could dig into the wreckage, and he couldn't do that in the middle of the wilderness with an injured arm.

"Not enough to tell anything," he said quietly. "I didn't really expect there to be, but I'd hoped."

"What are you thinking?" Becky asked.

He shook his head, staring at the scorched hull and what remained of the plane. "One engine stalling? Not the worst thing in the world. It can happen for any number of reasons. It still doesn't make sense, but I could explain it. Both? I—" He turned to her. "Honestly, I can't explain that."

She wrapped her arms around herself, and hell if he didn't want to be the one wrapped around her instead. "What does that mean? The plane belongs to the Swanson ranch. I know Mr. Swanson—he takes the maintenance of stuff seriously. The plane should have been fine."

"It should have. I did the inspection. You saw me do it. Everything looked fine. Believe me, if there was anything wrong with the plane, even a scratch, I never would have let you on it. I wouldn't risk your life like that."

"I know."

The words were soft. Dangerous. The moment hung between them until Derek broke it, looking away. "I...I can't lie, though. I was distracted during everything because you were there. I hadn't expected to see you, and then you appeared like some kind of miracle and—" He hauled in a breath. "Maybe I missed something."

And if he did, it was his fault she'd almost died.

Again.

"Maybe you did," Becky said, stepping forward and taking his face in her hands. They were so close, too close. But he couldn't force himself away.

"Maybe you did miss something," she breathed. "But it doesn't matter."

"Doesn't matter? I almost got you killed."

"Derek, if anyone else had been piloting that plane, we'd both probably be dead right now. The only reason I'm alive is because you're a damn good pilot. I'm here because of you. So, no, I don't care if you missed something because you still saved my life."

He looked down at her, captured entirely by her gaze. "Thank you." He wasn't sure it was true, but he appreciated she wasn't blaming him.

He turned back toward the plane. "Maybe there's something here. Anything that can point us to why it happened. I'm not hopeful, but…"

"But we should look now while we have the best chance," she finished for him. "What am I looking for?"

He shook his head. "I have no idea, honestly. Just anything that seems out of place."

They walked around the plane, examining things together. None of the burned pieces they found raised any suspicions, nor did any of the exposed plane parts. But Derek was a pilot, not a mechanic. He knew enough to understand it shouldn't have happened, but not enough to identify a problem in the wreckage.

They wouldn't have answers until the cavalry arrived.

He looked up at the sky. He hadn't seen any planes flying over. It had been hours since the crash. Someone should've already been out looking for them already.

They weren't so far away from the coordinates Becky had read to air traffic control. If there were planes in the area, he and Becky would've heard them.

Becky watched him examine the sky. "Do they think we're dead?"

He shook his head. "No. Not yet. They'd still be cautiously optimistic. Definitely wouldn't give up without earnestly searching for us. My helitack crew will be in on it at this location. They would never assume a member of the team was dead."

They would search until they had proof one way or another. Especially in the early hours when it could make a difference between dying and surviving.

"Plus—" he guided Becky back around the wreckage to get free of it "—I've flown them in and out of all kinds of crazy situations over the past year. Planes and helicopters both."

"You get to fly both?"

He nodded. "It's one of the reasons I took the job. And

what made me a valuable commodity for them. I can switch between both easily."

"You love it."

"I do." He shrugged, hoping the admission wouldn't upset her. "My team...my *friends* won't assume I'm dead. I wouldn't give up on any of them, and they won't give up on me. We've got more flying to do together."

He glanced at Becky to find surprise on her face, and he grinned. "Why do you look shocked? Because of the flying?"

Becky shook her head. "No, of course not. You're an incredible pilot. Of course you love to fly, and of course they wanted someone with your skill. It's just...you've put down roots with the team. They're important to you."

He hadn't expected it, but his team meant a lot to him. "Yeah. They are."

Becky swallowed, and her gaze slid away. "I'm glad you've found that. It's...important."

He wasn't sure what to say. Obviously, the fact that he'd become tight with his team hurt her a little. He wanted to tell her the truth—that he hadn't been looking for any sort of camaraderie when he'd taken the job. He'd just wanted to be able to fly.

And to be near Becky. He couldn't tell her that, and hell, he hadn't even been truly aware of it himself, but part of the biggest reason why he'd taken the helitack job had been because of her. He'd told himself it was the opportunity to fly both helicopters and planes, that it was the adventure and the danger the helitack job afforded.

But really, it was that he'd wanted to be as close as possible to Becky without actually being near her.

They looked at each other for a long minute. She finally nodded. "Helitack has been good for you. I'm glad."

He wanted to say more, to try to explain some of the details he'd been processing in his mind. But a cold breeze reminded him of their current situation. The sun was sinking. Here in the mountains, the dark would come quickly, and the temperature would drop fast.

"We need to find some shelter," he said. "But not too far. When the rescue comes, they'll be looking for the plane."

"Yeah, okay." Becky turned away, and he hated the distance still between them. But nothing could be done about it now.

"Let's move everything over here." He pointed to a bigger rock outcropping a little uphill from their current location. It was a little more enclosed, with wider rocks. Less distance for them to defend if they needed to for whatever reason.

"Okay."

Becky packed up the first aid kit and hefted his backpack onto her shoulder. It wasn't small, containing everything he'd been intending to take back to the helitack team. He reached for it out of habit, and Becky batted away his hand. "Your shoulder is in no shape."

"I have two shoulders."

She rolled her eyes, but she was smiling. "It's like two hundred feet, Derek. I'm fine."

He followed her and watched her as she dug through the backpack, removing the emergency supplies he almost never traveled without. A tarp and a compact sleeping bag. Some granola bars. The tablets for purifying water, though that wouldn't likely be a problem out here. She worked with singular focus, and something settled in him.

Being near Becky always did that for him—settled him, made him calmer, made him closer to the person he longed to be.

Question was, would he ever have the same effect on her?

Chapter 17

A snapping twig woke Derek. He kept himself still, only the years of military training allowing him to do that, and listened further. Morning light slanted through the trees above them. He hadn't been asleep too long, drifting off after light had broken. Maybe an hour or two. Becky still slept on the ground a few feet away, curled inside the sleeping bag.

He winced as he took his arm out of the sling and gingerly rolled his shoulder. It was still swollen and hurt like a mother-fucker, but it was usable. Which was good because he had a feeling he was going to need it.

Scanning the end of the ravine and the trees beyond, Derek listened for the source of the sound that woke him. Nothing seemed amiss. No sense of presence or an animal creeping through the underbrush, and no further sounds to indicate movement.

But above the ravine, up the mountain, the sky was dark. Too dark for morning. The storm that had been on radar yesterday was closing in—and faster than what was good for them.

Where the hell were the flybys?

The Wyoming wilderness was so silent it wouldn't have mattered if he were sleeping. He would have heard a plane going overhead. The fact that there hadn't been anything? It wasn't good.

They should have seen something by now. Or heard from an attempted rescue. Air traffic control had their rough coordinates, and it had been nearly twenty-four hours since the crash.

But there had been nothing. That wasn't right.

And now, they needed to move, and that was not ideal. Staying here at the scene of the crash would be their best shot at rescue. Leaving meant it would be harder for the rescue team to find them.

But with a storm moving in, they didn't have a choice.

Maybe if they'd crashed above the ravine instead of inside, it would be different. But staying here during a storm wouldn't be safe. Flash flooding could happen too easily here.

Moving slowly so he didn't wake Becky, he stood and looked more carefully around the space they occupied. There were marks in the dirt that spoke of movement, and piles of leaves built up where water might pool and catch. Both the dirt and leaves were soft enough to have been exposed to recent water.

Water would enter this ravine in the storm, and they had no way of knowing how quickly or how much.

They needed to move now.

He looked up, examining the sheer walls. They needed to go away from the plane and up, even if they traveled temporarily in the direction of the storm. It would give them higher ground and keep them in possible sight of flyovers.

"Becky." He crouched down and touched her shoulder.

She startled awake, looking around, and he immediately stepped back. She was afraid of him being so close as she woke up. How could he blame her?

"Sorry."

She looked distressed. "No, it wasn't you. It just took me a minute to remember exactly where I was."

He doubted it. "We need to move away from this ravine. A storm is coming, and this place has all sorts of signs of flash flooding."

She looked around and rubbed the sleep from her eyes. "What about staying close to the plane?"

"I wanted to wait for a flyover, but there hasn't been one. We can't be trapped down here when the storm hits, and it's moving fast."

Her face was pale and subdued, but she nodded. "Okay."

She got out of the sleeping bag, and they loaded everything up. He grabbed his pack and lifted it onto his back.

"Are you sure you don't want me to carry it?" she asked.

Rain started trickling down on them.

"No. I'm used to it. And if we need to climb, I don't want the weight throwing you off."

Despite his worries about leaving the plane, moving felt good. Movement cleared his head, and his instincts told him this was the right thing to do. Granted, his instincts hadn't always served him, especially around Becky. But they were all he had.

The soft, skittering sound of wind rushing through leaves rose up above them, growing stronger. He looked up ahead into the clouds. The sky was darkening quickly. What were currently scattered drops of rain falling on them would be a downpour soon.

Last time he'd faced a storm that looked like this had ended with him nearly crashing the helicopter into a cliff. Getting out of this ravine right now was even more important.

He settled the pack more evenly on his shoulder and reached for Becky's hand. "Let's go."

"We're probably okay, right?" she said, not pulling away from him. "It still looks like it's pretty far away."

He shook his head. "It's moving faster than it seems."

"Do you think we'll need to get all the way to the other end in order to find a way up?"

"Hope not."

But it might be their only option. Right now, the walls stretched twenty to thirty feet above them and were too smooth to climb without equipment. If they had actual rope and anchors, it would be a different story.

Around them, the temperature was dropping and the rain becoming steadier. They needed to get to higher ground.

"Start looking for anywhere you think you'll be able to climb," he said.

"Okay."

He was moving faster and knew his longer legs would make Becky rush to keep up. The knowledge their situation could change at any moment kept him from slowing down.

It didn't take long to realize they were going in the wrong direction. The walls were only growing higher as they headed uphill and toward the bigger mountains. The surface of the ravine walls here was rougher, but every extra foot was another foot they'd have to climb.

Rain began to splatter on them in earnest.

"Holy shit," Becky said. "You were right. It is moving fast."

Being right didn't make him feel better. There were no good places to climb here, and without the gear they needed, the rain made it so much harder.

He turned and looked at her, letting go of her hand. "How are you holding up?"

"I'm fine."

"If there's anything wrong or hurting, I need to know right now, in case I need to—"

She poked him in the chest with a single finger. "I'm fine. You're the one injured. We need to get out of here, so let's go."

Thunder cracked overhead, earsplittingly loud. The rain fell harder. Shit. He nodded at her. "Okay. Faster."

He began to jog, Becky right behind him. There had to be somewhere for them to get out. Already, the floor of the ravine was slick with the rain, and rivulets ran in patterns too well established to give him comfort.

"What about that?" Becky raised her voice to be heard over the rain.

A fallen tree hung over the edge of the ravine. Some branches hung lower, still too high for them to reach without climbing. Plus, no guarantees the tree would hold their weight.

"If we have no other choice, we'll come back," Derek said.

Water splashed under his feet, the rain falling harder. The ominous black clouds were now directly overhead. Living in Wyoming most of their lives, both he and Becky knew how ugly these types of storms could get.

Being caught outside in one was not where anyone would choose to be.

Light flashed, followed by thunder almost immediately. His foot slipped on wet stone, and he barely caught himself.

"Derek," Becky called. "Are you okay?"

"Yeah."

Come on. He begged the universe. *Give us something.* They couldn't have crashed in the only ravine in the Tetons where there was nowhere to fucking climb.

They kept running forward, as much as the wind and precarious footing would allow. Water was now coming up to their ankles. This place would potentially be filled with water —past their heads—in the next thirty minutes. And even if they didn't drown, it wouldn't take long for hypothermia to set in if they were soaked and exposed to the elements for a long period.

A cutoff from the main section of the ravine caught Derek's attention. The crevice was narrow, but the ground in it was a little higher—it would get them out of the water. He had to take off the backpack and twist sideways to squeeze through the opening.

He turned to make sure Becky made it through, and thunder hit again. Like the sound was a signal, the rain poured. The kind of rain that fell straight down. Brutal, stinging the skin and soaking through their clothes as they made their way through the crevice. So much for staying dry.

As they made it back out the other side of the crevice, Becky reached for him and pointed. "Derek, look."

Through the downpour and darkened sky, a cluster of boulders was visible. Not high enough to get them out, but it was at least higher ground. It was this or try to go back and take their chances at the other end, and he already knew climbing those walls would be impossible now.

Grabbing her hand, he pulled Becky along to the boulders, yelling over the storm on the way. "I'll go first to find the path and help you if you need it!"

"Give me the bag," she called, blinking away the water. "You need your balance and your hands."

His hesitation was momentary. She wasn't wrong. He passed her the pack and started to climb carefully. Moss covered the rocks and made the surfaces slicker than they would normally be. More than once, he almost fell picking out the safest path for them.

Becky was right behind him, following where he stepped and placed his hands, once he'd determined them as safe. Water seeped through the cracks in the rocks like small water-falls, making purchase even more treacherous. More than once, he stopped and turned to Becky, taking the backpack from her as she made it through a difficult patch.

They reached a fallen tree wedged so tightly between two

rocks, it looked like it had been there for years. He couldn't see what was on the other side, but they were climbing, and higher gave them a better chance.

Another lightning strike, followed by thunder that shook the earth. The rain fell so heavily he had to blink away the water from his eyes. More and more water flowed from the rocks, more than there should be. Almost there. He grabbed a branch and hauled himself upward, the wood straining with his weight.

They were almost out of the ravine and no longer in danger of flash flood, but that didn't mean they were out of danger. They needed shelter from this storm.

Barely over the top of the tree, he spotted an outcropping of rock that looked like it could fit the both of them beneath it and protect them from some of the elements. Not ideal, but waiting out the storm there would be better than being exposed.

Derek realized his mistake immediately. One more pull upward showed him what was behind the boulders and tree: water.

A buildup of water that seeped through the rocks and drained when something wasn't pouring into it, like the current storm. And the only reason it was contained was because it had settled perfectly, without any extra weight on it. Like his weight.

The tree shifted, and he moved, turning and reaching. "Becky."

It was too late.

The wood gave way, water sweeping through the gap and slamming into both of them. He grabbed Becky, scrambling for purchase on the rocks and just managing to wedge his foot into a crevice.

Fuck.

It hurt, and he didn't care. Becky's hand was in his, water

crushing her. It was all he could do to hold on to her. She pushed with her legs, keeping her head above water, but her body wasn't moving. "Derek," she gasped. "I'm stuck."

Now stable, he pulled. She cried out and didn't move. The sound crashed into his head, so familiar, so brutal. Darkness and her blood on his hands, crying and fear.

He ground his teeth together. Not now. Not fucking now.

If he lost his mind to the darkness of the past right now, Becky wouldn't make it.

Lightning blinded him momentarily, but it also illuminated them both in the dimness. Becky wasn't stuck. It was the backpack, wedged between two rocks where she'd fallen.

"It's the bag," he shouted. "I'm not going to let you go. Get one arm out of it if you can and let it drop."

"We need it."

Derek tightened his grip on her. Her skin was slick, and he could only fight the force of water and the stuck backpack for so long. Enough water poured through the crack that if they let go, they'd be swept away, possibly trapped against the rocks at the other end to be drowned.

"It's you or the bag, Button, and I'm not letting you go."

He saw the shift in her gaze, from fear to determination. Becky firmed her grip on his hand and turned, trying to find a place for her feet while twisting one arm out of the strap. As soon as she was free, she switched her hands, and he hauled her up and away from the water.

They still had to get to the outcropping, or they would never survive this. Tingling on the back of his neck made him shiver. The crack of lightning was physical, the sound and noise so loud, he felt deaf. But he didn't look around for the strike.

He pushed Becky in front of him, making sure she couldn't fall again. "There."

Becky saw the outcropping and crawled toward it. The

flow was ebbing just enough to allow them over the tree and along the boulders to the little space of bare rock that was their salvation.

Barely big enough for the two of them together, it would work. High enough the water wouldn't reach them, and deep enough to shield them from the worst of the rain.

Together, they collapsed on the stone, pressing their backs to the wall, heaving in breaths.

"The bag," she said. "That had everything we need."

"The bag is replaceable. You're not."

"What are we going to do without it?" The question wasn't an accusation; it was borne of genuine fear. He heard it in her voice.

If he was honest with her? He had no idea.

"Let's just make it through the storm," he said. "We'll figure it out."

Another crash of thunder shook the world around them, and Becky pulled her knees up to her chest. Derek closed his eyes and tried to calm his racing mind and heart.

They would figure it out.

Chapter 18

Becky didn't know how long it took for the storm to pass. It was at least a couple of hours. Watching water rush through where they'd been walking just a few minutes ago was a sight she couldn't look away from.

If they hadn't gotten out when they did, they wouldn't have made it at all.

She thought the water would run out of the ravine somewhere, but it didn't. Water poured into the crevice from above, racing down the mountain. It fell over the edge of their hiding place, nearly concealing them from the world. Like being behind a small and violent waterfall.

When a break in the rain came, it was too quiet. After hours of echoing noise, Becky felt as if she'd just gotten off the small plane all over again. The world felt fresh and new, even though it had tried to kill them.

Everything was lighter, and peeking out from the rocks showed the bulk of the storm moving away now. Tension she'd been holding in her body eased and left her even more exhausted. "Do you think we're in the clear?"

Derek's eyes fixed on the sky as well. "For now? Yes. But not for long."

"God, I could go back to sleep for a hundred years."

"Me too." He gave a choked laugh. "But we can't stay here."

She was thankful their little outcropping had kept them from drowning, but she definitely was ready to leave. Although… "Where do we go?"

He sighed. "Let's start with getting the hell out of the ravine. Then we'll deal with the next steps."

They picked their way back across the rocks to where they could see down the ravine to the plane. Water still filled the lower section, the thin hole in the rocks they'd seen now blocked by the fuselage. The backpack was nowhere to be found.

Becky shivered and wrapped her arms around herself. Whatever they did, they needed to get dry sooner than later. It was still early in the day, but once night fell, if they were still soaked through like this, their chances of surviving dropped significantly.

Derek was quiet as he helped her toward the top of the ravine on a barely climbable path. She almost fell a few times and had to rely on Derek more than she would've liked, given his injuries. Her palms were scraped, and her fingers ached when Derek pulled her over the final edge.

Her whole body hurt. She was in decent shape, but she liked to think anyone who survived a plane crash and a full day in the wilderness would be exhausted.

Derek, on the other hand, seemed fine. If she hadn't patched him up herself, she wouldn't even have known he'd been injured. He was focused, intently concentrating on their surroundings.

He looked up at the sky with a frown. "I don't like it."

"Don't like what?"

"That no one has come for us. The storm would have slowed things down, of course, but we should've seen someone by now."

She pressed a hand to her stomach, fighting against the hollow sensation there. "Are you sure? What about the storm? Or maybe they're looking and just have the wrong location? We did veer pretty far off after we talked to air traffic control."

Derek continued to look at the sky. "No. As soon as we broke contact, they should have put things in motion. Even if they weren't close, we would have heard a flyby. It's not right."

"Okay, so what are the odds they come now after a full day?"

"I want to say they're good, but my instincts tell me something's wrong. Helitack should be all over this, especially with me out here. If they're not?" He let the question hang in the air. "I don't know exactly what's going on, but we're going to have to handle things ourselves."

"How?" It wasn't raining now, but more storms were rolling in. And their bag with their few supplies was gone, probably buried underwater. "We're wet, and it's going to get colder. We have no shelter. No food or supplies."

"First, let's get some distance from here." He extended a hand and helped her up. "Climb higher, see what we can see and figure out a plan."

She didn't have arguments against that.

Derek turned and started up the hill. He knew what he was doing. She wasn't going to question it.

Two hours later, she was a lot closer to questioning it.

The day was passing, and they were seemingly no closer to getting somewhere they could sleep. Or have food. Her skin was irritated from hiking in damp clothes, and her body still ached.

Up ahead, Derek froze, momentarily ducking down to check out something on the ground that looked out of place.

Sort of like someone had dumped cranberry sauce on the ground.

"Here," he said with a grin, moving quickly to a bush. "Huckleberries. Not much, but it's something."

By the time she reached where he was standing, Derek had a handful to give her.

"Oh, thank you." She took the fruit he offered, and then they both ate more, pretty much stripping the bush of the little, dark berries. The fruit was like someone had shoved a raspberry and a blueberry together and, honestly, was the most delicious thing she'd ever tasted.

Derek had juice dripping down his chin, and she laughed. "You've got something here." She tapped her own chin.

"Yeah?" He smiled, and his teeth were colored with the juice, and it only made her laugh more. She was sure she looked identical. He nodded. "You look a little like a serial killer yourself."

Bending over, she let her torso hang forward to stretch her back. "I'll own that. Depending on who we meet out here and how hungry I am, I might turn into one."

Derek chuckled, and Becky smiled. This felt more like old times, when she and Derek had been free and easy and there wasn't nearly as much...angst between them. "How did you find these?"

"Back there was a pile of bear scat that had huckleberries in it. Knew there'd be some close by."

She made a face. Scat wasn't something she wanted to think about. But the berries took the edge off her hunger, so bring on the poop.

Why did Derek feel so different right now? The contrast between yesterday—and all the days before that—and today was shocking. He seemed far more at ease and relaxed. Which was strange, considering the chances they were going to die rose with each passing hour.

"Let's keep going," he finally said.

She began to follow him again, but her mind kept working on the problem. What was different? Being in the wilderness didn't seem like the answer. Derek enjoyed the outdoors, but he wasn't one to go out and spend long weekends camping.

Even the way he moved seemed filled with energy. Less weighed down.

Then it hit her.

Out here, Derek had no choice but to use all of his mental and physical energy to keep them both alive and safe, instead of dwelling on the past. He was so busy making sure they survived that he was forgetting to hate himself for a few hours.

And as soon as they got back to civilization, he would disappear into the dark void in his mind and not want to talk about it at all. He would go back to running and avoiding, and the thought devastated her.

There were things they needed to talk about. And now, while they were stranded, though the setting wasn't ideal, was the best time to do it.

Derek would focus his efforts on getting them home, and Becky would focus her efforts on getting this mountain-sized elephant out from between them. He wasn't going to do it, so she had to. It was long overdue.

They climbed up a little crest of rocks, and there was a break in the trees. Above them, the sky was visible, and the surrounding area spread out around them like a lush blanket. Derek looked around, face hopeful.

Was this a better place to be rescued?

Sure, they were more visible, but with more weather on the way and the temperature dropping as evening came, it wasn't likely.

"This is much better," he said. "I can actually get a look at where we are now."

"Oh," she said. Looking around didn't help her at all. All she could see were trees and rocks.

He chuckled. "You thought I was dragging you all over the place for nothing?"

"No." She made a face. "Well, maybe."

"I've studied maps of this area extensively for helitack. There." He pointed, and Becky stepped up beside him. A river nestled in one of the lower areas they'd crossed snaked through the foothills. "See that bend?"

"Yes." She couldn't tell how far away it was. Maybe a mile? Estimating distances wasn't a strength she had.

Derek dropped his hand. "There's a registered hunting cabin there. We've actually sent lost hikers to that location before. It will have supplies and a radio."

Thank God. "That sounds great to me."

Becky's stomach growled at the same time thunder sounded from over the mountain. She'd been ignoring the way the sky had darkened ahead of them, trusting Derek to get them where they needed to go. She'd trusted him before he'd pointed out that cabin.

She *trusted* him. She wished she could make him understand that.

"Want to get the hell out of here?" He gave her a smile that made her heart want to beat out of her chest.

"Yes, please."

They started the trek back down the hill. At least it wasn't too far this time. Having a destination made hiking seem easier.

Around them, the wind picked up, whistling through the trees. Where her clothes were still wet, the wind tore through the fabric, and she shivered. She looked up, and what was left of the warmth in her body disappeared.

Black clouds billowed over the peak, spreading over them like a twisted form of déjà vu. "Derek."

He looked and swore. "I see it. Keep going. We'll be there soon."

Soon wasn't soon enough.

The sound reached them first. Like rain amplified. But there was no water, only ice. *Hail.* Of course it would fucking hail. Everything else for the past day had tried to kill them. Why not this too?

"Come on," Derek called over the coming sound. He grabbed her hand, and they ran. It was too fast, and she almost fell what felt like a hundred times while the sting of hail pelted down on her.

They slogged through the river, thunder once again shaking the air around them. Thankfully, it was shallow enough to move through. She was already so cold and wet it didn't make a difference now. And finally, there ahead of them, was the cabin.

Small and unassuming, it was the most beautiful thing Becky had ever seen.

Derek burst through the door, and she followed, slamming it behind them to keep out the weather. It was dark in the small space, but they were at least out of the bruising ice outside. "Is there power out here?"

"No," he said. "But they'll have extra batteries for the radio and plenty of firewood. You know how seriously people take hunters' cabins around here."

Keeping them supplied was crucial—you were in charge of replacing whatever you used. That way, the next person who came in also had better chances of survival.

"Okay." She leaned against the door, hardly able to move. Now that she was inside, every bit of energy she had was disappearing. If she didn't move soon, she would fall asleep right here.

"I'm going to get the fire going," Derek said. "The food should be in those cabinets." He pointed to a kitchen in the

165

corner, complete with an old-fashioned potbelly stove and cabinets.

A couch and armchair sat in front of a large fireplace in the other corner, and a huge, soft rug filled that space. It was begging to be stretched out on. But all Becky could think about was food and warmth. They needed to get out of these clothes before the cold fully settled in them and made them sick.

She went through the cabinets, seizing on the first quickly edible thing—meal bars. A groan burst out of her when she took a bite. Never in her life had a nutritional bar tasted this good. She took one over to where Derek sat in front of a desk, messing with the radio.

"Thanks." He set the bar on the desk and moved the dial a little more. "Mayday, mayday, mayday, this is Derek Bollinger, pilot of Cessna one-two-six-five-zero en route to Swanson Valley Ranch. The plane went down, and we need immediate assistance. Over."

"Mayday?" she asked quietly.

He shrugged. "Since we were flying a plane. There's not a universal ground emergency call, and the firefighter call doesn't apply here."

Fair point.

Derek started to repeat the spiel one more time, and Becky went over to the fireplace. If there was one good thing about growing up with a bunch of men who taught survival skills, it was that she knew how to build a fire. Wood and kindling were stacked nearby, along with matches. It took no time at all for her to get a small fire going and add logs for it to grow.

"Over," Derek finished for the third time.

The radio crackled. "Holy fuck, am I glad to hear your voice. Over."

"Sam?" Derek said. "Same, buddy. Over."

"Give me your status," Sam said. "Becky's with you?"

Derek glanced over at her, smiling briefly. "She is. We're

both okay. A little worse for wear, but no injuries. Double engine failure on the Cessna and crashed in a ravine. Storms made it difficult, but we're at the hunting cabin by the Yellowstone River, south of Hawk's Rest Peak. Over."

A crackling silence followed. "Double engine failure? Over."

"Correct. I have no explanation for it, and given where we landed, plus the weather, I'm not optimistic about recovering much. Over."

Becky could almost feel the shock rolling through the radio. "Well, we're all glad you guys are safe. It's a good thing you made it to the cabin. The storm system we're facing is a mess, and we're grounded for safety reasons. Since you guys are safe and uninjured, I can't push through that. Over."

"Not a problem. Over."

"Based on satellite, I'm guessing it will be about thirty-six hours until we can get to you. You have enough supplies?"

Derek looked at her, and she nodded. There was definitely enough food for that amount of time. "Yeah, we're good, Sam. Thank you. Over."

"Stay safe, and stay warm. Radio if your circumstances change. Over."

"We will. Over and out." Derek slumped back in the chair and leaned his head back, relief clear on his features. Then he picked up the nutrition bar and began to eat it.

Becky crossed over to the stuff piled in the corner. There was a stack of blankets. Perfect.

She started to undress and lay her clothes out on the floor. She and Derek needed to be closer to the fire than the clothes right now, but tomorrow, they could make sure their clothes were fully dried.

Every single thing she wore came off, and she wrapped herself in one of the blankets like a big towel. Grabbing two more blankets, she tossed one on the rug in front of the fire and took the other one to Derek. "Here."

He looked over, blue eyes slowly tracking up her body. Becky tried very hard not to react to the way he looked at her. It was rare to get such an unguarded look from him, so she savored it and pretended she didn't.

"You need to dry your clothes." She nodded toward her own. "It'll be warmer."

Derek swallowed and nodded. "Right."

Resisting the temptation to watch him undress, Becky went over and lay down in front of the growing flames. The second blanket and the softness of the rug more than made up for the fact that she was on the floor. The heat felt so good.

Amazing how her body had convinced her she was fine until she felt this. Now it was like she'd never experienced heat before. Her whole body shuddered.

Soft footsteps crossed the floor behind her, and then she heard the shuffling of a blanket. Derek didn't touch her, but he was close.

So close, and so far.

Now warm, now safe, she couldn't resist the sleep that was rising to claim her like a tide. "Derek," she said. "I'm glad you're the one out here with me."

Becky fell asleep before she heard his answer.

Chapter 19

Becky was in his arms.

It was still light outside—barely, so by his guess, it had been a couple of hours since they'd settled by the fire. Derek hadn't slept, and he had no intention of sleeping. Not while Becky was next to him.

She hadn't had that same problem. She'd fallen asleep almost instantly, and as if she was drawn to him like a magnet, she'd turned over and slipped into his arms moments later.

He felt like he could snap, his body was so stiff. The temptation to close his eyes was way too strong, so he forced himself to think about the map of the area and tried to recite the mountain peaks in alphabetical order to keep his mind active and in the present.

Not in the past with blood on his hands. Becky sobbing on the floor, staring up at him in horror. Like he was a monster.

"Fuck," he muttered.

There didn't seem to be any way out of the nightmare. If he fell asleep beside her, he risked reliving the worst memory of his life, but even awake, he couldn't stop reliving it.

He must have tightened his hold on her, because she

stirred, her eyes opening. He watched her realize how they were positioned, but neither of them moved. Her throat bobbed as she swallowed. "How long have we been out?"

"A couple of hours."

Her eyes narrowed, and she looked at him. Really looked at him. In his darkest moments, when he couldn't shove logic or longing aside, he'd imagined her looking at him like that. Like she knew who he really was, accepted that, and wanted to be there in his arms.

Then anger grew in her brown eyes. "You haven't slept at all, have you? Because you were next to me."

"It's fine, Becky. I'm all right."

"The hell you are. You were actually hurt in the crash. I know you're okay, but I still had to help haul your body out of there. You need sleep even more than I do."

He wasn't going to have this argument. She needed the rest, and if she wasn't going to do that while he was beside her, he'd sit over in one of the chairs.

But when he went to move, Becky's hand snapped down on his wrist. "Where are you going?"

"I'll sit in the chair, so you can get some rest."

Something between a sigh and a hiss came out of her. "Of course you will. Running. Again. I thought out here you might actually be distracted enough to talk about this."

Derek pulled on his hand, but she didn't let go. He pulled again, and still, she held on with strength he didn't anticipate. When had that happened? One final pull released him, but he stopped trying to move away.

"I don't trust myself, Becky. I don't, and you shouldn't either. For good reason."

She groaned and rolled onto her back, covering her face with her hands. "That's it, huh? No discussion, no figuring out a way through it. You just decided you weren't trustworthy and decided to cling to the feeling like a life raft."

Anger and shame surged through him. Now he did move away, standing so he could pace off the energy. "A life raft? I don't deserve a fucking life raft. I deserve to drown. I *beat* you, Becky. On our wedding night. I woke up with your blood on my hands and your eyes proving to me I'm a monster. I can't be trusted."

Becky sat up, her body haloed by the fire, giving her an almost unearthly look. "I never blamed you for what happened. But you didn't stay long enough for me to tell you, and you never asked."

"You should blame me."

"For fuck's sake." She struggled to her feet, momentarily caught in her blanket. "Do you remember when we were seventeen? You and I were on a date, and I shut the car door on your hand? Do you blame me for that?"

He rolled his eyes. "That's not even remotely the same."

"Why not?"

"I didn't end up in the hospital because you shut the door on my hand, Becky," he roared, the sound filling the cabin.

"It's not about what I did when I shut the door on your hand, or what happened when you woke up from a nightmare. It's how it was *intended*. Did I mean to shut your hand in the door?"

Derek said nothing. Obviously, she hadn't, and he knew the point she was making. He hadn't meant to hit her; therefore, she didn't blame him.

But it had been so much more than that. He hadn't even recognized her that night. His brain had thought she was an enemy to be eliminated.

They were both extremely lucky he had stopped at all.

She stared at him, more strength in her eyes and body than he ever remembered seeing. And somewhere, in the part of his mind he'd shut down, he loved it.

"If you were still in the military and your commanding officer ordered you to hurt me, would you do it?"

He scoffed. "Of course not."

"If someone put a gun to your head, would you hurt me?"

"No."

"Exactly. What happened on our wedding night was an accident, Derek. Just like my closing the door on your fingers was an accident. I know one impacted you more than the other, and I know you're terrified it's going to happen again. But what you don't seem to realize is I'm still your wife, and you won't even talk to me about this. Do you honestly think you're the first veteran to mistake a loved one for an enemy?"

"You think that makes it better?" he spat. "Because I'm not alone in abusing you, I should feel less guilty?"

"Say you *abused me* again, and I will slap you." Her tone was matter-of-fact. "A mistake is not abuse. You didn't pin me down and punch me repeatedly while I begged you to stop. You woke up with your mind confused and trapped in hell and had a reasonable reaction."

"Reasonable? What sort of reasonable reaction?"

"To protect yourself. The second you realized the situation wasn't as your brain had interpreted, you stopped."

"After I'd broken your nose and was choking you." The thought ate him alive. "I'm a monster."

"I saw the shift, Derek. I saw you recognize me and come back. That alone is what makes you not a monster. Why can't you see it?"

He shook his head. "It doesn't matter because it can still happen again."

"You're right, but here's the thing. You haven't spoken to me long enough to know that I'm not the same woman I was a year and a half ago." She crossed the room, dropping the blanket and walking toward where their clothes were drying. He looked away. They were married, but he didn't have the right. "I've done the hard work that was required after that night. I worked through both the fear I had and the pain of recovery."

He scrubbed a hand down his face. "I'm sorry you had to do that at all."

If there were anywhere else for him to go right now, he would.

"Actually, working through those wasn't as difficult as working through the fact that you abandoned me."

What? "I didn't—"

"You did," she said. Her voice told him she'd turned back toward him, and he looked. She was in her bra and underwear now, but it didn't look like she was going to dress further. "You left to protect me. I know that. But that's not the way it felt. It felt like my husband abandoned me and left me to deal with the scariest night of my life alone."

He pulled on his own boxer briefs so he could move around without the blanket he, too, wore around his body. Her words ripped at him.

"I'm sorry for that too."

"Don't be. Because in the middle of all of it, I started training with Lilah."

Derek spun back to her. "What sort of training?"

She looked at him with one eyebrow raised. "Self-defense. Hand-to-hand close-quarters combat. MMA."

He stared at her, trying to wrap his head around his petite wife...*sparring*.

"I started training with Lilah a month after you left, and I never stopped. I've gotten good, and I want to show you."

"Are you serious?"

"Yes."

"You want us to fight?"

"Yes."

She could not seriously be asking him to *strike* her. There was no way in hell. "I'm not going to do that, Becky."

She came to him, standing only inches from his body. His fingers itched to grip her hips, but he forced the urge down.

"You know why I started training with Lilah? Because I felt out of control. I hadn't been able to do anything to defend myself that night, and I didn't want to feel like that ever again."

"I don't blame you."

"I know you don't. You blame yourself for making me feel that way."

"Yes." Because it was his fault.

"It took me a while to realize I wasn't just doing all the work with Lilah to make myself feel better. I was doing it for you too."

He blinked out at her. "For me?"

"I thought it would make you feel better. I wouldn't be a defenseless woman you had to protect, I would be able to protect myself and fight back if anything like that night happened again."

"And what if you fighting back makes it worse?" He growled. "If it makes me think you're more of a threat and I kill you?"

Becky reached up and grabbed his face with both hands and made him look at her. The brown eyes he loved so much were full of desperation and determination. "I see you, Derek Bollinger, and I am not afraid."

The words were everything he'd wanted to hear from her, but still, he couldn't accept them.

"Do you hear me?" she whispered, a shine of tears in her eyes. "I am not afraid of you."

"I am." He took a step back.

"I know. Which is why I'm going to show you I'm not made of glass. I'm strong. Strong enough to stand by your side.

You've been through hell, and you have scars—emotionally, mentally, physically. Before our wedding night, we tried to pretend they weren't really there. That was a mistake."

"Obviously, since you ended up in the hospital."

She rolled her eyes but kept going. "We thought it would go away if we ignored it. We were wrong. Then you've been ignoring it again by running away from us."

"Button—"

"The one thing I won't do is accept your absence from my life because of what happened eighteen months ago. The people we were then and the people we are now are not the same. We have a day and a half in this cabin, and for better or for worse, we are going to break through this wall between us by the time we leave."

Derek acknowledged the fear coursing through him. Both the fear of hurting her again and the fear of losing her. There was a reason he hadn't let Lincoln go through with dissolving the marriage. A reason he was living an hour from Oak Creek. Becky Mackay was the love of his life, and it wasn't going to change.

If he'd wanted to disappear, he could have.

But he hadn't.

She was right; he had to face that.

"Now, fight me," she said quietly.

Chapter 20

Derek stared at her. Fight her? There was no way in hell. "No."

She took a step back and threw her arms wide. "This is the only way to show you what I'm talking about."

He took a step back. "How about you use words instead?"

"No." She crossed her arms over her chest, reminding him they were both standing there in their underwear. "I've known you my whole life, Derek Bollinger. Words have never been the best way to convince you of something. You're a man of action."

"And fighting is the way to convince me of what, exactly?"

"That I want you. That I want us. I wouldn't have struggled and trudged through all of this if I wanted to divorce you. I wouldn't have waited for you to come back."

Turning away from her, he pulled on the back of his neck. She made a good point. At any time in the last eighteen months, she could have dumped him. He'd been hard to find, but if she'd sent divorce papers to his command or tried to eliminate the marriage, there were ways.

"I'm still not going to hit you, Becky. That's not the way to solve this."

"You're not going to hit me," she said mildly. "You're going to *try* to hit me."

"Still." No way in hell.

She huffed out a sigh. "Fine. Baby steps. Don't 'hit' hit me. We'll do some self-defense drills. You know them, we all know them. Try to grab me, and I'll show you exactly what I can do. Then maybe you'll see I can spar with you without getting my ass handed to me."

He turned back toward her. She was definitely serious. Could he do this? Given his wounds, in this situation, he'd be the only one in any pain. That was an outcome he could live with. "I still don't know what this is going to prove. You're sure you want to do this?"

"No." She let out a dramatic sigh while rolling her eyes. "I'm begging you to do this when we both could be sleeping by the very nice fire I built because I'm unsure."

Derek smiled in spite of himself. God, he'd missed her. More than he would ever let himself say to anyone. This fire-cracker of a woman was perfect for him. She always would be, no matter what happened between them now.

"Okay," he said. "We'll try."

"You want me to put down a blanket?" she asked. "Or some cushions from the couch for when you hit the ground?"

He raised an eyebrow. "You're so sure you're going to take me down?"

Becky said nothing, just waited for the answer to her question.

"Let's put down a blanket," he said. "Because I don't want either of us getting splinters from this floor."

"You're the only one getting splinters," she muttered under her breath.

"What?"

She just smiled while she pulled another blanket from the pile and spread it on the floor.

"Nothing, nothing." Then she stood and turned her back to him. "Okay. Whenever you're ready."

He took a second to look at her. Doing this while she was in nothing but underwear wasn't exactly going to help his focus. Then again, it was Becky. Just being around her hurt his focus. He was so *aware* of her—every move and every breath.

It wasn't the desire to fight her that drove him forward; it was the impulse to hold her, even if he was playing the aggressor. Right now, he was completely in control of himself and posed no danger to her.

Stepping forward, he threw his arms around her roughly, the way instructors who were playing an attacker would in a self-defense class. Nothing about the move would hurt her. If she got tired of trying to break his hold, he'd be able to let her go immediately.

His arms had barely made it around her when she moved faster than he'd expected, shoving her hips back to put him off-balance. A split second later, she'd used all of his and her momentum to toss him over her shoulder. His back hit the blanket, breath going out of his chest.

Shit.

Becky looked down on him from above. He expected a smug grin on her face, but there was none. She simply extended her hand to him to help him up. "Want to try again?"

"I think you've made your point."

"I haven't even begun to make my point. That was a basic move that our dads all taught us when we were kids. If we stop right now, it'll defeat the purpose."

"And what exactly is the purpose?"

"Less talk, more action, Bollinger. We need to work up to the stuff you think I can't do."

"You think I think you can't do this?"

"I think you're treating this as a training exercise. You're coming at me like an instructor would someone in a beginner's class, slow and clunky to help build confidence."

He got back onto his feet. "And that's not what you want."

"We both know that's not how real fighting works. We both know that a few hours in a self-defense class will help someone in a dangerous situation to a degree, but it won't do much against a trained fighter. Won't do much against someone like you if you came at me in your sleep."

"All right," he said slowly. "I'll spar with you."

"Really?"

"I'm…" He struggled for the words. "I'm not going to hit you. I can't."

"Derek." Becky stood in front of him again, such trust and love in her eyes. He deserved none of it. "I'm not asking you to clock me in the face while I'm defenseless. I'm not asking you to hit me at all. I'm asking you to let me show you that if someone's coming at me, even if that person is you, I can handle it."

She raised her hand and placed it lightly over his heart. "It's good that you don't want to hurt me. But it's also important you understand that I'm not as fragile as when you left."

It was impossible to make her understand the image of her that constantly battled for dominance in his head. Her on that hotel floor, blood streaming from her face, blinking up at him in confusion and terror.

"Stop," she whispered. "We're not there. Stay here with me. This moment is the most important, not what happened in the past."

"How do you want to do this?" he finally asked.

She thought about it carefully, and Derek appreciated it. This was hard enough, and her putting thought into every second helped him.

"My first question," she said, "is if you need me to hold back with you? I know you'll be holding back with me, regardless."

It wasn't the statement he was expecting. He couldn't help his raised eyebrow. She was right—there was no way he'd be coming at her full force. But her having to hold back with *him*? Not necessary.

He shook his head. "You don't need to hold back."

"Okay, then let's do a modified version of what we just did. You try to take me down, and I'm not going to let you. Can you do that? We'll escalate from there."

Derek nodded once. He wasn't attacking her if all he was trying to do was take her to the floor. "Yes."

"Okay. Then let's do it."

Chapter 21

Watching Derek struggle wasn't Becky's favorite thing to do. But it was the furthest they'd come. Something cracked open, and he was listening. She couldn't let up, or it would all slip away.

Stepping back onto the blanket, she squared up across from Derek, a sense of rightness settling over her. She wasn't sure she'd even realized it until that moment, but *this* was what she'd been waiting for since she'd started sparring with Lilah.

Yes, the goal had been to learn how to protect herself, especially early on. To give her confidence in case she ever found herself in a situation again where she needed to be able to fight her way out long enough to get away.

But she'd passed that stage long ago.

It had never occurred to Becky to stop after that. She'd wanted to keep learning, keep doing, keep becoming more competent.

She hadn't just wanted to know how to survive; she'd wanted to know how to *kick ass*. Hadn't realized it was all for this moment.

To prove to Derek that she was strong enough to take on

his demons. She hadn't been eighteen months ago, but she was now.

Moreover, to prove it to *herself*.

This was going to be a moment that changed everything, one way or another.

Derek stepped farther onto the blanket, and she still saw his hesitancy. He didn't want to fight her. But he was willing, and that was all that mattered.

Her mind shifted, and she lowered her body a little, allowing for more balance. Derek's stance changed as well, awareness crackling through the room. The man across from her no longer regarded her as Becky, but as an opponent. She knew he would never intentionally hurt her, but she wondered as they circled each other if this was what it was like to be his target.

When someone was in his crosshairs, did they feel a shiver on the back of their neck?

Stepping toward her, he reached, a move she easily slapped away. He wasn't really trying yet. That was fine. He needed to work up to it. Then came a couple more very mild attempts to touch her, which she dodged and avoided.

Finally, he moved. *Really* moved. And he was so fucking fast. Derek's arms came around her waist, the momentum meaning to carry her off her feet and onto the floor.

This was something she and Lilah had practiced since it was common for larger opponents to attempt to use brute strength when first attacking. Men, in particular, reverted to that.

So they'd worked for weeks on how to get out of holds or avoid them to begin with. That was what Becky did now, moving with Derek so he couldn't wrap her in a restraining hold. She immediately took the extra second the movement gave her to bring her elbow into his jaw with a crack.

He released her immediately, and she put distance between

them and took up her ready stance once more. Derek rubbed his jaw before turning to look at her. Surprise had replaced worry in his blue eyes as he took up his own fighting stance again.

They moved together, circling each other.

Once again, Derek moved lightning-fast, catching her wrist and spinning her, trying to pin her against his body. But once again, she used momentum and continued the spin, hooking one leg around his calf, getting away before he could restrain her.

She could have thrown her head backward instead, but she didn't want to break his nose. A fountain of blood wasn't helpful in the middle of an exercise meant to help him let go of the memory of her blood.

They continued with him on the offensive, attempting different moves and means of attack. Most blows, she was able to block before they connected. The ones she did take, she quickly recovered from and offered her own blows in return.

It wasn't long until he was barely holding back, his attempts growing more forceful as both his mind and body learned the truth: Becky could handle him.

She wasn't even overthinking it or trying to show off. She was merely relying on training she'd put herself through week in and week out for the past year. At this point, a lot of it was muscle memory combined with the way Lilah had trained Becky's mind to come at a fight.

Becky knew what she was doing.

Could she overpower him if he unleashed himself? No. But she would never need to. If worse came to worst and she had to fight him when he was in the middle of a PTSD episode, she wouldn't be trying to defeat him. She'd just be trying to survive long enough for him to rouse himself from his nightmares and realize what was going on.

What they were doing now was much more complex than what she would need to do to protect herself.

They went at it for a long time—longer than she even normally sparred with Lilah. They were both breathing hard, and Derek had a darkening bruise near his eye. Becky had bruises of her own, but she hadn't had to tap out at all. She'd been able to defend herself from nearly all of his moves.

She wasn't sure exactly when things shifted, but at some point, his grabbing her felt more like an opportunity for them to touch each other without everything piling up in the space between.

The next time, when his arms circled her waist to try to take her to the floor, she let him. It was a move she could've countered without a thought. They both knew it.

The blanket scratched her back, and the firelight painted Derek above her in delicious shades of orange and gold. He stared down at her with more life in his gaze than she'd seen since before their wedding.

"Did I do it?" she asked, breathless.

His voice was rough. "Do what?"

"Prove to you I can handle this."

"More than. You're—" His face lowered toward hers like an instinct before he stopped. "Fuck, Button. You're incredible."

Tears flooded her eyes, though she didn't want them to. She wanted to stay in this perfect moment because it was all too much, and no matter how she pretended, she was still so sad they had missed so much time.

"Are you going to leave again?"

Derek sighed, and she closed her eyes, dreading the words out of his mouth. It hadn't made a difference. She'd done everything and hadn't convinced him.

"I don't want to," he finally said. The words sounded like they were dragged out of him—like they were admitted against his will. She supposed they were, given how he felt about himself.

"But you feel like you should?"

His whole body shuddered, and he nodded. "Yes. I do. I don't want to, but I feel like I should. Everything is so complicated between us."

She slid her hands over the skin of his shoulders. "I don't need easy. I just need you."

The words snapped something between them. Derek's mouth came down on hers, hard and hungry. No hesitation in this kiss, and it didn't feel like the moments they shared in the bathroom either. This was Derek surrendering to what they both needed.

A rough sound came from the back of his throat, and he pulled away.

"Wait—"

He lifted her off the floor, taking her back to their blankets near the fire. "If we're doing this, I'm not going to do it in the dark. I want to see you."

Part of her wanted to give in to the temptation to go fast. The way they had when they were teenagers and they could barely keep their hands off each other. The other, louder part of herself wanted to savor every moment of being seen and loved by Derek. He was here with her, and Becky was going to enjoy it for as long as it lasted.

And pray it might be forever.

Derek kissed her again, spreading her out on the blanket in the delicious warmth of the fire. As always, it felt as natural as breathing. Their bodies had never had any trouble finding each other.

The way he kissed her wasn't fast, but it was urgent. Pressing deeper, consuming her like she was the only oxygen he had left. One hand slid beneath her neck, tilting her face where he wanted it—where he needed it.

Becky moved, trying to get her underwear off, and Derek didn't let her. Without breaking their kiss, he grabbed both of her hands and wove their fingers together, gently pinning them to the blanket. She smiled through the kiss and decided to tease him. "You don't want me naked?"

"You have no idea how much I want that." Derek kissed along her jaw. "But I'm going to be the one to do it, and I'm going to take my time."

His lips brushed over that sensitive spot she had just below her ear, and Becky shivered. Felt him smile. One thing hadn't changed. Derek still knew every secret spot that made her body sing.

"You made me wait eighteen months, so you could go a little faster," she said on a sigh.

"I starved myself for eighteen months, so I'm going to enjoy it," he countered.

They would both enjoy it.

Derek slipped one bra strap off her shoulder and then the other. She loved the way he looked at her, like she was a marvel or a wonder.

But then emotion struck her deep down in her chest. He was looking at her like this because he genuinely thought he would never see her or touch her like this again.

She would have pulled his face back to hers and kissed him again if he hadn't already had his mouth on her skin. He moved her as he touched her so he could take her bra off.

"Fuck." He murmured the word into her skin before he brushed his lips over the tip of her breast, only pausing for a moment before taking it between his lips, teasing it long and slow. Her nipples hardened under his touch, hands going to his hair.

"Derek," she gasped his name. "I know you want to go slow, but we're going to have to meet in the middle. I need you."

As if he hadn't heard her, he moved to her other breast. Just that feeling had her arching into him, hips begging for more.

"*Derek.*"

He lifted his head and smiled at her. The new light was still in his eyes. It made him look like the old Derek. "So demanding."

"You've always known that about me."

The grin deepened. "And have I ever once given you your way?"

He had, but it was always a push and pull between them. It was one of the things she loved—and one of the things she missed. Raising her legs around his waist, she gripped his body and used her newfound skills to take him by surprise, rolling them so she was on top. "I'm strong enough now to make you."

"Is that so?" He smiled. "Maybe this is exactly where I want you."

Hands on her hips, Derek lifted her and moved her so her knees rested on either side of his head. Now he didn't go slowly—he moved her panties to the side and consumed her. "Oh my God."

Derek groaned like he truly had been starving and couldn't hold himself back any longer. She fell forward, bracing on her hands, unable to do anything else with his hands holding her firmly against his mouth.

Pleasure swirled through her, building faster than should be possible. Becky wasn't one of those women who had an easy time finding her orgasm. But with Derek? It came out of hiding. Maybe it was because it had been so long, or maybe it was just him.

He knew exactly what she liked and where she needed to go, his tongue circling and focusing on that one spot that always made her turn into a supernova.

And just like always, she turned into one again.

One second, she was catching her breath, and in the next, she was shaking, crying out her orgasm into the mountain silence. It was a damn good thing no one was out here with them, because they probably could have heard her for miles.

Derek didn't stop, merely slowed, dragging out her orgasm with his lips and tongue, every tiny movement shooting off flickering sparks that felt so good.

Eventually, he gathered her up, holding her limp, sated body, stretching her out on the blanket again and stripping them both completely naked. And no matter what anyone said, cuddling for warmth while naked was not nearly as sexy as being with someone while you had no walls between you.

Hitching her leg around his hip, Derek pressed his forehead to hers, breathing deep. "Are you sure you want this?"

"Why wouldn't I be?"

Becky met his gaze, and the vulnerability there stole her breath, the pain and the reality of what he felt about himself and what had happened. It would take more than this one night to heal, for both of them.

"Yes," she whispered. "Yes, I am sure."

He pushed inside her, both of them shuddering. It ached in the best way. When Derek had disappeared, after a while, she'd tried to use internal toys to satisfy herself, and then she'd stopped, because it wasn't enough. Nothing would ever feel like him.

But because it had been so long, her body was no longer used to him. Derek dropped his face into her neck, breath hot on her skin. "Button, I—"

"I know," she said. "I know."

It felt more momentous than they acknowledged. Because if they did, they'd fall down into the hole of emotions it was too easy to get lost in.

Instead, she looped her arms around his neck and kissed

him. She wouldn't let them get lost. The man above her could lead their way through the mountains, and she would lead their way through this. "Don't stop."

Derek stayed still for another eternal moment before he began to move, slowly easing back before thrusting forward again, gradually finding a rhythm. She smiled, meeting his eyes and showing him her happiness. For all she cared, they could stay like this—connected and content. The pleasure was all a bonus.

Finally, Derek broke, the momentary darkening of his spirit lifting when he saw her smile. He laughed softly. "This might be the part where we relive our first time, and I tell you I'm not going to last because you feel so fucking good."

Becky laughed. "I don't care."

"I do." He brushed his mouth over hers and spoke against her lips even as he moved. "I want to last forever so we never have to move from this spot."

She raised an eyebrow. "I'll let you in on a secret."

"What's that?"

Pulling him down so she could whisper in his ear, she said, "We're allowed to have sex again."

"Really? I had no idea."

Their shared smiles and laughter made all of this so much better.

"Fuck, I missed you," he said. "Even when I didn't let myself miss you, I still did."

Arching up against him, Becky urged him faster. "I missed you too. So much, I can't even try to express it, because if I do, I'm going to get all emotional. And right now, the only thing I want to do is feel you."

"We can do that."

Derek's lips came down on hers, and they gave themselves over to the rhythm they'd forgotten. Learning each other like they were new lovers, but instead awakening memories they both had pushed aside. The sounds of them coming together and Derek's soft groans each time he entered her. The feeling of his breath on her skin. The way he coaxed her own voice from her with every movement, reaching between them to aid her pleasure before he reached his, even though he struggled to hold it back.

This orgasm was a rolling tide, rushing in with the new sound of rain on the roof above them. It stole her breath and filled her up, washing away so much of the pain and loneliness that had made up the last year and a half.

After their bodies calmed, they lay together in stillness, neither one of them wanting to break the bubble they'd created, protecting this moment from everything else. Becky kept her arms around him.

Watching Derek come undone above her was a sight she'd never take for granted again.

Chapter 22

Screaming echoed in Derek's head, followed by pain. Slicing, burning, broken bones.

They were going to try to hurt him again, but this time, he would fight back. He couldn't let them take him. Not again. Never again.

He waited, crouched by the door in the darkness. Had there been a door? He didn't remember. It didn't matter; he was taking them down.

Footsteps echoed, coming for him, and he pounced—

"*Derek.*"

He blinked, his eyes coming to focus on Becky, who was on top of him, looking down. Her naked body straddled his chest, her hands holding his away from her body as they reached for her.

Reached for her neck.

He'd been about to try to choke her again.

"Oh fuck." The words sounded blurred to his own ears, but he shifted, getting her off him and moving away as fast as humanly possible.

Scooting back against the nearby couch, he closed his eyes.

Fuck. *Fuck*.

He'd barely closed his eyes, and he was already having the flashbacks and lunging for the closest thing to kill. Even if that thing was Becky.

This had been a bad idea. He'd known it was a bad idea, and he'd done it anyway.

"Derek," Becky said from where she sat on her knees next to the fire. "Look at me, please."

"I'm sorry. I shouldn't have slept next to you."

His thoughts were racing, his heart pounding, skin covered in sweat. He covered his head with his hands. The need to move and do something other than sit was so strong, but he couldn't risk movement with her here. He wouldn't put her in danger again. He couldn't.

He didn't realize she'd moved until she was crouched in front of him. "Derek, look at me."

He didn't move his hands from his head. He didn't want to see the blood on her skin—couldn't take it again. They were in the middle of nowhere, and he couldn't get her help. He couldn't—

"Derek." Becky's voice cracked into his thoughts, and he looked at her out of instinct. "I'm fine. You woke up. Look at me."

Her words finally got through to him. He lowered his hands and looked at her.

No blood. No bruises. No tears. She looked fine.

Still… "You shouldn't be so close to me."

The determination hardened in her brown eyes, and before he could stop her, she was forcing his arms back and climbing over him, straddling his lap. His body responded to hers, naked as they were, the visceral feeling of her so close helping to relax him, though relaxing was the last thing he should be doing.

Becky took his face in her hands and locked their gazes together. "Take a deep breath with me, okay?"

He obeyed, filling his lungs. She was so close, he could still smell her skin.

He craved that scent more than anything.

"Another breath," she said quietly. Evenly.

Derek took one.

"Now, I want you to look at me. Am I hurt?"

He blinked and looked at her again. There was no blood on Becky's skin. In the warmth of the dying fire, the only thing on her skin was dirt from their ordeal. No blood. No marks or injuries. Just her.

"No, you're not."

She smiled. "No, I'm not."

"But did I try? I was having a nightmare."

Looking at him, she nodded. Her eyes held no sadness or grief; they were just matter-of-fact. "You made some moves that suggested you might try to hurt me. But I'm fine."

"I could have killed you, Becky."

"And yet here I sit—no bruises, no blood. Healthy and fine."

"And lucky." Derek huffed out a frustrated breath, and she didn't let him get away with it.

"I know this is hard, and I know that this is literally your worst nightmare, but I need you to be here with me right now. You took a chance when you let me fight you, and I proved to you I could handle that. Let me show you I can handle this."

She wasn't wrong.

He knew she wasn't wrong in what she said, and still, every instinct screamed in his head to get as far away as possible.

"If you want there to be any chance for a future between us, we've got to move forward," she whispered.

He didn't know if a future was a possibility or not, but if it was possible, he would do anything to try.

"Tell me what happened," he finally said. "What did I do?"

Becky released his face and let her hands drop to his shoulders. "We were huddled together, and you pulled away from me very fast—that's what woke me up." Then, softer, she added, "You sounded like you were in pain and angry. You rolled on top of me, and that's as far as I let you get. I flipped us. As soon as I pushed you over and called your name, you woke up."

"Did I—" He swallowed. "Did I try to hit you at all?"

"You might have if I hadn't stopped you." He tensed, but she didn't let him shut down or push her away. "And that's okay."

"That's *okay*? For Christ's sake, Button, it's the furthest thing from okay."

For the first time, she looked angry. "I don't care how many times I have to tell you this, and I don't care how many times we end up in this exact position. Hell, Derek, I don't care if we come up with a system where we do this and I help you talk through it, but I need you to hear me when I say *I am not afraid of you*."

Before he could say anything, she continued. "And before you tell me I should be afraid of you or that you're a monster or whatever other bullshit your mind is lying to you about— no. I reject that. You're not the first veteran to struggle with this, and God knows you won't be the last."

She pressed her forehead to his. "And I know you don't want to think about this, but there's every chance you will hit me again on accident."

His whole body went stiff.

"If that happens, it's not the end of the world. It's an accident we will deal with together. Did it upset you that I took control and stopped you?"

"Of course not."

"Would it upset you if I'd needed to get in a couple of blows in order to stop you?"

"No. Definitely not." He wished she would.

She smiled gently and kissed him, showing him every bit of love he felt he couldn't possibly deserve. "Good. Does the fact that I woke you up make you feel any better?"

"A little." That was good. Derek scrubbed his hands over his face. "It happened so fast," he said. "What I hate is that I haven't had an incident like this in a while, then it happens the first time I'm sleeping with you?"

"I think it makes sense."

He looked up sharply. "How?"

"When you're sleeping alone, you're not worried about hurting anyone. It doesn't matter if you roll over and punch a pillow. Or even a wall. So, you're not focused on it, and you let it all slip to the background."

He shrugged. That made sense.

"But while you're with me, you're thinking about it and so worried about whether you're going to come out swinging that it's all your mind is focused on. It brings the PTSD so much closer to the surface."

He hated that it made sense, because he would rather it be the opposite. Still, he had to admit the theory was sound.

Regardless, was knowledge enough?

"I'm sorry," he said.

"For that time you buried my Barbie doll when I was six? You should be sorry." When he glanced up, he spotted a twinkle in her eye.

They both knew he had plenty to be sorry for. The fact that she had the capacity to tease him right now? She really was so much stronger than he'd ever given her credit for. That didn't make him feel better about himself, but it gave him hope for their future.

"For all of it," he finally said. "For everything. I know you don't blame me, but I'm so fucking sorry, Becky."

"I know." Those brown eyes of hers were all he could see. "And I forgive you. But I need you to try."

"Try to what?"

"Forgive yourself. To give us a chance." She kissed him.

He allowed himself to touch her, dragging his hands down her ribs, marveling at the feeling of her skin under his hands, and realizing...he was okay.

The feeling of being out of control was absent. He was exhausted and suspicious of himself, but he didn't have the urge to go pound himself into the floor until he couldn't stay awake. He didn't even have the urge to paint out his demons. There was an ease in his mind he didn't usually have after a nightmare, and he didn't fully understand.

"Do you think you'll be able to go back to sleep?" Becky asked.

"Maybe."

Her eyes glimmered with amusement and arousal. "And what if I do this?"

She dropped her hand between their bodies, stroking the length of him. He was already half hard because it was Becky, and he couldn't be within feet of her without his body responding. But now his arousal raced clear to the surface, need exploding.

Becky sank down onto him, both of them closing their eyes at the sensation. New and old. Familiar and not. So fucking good, it was hard to breathe.

"You don't have to fuck me to sleep, Button."

She grinned, rising up and sinking down again. "And what makes you think it has anything to do with you? Maybe I've just been deprived and I want you."

He'd tried to go slow the first time, but God, hearing her say things like that made him feral. His guard was down, and frankly, he was tired of resisting. Becky had done more than she intended by showing him what he refused to see.

She wanted to show how strong she was, and she had.

But she'd also cracked through the stone walls he'd erected around himself over the past eighteen months. Those walls had been solid, tight, and kept out anything that would make him feel.

Now that they had a crack, it felt as if the whole ocean was ready to burst through.

Derek couldn't handle that yet, so he would keep it light and easy. Yet he wouldn't keep at it alone.

The slow, rolling motion of Becky's hips wasn't nearly enough for everything he craved, and they wouldn't make it back to the blanket. He held her, shifting them both to the floor so she looked up at him with those stunning eyes.

He didn't let himself think about all the time they'd lost or anything about the tangle of emotions that still separated them. Not about how his mind was still broken and would likely never be whole the way he wanted it to be.

All Derek let himself think about was Becky.

This wasn't the soft and easy lovemaking of coming together for the first time. This was hard and fast and the other side of what they both needed.

But he couldn't help himself. He'd had his mouth on her a few hours ago, and it was still all he could think about. Pulling out, he moved them again, so Becky's back wasn't on the bare wood of the floor, before he threw her legs over his shoulders and consumed her.

Before Becky, Derek hadn't known what it meant to want someone so badly you dreamed about the taste of them. It wasn't anything he could describe either. It was just her, and as long as he lived, he would never have enough.

"Derek," Becky gasped beneath him. He was blind with need, barely holding himself back, but he needed to feel her first. Needed to taste her orgasm more than he needed anything else in this moment, and he knew exactly how to give it to her.

With a groan, he grabbed her hips and held her more firmly against his mouth, using his tongue in the ways he'd learned drove her crazy. Even after all this time, he'd never forget how to make Becky Mackay come.

She twisted her hands in his hair, pulling almost painfully, and he welcomed the pain. Derek would take any pain she gave him for the rest of their lives.

Her cry bounced off the walls, her sweet flavor flooding his mouth, her body shaking where he held it. He didn't hesitate either, thrusting back into her body and taking her hard.

With her eyes closed, Derek braced himself above her as he moved, driving them both to the brink. "Open your eyes, Button."

She did. They were hazy with pleasure and comfort and trust. It was the utter openness, grace, and faith that undid him. Lightning barreled down his spine, and he covered Becky's mouth with his so he didn't roar so loud he shook the mountaintops.

He felt her squeezing down on him so hard he saw stars. It took everything he had left not to collapse on top of her. Instead, he turned, falling to the side and pulling her to him. Exhaustion came over him so quickly, he couldn't keep his eyes open.

But as he slipped into slumber with Becky at his side, he wasn't completely afraid, and that was everything.

Chapter 23

He woke when the sky was first lightening. As much as it could lighten with the storm still raging. Rain fell outside the windows, and Becky still slept peacefully beside him.

Slowly, he untangled himself from her, doing his best not to disturb her rest. The fire had died down to cinders. He pulled on his boxer briefs and crouched in front of the fireplace, tucking more kindling into the ashes and piling on a few more logs so it could rise up again.

It wasn't cold, but with the storms, the air held a distinct chill, and with nothing for them to do but wait, he imagined he and Becky would spend a good portion of the day in front of the fire.

There was nothing he wanted more.

He used the cabin's small outhouse, then came back in and cleaned himself up with some of the disposable wipes in the cupboard. He couldn't wait to have a proper shower when they got back to civilization.

The mirror showed him what he felt but hadn't bothered to examine—he had bruises.

Across his chest where the plane's harness had caught him

in the crash were ugly purple marks. They ached, but not as much as they looked like they did. Then there were the stitches Becky had done on his side. He was aware enough of his body to know nothing was deeply wrong, but he was sure Sam would want both of them to get checked out when they were back.

He came back into the main room, where Becky still slept. He sat on the chair and watched her. He'd made it through the rest of the night without waking again and without endangering her. Maybe that was a good sign.

There was no denying his instinct to go back to the way things had been—keeping away from her to make sure she was safe. But he saw now that her physical safety wasn't the only thing he needed to account for.

When he'd left, he made sure she wouldn't come to physical harm. That had been his only thought: her physical safety.

Her mental and emotional safety hadn't been on his radar. Not because he was unaware they existed, but because he'd assumed Becky would never want to see him again after what had happened. Even with all the calls and messages, somewhere in his mind, he convinced himself that his staying away was for the best.

It would take time to undo that belief.

But here, where it was just the two of them and the rest of the world wasn't pressing down, being together felt as easy as breathing. It was just the two of them smiling, talking, laughing.

Even sparring.

Half of him wanted to spar with her again. It had been one of the most arousing and humbling experiences of his life. At the end of their session, he hadn't been holding back as much as she thought. Becky had turned herself into a warrior, and he would never be able to tell her how proud he was.

Hopefully he could show her by trying. Working through

his own shit and finding a way of getting back on track. It wouldn't be easy. Derek knew himself and he knew her, and it would be ugly and messy. He was a stubborn fucker, and his mind had permanent damage.

The miracle was, Becky knew that, and she still wanted him.

His *wife*. He shook his head in amazement at it all.

They needed to call on the radio and check in with Sam, but he didn't want to do it until she woke on her own. She needed the rest. So did he, probably, but this wasn't about staying awake for Becky's sake. He just didn't see himself going back to sleep.

As he watched the rain fall outside the windows, his thoughts turned back to the crash. He went over the flight in his mind. The plane had looked good. Every inspection point clear, everything behaving normally. So how in the hell had both engines failed? They hadn't even been flying in bad weather.

There was no logical explanation for it, and that set his instincts aflame. As fun as the idea of spontaneous combustion was, that didn't happen. Something was always the reason. He just didn't know what it was.

And given where the wreckage was, he doubted they'd be getting much information now. He'd be lucky if anything was left after being pummeled by water from multiple storms. Right now, they just needed to get home. The rest could be figured out later.

Across the room, Becky stirred and turned over, reaching for him, freezing when he wasn't there. She looked around, smiling when she found him and relaxing back down into their makeshift bed. "How long have you been awake?"

"Not long. Promise."

She narrowed her eyes playfully. "Better not have been, Bollinger."

He chuckled. "I was waiting for you to wake up so I could call Sam and check in."

"Yeah, good idea." Standing, she crossed to the kitchen completely naked, which had him distracted. It took him a few seconds longer than it should have to get himself moving to the desk. Becky got herself some water.

Derek fixed the frequency. "Helitack, this is Derek Bollinger, over."

A few seconds later, a voice crackled. "Loud and clear, Derek." Scarlett's voice. "You guys okay? Over."

"Hey, Scarlett. Yeah, we're good. Just checking in, over."

"Good. The weather's moving faster than anticipated, so we should be able to get to you this afternoon. Keep the radio on. We'll let you know when we're close, over."

"Sounds good. Over."

"It'll be good to have you guys back. Over and out."

He put down the receiver and looked over to where Becky leaned on the kitchen table. She'd put her underwear and shirt back on, but her bare legs were still visible and still a distraction now that he'd spent time between them again.

"How do you want to do this?" Derek kept his breath even.

"Do what?"

Gesturing between the two of them, he shrugged. "Us."

"I'm not sure what you mean," she said, coming over to him and perching on the desk in front of him. "But talk to me. We have the time."

Derek swallowed, putting his words together. "I know there's a lot to deal with and a lot we have to work out. But one thing hasn't changed. I'm not going to fuck up your life. So you tell me how you want to handle things in public. You know, us being married."

They were married, and no one knew about it. It seemed like a lot. Everyone finding out they were married would come with all kinds of questions and well-meaning probing from friends and family. Derek didn't know if he was ready for it, but if she was, then he would find a way to handle it.

Becky watched him carefully. "Tell me what you want. Not what you think I want, and not what you think is best for me or even us. Tell me what *you* want. Let's start there."

"It doesn't matter what I want."

"Of course it does. If we're going to do this, we're doing it together, and it has to be a partnership."

He looked away out the window. Plenty of times, his therapist had said something similar.

"That's not what I meant," he finally admitted. "It doesn't matter because I can't have what I want. It's not possible."

Fear rose in Becky's eyes, and he touched her arms, trying to reassure her.

"I don't mean it in the sense that I don't want to be here. I mean the thing I want most is for this never to have happened. Everything that night, and everything that led to it—me being held in that prison camp. I'm not the same. I'll never be the same, and I fucking hate it."

"That's understandable." She stroked her fingers gently through his hair.

"So, like I said, it doesn't matter."

"It does to me," she said quietly. "Whatever we need to do to make this work, I'm in. Whatever you need to make it better and easier, I'll do it. Anything except for walking away from you. I won't do that."

He didn't know what to say, so he just nodded. There was still the voice in his head saying this wouldn't work and he shouldn't be here, but he ignored it.

It was time to stop running.

DEREK WAS TALKING. It was all Becky could ask for.

But still, they needed to keep this practical. It would have to be small steps for them together.

"I don't want to tell people we're married yet," she said, following a hunch. "While we're working on this together, it'll be better if it's still just the two of us and not everyone in Oak Creek."

Part of her hated that idea. She wanted everyone in Oak Creek to know he was hers permanently. But finding their way forward was already hard enough without so many curious eyes.

As she suspected, she saw the slightest relaxation in his body. "I'm good with that." Then he paused. "I'm still with helitack."

"And?"

"And I like it there. I like the work, and I like the team. But if you—"

Becky reached out and put a hand on his shoulder. "I'm not expecting you to drop everything to move back to Oak Creek and become a house husband, Derek. All I want is this. You here. Talking. Us figuring it out. It's only an hour drive for either of us, and we can make it work."

"Really?"

She let out a small laugh. "Of course. We're going to take this slow, Bollinger."

That finally brought out a small smile. It was strange to be starting from zero, while at the same time knowing almost everything about someone. But if that was what it took, then that was what it took.

"So, let's not overthink it," she continued. "That's all we need to know. I'm proud of you for doing all of this."

He met her eyes. "It's not going to be a straight line."

"Recovery is never linear. One step forward, eight steps back. My parents told me that more than once."

Reaching out, Derek grabbed her hand and held it. Silent

thanks and more emotion than she could name with that one simple movement. "Now, you know what I found while I was poking around yesterday?"

"What?"

"Board games." She grinned, hopping off the desk and going to the cupboard she'd found them in. Pretty basic ones. Chess and checkers, Sorry, Monopoly, and a deck of cards.

She left Monopoly in the cupboard.

"You scared of my Monopoly skills?" he asked with one eyebrow raised.

Becky made a face. "Monopoly isn't fun with two people, and I'm not scared. I'm just not willing to have my ass handed to me this early in the day."

He had an uncanny way of winning Monopoly. Even his family wouldn't play the game with him. He'd been undefeated for as long as she could remember, but they could never prove he cheated.

Instead, she set checkers out on their blanket and grabbed more granola bars and a can of nuts. Derek joined her on the blanket, a look of amusement on his face. "Do you think you're going to win more because it's not Monopoly?"

"I think I have a chance."

Derek bit into his granola bar. "Well, I'm not going easy on you. Now that you can almost put me on my ass in sparring, I need to be able to win something."

"Do your worst."

"You think you can handle my worst?"

She heard the double meaning in the question and met it head on, moving her first piece on the board. "I can handle anything you throw at me."

He smiled. A real one. Small, but there. "I think you can."

They played games, keeping everything else light and easy and free of anything but fun. If she had to be in a plane crash and stranded, there were worse people to do it with.

Becky stopped short of being grateful for whatever the hell had been wrong with the plane. But without the crash, she and Derek wouldn't be here. It would have been over for them.

So yeah, she was pretty damned thankful for the plane crash.

It was well into the afternoon when the radio crackled with Sam's voice. "Derek. Becky. Come back, over."

Derek went to the desk, and Becky grabbed her pants, which were now dry. Stiff and dirty, but dry.

"We're here, over."

"We're getting close. Ten minutes out. Not enough room to land, so we'll have to lift you. You guys ready for that?"

He looked at her, and she nodded.

"We are," he confirmed. "We're ready to go home."

Chapter 24

Two days later, Becky woke up in bed. She stretched and reached for Derek but didn't find him there.

She sat up and listened in case he was in the bathroom or kitchen. But...nothing.

She lay back down with a sigh. She wasn't surprised she was alone. In the forty-eight hours since their rescue, it seemed as if Derek had been on the verge of panicking.

The only time he hadn't been tense and anxious was when anybody else *would* have been. Like when the helitack team had arrived with the rescue helicopter for them at the cabin. Sam had been right—landing hadn't been an option, so the team had lowered some kind of basket contraption. Derek had calmly hooked them both in, then signaled up to his team that they were ready. Before Becky could even scream her head off, they'd been winched up to the helicopter.

Derek had looked happier and more carefree hovering in the air in that moment than he had since. So she wasn't surprised to find him not in bed with her now.

"Derek?"

No response. Not that she'd expected one.

She got up and pulled on her clothes for the day. She hadn't done much since they'd gotten home besides eat, spend time with Derek when he was around, and explain over and over again what had happened. It had been pretty much a nonstop line of people circling in and out of her house wanting to check on them.

Most people hadn't batted an eye that Derek was back in town. They certainly hadn't asked questions about where he'd been for the past eighteen months—just assumed it had something to do with work. Talking about a plane crash was much more interesting than a Bollinger being back in town.

She checked the bathroom and kitchen, just in case she was wrong about Derek not being here. She didn't have to worry about him being in her home office—that was still sectioned off with plastic because of the fire damage and would be for a while.

There was no sign Derek had been here at all.

Becky had to force herself to stop and swallow down her panic. This wasn't like all her other nightmares, when she'd woken up reaching for him, only for him to be somewhere on the opposite side of the world where she couldn't reach him.

Yes, he wasn't here, but that didn't mean he *wasn't here*.

But also, he hadn't slept with her either night. They'd made love multiple times, but he hadn't stayed to sleep. She assumed he'd gone to his parents' house to sleep. Since they didn't know Becky and Derek were married, they probably expected it. And that was okay with Becky.

Still, she had to rub the heel of her hand against her chest to ease the ache there, feeling almost hollow. Derek had his triggers, and they were ugly and scary and real.

But Becky had triggers too. Derek being gone without warning was definitely the biggest one.

She heard a car pull up in the driveway and rushed over to

the window, hoping it was him. But it was Callum Webb. She forced a smile onto her face and opened the door for him.

"Morning, Sheriff."

He offered her a tight smile. "I hope it's not too early for me to stop by. I know you need rest."

She glanced down at her watch. "It's nearly nine. I've got to start getting back to a normal schedule at some point, or my clients are going to revolt. Animals are not interested in whether their vet needs rest or not."

"Well, don't rush it. You may not be injured, but what you went through is still pretty traumatic."

She held the door open so he could walk inside. Callum wasn't here to chitchat. It wasn't the older man's style. If he was here, it was because he needed something.

"If I'm the one who's been through something traumatic, how come you're the one looking like they haven't had any sleep for days?" She put on a pot of coffee as they walked into the kitchen and gestured for him to sit at one of the island barstools.

He swiped a hand down over his face. "I've worked as sheriff here for over a decade and don't recall things being this crazy. All hell broke loose at once."

"Oh yeah?"

"First, Eva getting kidnapped, the fire here at your place, then the plane crash."

The coffee finished, and she poured him a mug, hiding a smile when he put enough cream and sugar in it to have a toddler zooming around for a week. Callum was one of the gruffest men she'd ever known, and that was saying a lot, given that she'd grown up surrounded by the men who'd built Linear Tactical into one of the leading self-defense, survival skills, and weapons-training centers in the country.

"Sounds like you've had an exciting week too."

He took another sip of his coffee as she poured hers. "And

then it gets even worse. I'm working with Teton County, trying to find a missing woman. Woman's mother is hysterical. Last seen up near Alpine."

Becky knew Alpine; it wasn't too far from the Swanson ranch. "There's not much out in that area besides trees and ranches. Was she hiking?"

"Not that we're aware of. She was last seen in a bar outside of Alpine. We're keeping an eye out for her here too. Her name is Elena Rodriguez."

He took his tablet and spun it so Becky could see an image of the woman. Young, attractive, with deep black hair and a wide smile.

"I'll keep an eye out for her, of course. I'll be headed up to the Swanson ranch soon too. If you send me her picture, I'll be sure to show it around up there. Maybe Mr. Swanson knows something."

"Thanks, I'll take you up on that offer. I'll be showing her picture around here too, although I'm fairly certain I would've already heard about it if someone as pretty as Elena Rodriguez showed up."

"That's true." In a town the size of Oak Creek, someone who looked like that would be talked about.

"So, between working with the National Transportation Safety Board about the crash, the fire marshal about your office, the Feds about Eva being kidnapped, and multiple local agencies trying to find Elena Rodriguez, I feel like my people skills are being stretched pretty thin." Callum was blunt, as he always was. "Not that those skills were great to begin with."

"What can I do to help?"

"Actually, I was hoping to find Derek here. The NTSB is sending out a representative next week for a full report of the crash, and I was hoping to go with Derek to the crash site so we could get the info they'll need. Plus, Mr. Swanson needs it for insurance purposes."

"Derek's not here."

Callum's eyes narrowed. "I'm sorry. I heard you two were back together. But I should know better than to listen to town gossip."

"We are back together." At least, she thought they were back together. "He's just at his parents' house or maybe his cousin's."

"I was going to ask Lincoln to come to the crash site anyway, so that works out. Do you want to come with us?"

She took a sip of her own coffee. "No thank you. I wouldn't be able to provide any useful info about that plane anyway, not to mention I have no desire to go back to that ravine. Plus, I've got to get back to the Swanson ranch."

"Does the thought of flying again scare you?" He finished his cup and set it down, waving his hand when she offered him more.

"Believe it or not, not really. I figure the chances of anything like that happening again have to be pretty much nonexistent, right?"

"Hell, from what I understand, the chances of it happening *once* were pretty slim. I'm hoping we'll be able to piece together what happened."

"It wasn't Derek's fault." That much, she was sure of. "If it had been any other pilot, I'm not sure I'd be standing here talking to you."

"I'm well aware of how good of a pilot Bollinger is. That's the reason I wanted to be part of the investigation—in case someone insinuates he was at fault."

"Thanks, Callum," she whispered. The last thing she wanted was people doubting Derek's skills as a pilot.

"I've known you both a lot of years—watched you grow up." Callum stood. "Derek's a top-notch pilot and a good man, even if he's got his demons."

"Yes, he is." And yes, he very definitely had his demons.

"Thanks for the coffee." Callum headed toward the door. "If you see Derek, let him know I'm looking for him. I've left him a message, so I know he'll get back to me soon."

Becky smiled, but it was forced. Yeah, Derek would get back to Callum.

The question was...when would Derek get back to *her*?

Chapter 25

A couple hours later, unwilling to sit alone in her house any longer, Becky headed to the Frontier Diner in town.

She hadn't heard from Derek, nor had she tried to message him herself. It wasn't that she was playing games; she just didn't know what to do in this situation.

Derek wasn't playing games either. He was trying. Since the moment they'd left that cabin in the wilderness, he'd been trying. He'd stayed with her as much as he could, but there had been some moments when that obviously had become impossible for him.

She'd been expecting it when they were trying to sleep… Him waking up in the middle of a PTSD episode was always going to be something they needed to be aware of. But she hadn't really considered that his PTSD might affect him at other times too.

Part of the problem had to be that he was constantly trying to hold himself in check. She could see the stressors on his face and feel the tension in his body, even when they'd made love.

Yes, he was trying. But he was paying a big price for it, and that price was probably making his symptoms worse.

How were they going to live like this?

She walked into the Frontier and was about to grab a small table when she saw Finn and Charlie Bollinger, Derek's parents, over in a booth. She gave them a little wave then headed in their direction when Charlie gestured for her to come over. Becky knew it would be completely rude not to go say hello.

Charlie had been best friends with Becky's mom, Annie, for decades, just like Finn had been best friends with Becky's dad, Zac. Becky had known the Bollingers her whole life.

"Hi, Mr. B. Hi, Mrs. B."

Charlie patted the booth next to her, and Becky took the seat. The woman was barely an inch over five feet, but no one told her no very often. Charlie Bollinger was, and always had been, a force to be reckoned with.

"How are you feeling, sweetheart?" Charlie asked as she wrapped an arm around Becky. "We are so thankful you and Derek are all right."

"Yeah, it was definitely scary. I'm lucky your son is such a good pilot, or I probably wouldn't be here right now."

Finn reached across the table and grabbed her hand. "That he is, but some situations you can't get out of, no matter how good the pilot is. So we're grateful."

Becky nodded. They had a lot to be thankful for.

"Derek hasn't given us many details about exactly what happened," Finn continued.

Becky tensed. Had the crash affected Derek more than he'd let Becky know? "Is he not talking about it?"

Charlie rolled her eyes. "He hasn't been around enough to talk about it. I know I should be used to that, seeing as how he hasn't been around at all for eighteen months, but I guess I thought since he was back, maybe he'd be…*back*, you know? I don't expect him to come running to us every time something happens, but it would've been nice to hear the details from him."

Becky nodded, mind racing. Evidently, Derek hadn't been staying with his parents either. If he hadn't been with them and he hadn't been with Becky, where had he been?

"He's a grown man, and he has to handle his issues the way he wants to." Finn looked pointedly at Charlie. "I keep trying to remind someone of that, but she doesn't want to accept it. But God knows that kid of ours has been through a lot. As long as he's talking to you, we're fine with it."

But that was it, wasn't it? Derek *wasn't* talking to Becky.

"Could he be talking to his brothers or Lincoln?"

Finn and Charlie shot concerned looks at each other.

"Is he not talking to you?" Charlie asked.

Becky forced a smile and shrugged. "You know Derek, always so protective. I'm sure he doesn't want to burden me with anything he might be thinking."

Derek was never willing to share his burdens. That was the problem.

It was all starting again. He was already running.

So when Becky happened to look out the window and see Derek walking down Main Street, head tucked low, she knew she had to talk to him right now. She couldn't live like this any longer.

"Do you mind excusing me? I've got some things I need to take care of." Becky slid out of the booth and stood. "I'll make sure Derek is talking to someone, even if that's not me or you guys."

Charlie reached out and grabbed Becky's hand. "We're thankful to have him back. We don't want to lose him again. I know that's true for you, too."

"It is. I love him."

Charlie nodded. "I know you do, sweetie. And he loves

you. I hope you've always known that. That even when he was staying away, it was never because of lack of love."

Becky nodded. She did know that. But love wasn't going to be enough if Derek was running.

She couldn't go through this again.

The waitress came over to talk to Finn and Charlie, and Becky was able to make her escape. A couple more people tried to engage her in conversation, but she just smiled and gave a brief wave.

Her attention was focused solely on getting to her husband.

By the time she got outside, he was much farther down the street. Where was he going? The only thing in that direction were a few houses on the outskirts of town. She thought about calling out to him, but curiosity overrode the urge. Instead, she followed him.

When he passed the hardware store, the last retail building in town, she got a little concerned. Where was he going? Oak Creek was small, but it wasn't so small that she knew who lived in every single house. She racked her brain for who lived out here, but no one came to mind. None of his brothers, none of his friends.

He was going to a house.

For just a second, her steps faltered. It had never occurred to her that Derek could possibly be seeing someone else. Even when he'd been completely absent from her life for the past eighteen months, him having someone else had never even crossed her mind.

For the first time, it did now. Her heart threw itself against her ribs as he walked up the driveway of a tiny bungalow.

When he didn't stop and knock on the door, she thought she might be sick. Obviously, this was a place he'd been welcomed into before.

. . .

AS SHE WALKED CLOSER to the house, anger replaced the anxiety coursing through her body. There was so much she was willing to work through with Derek. So many things she was willing to forgive.

But this? Whether it was some sort of secret hideaway he'd been keeping from her or someone else's house he was visiting, either way, it felt like a betrayal.

She was fuming by the time she made it to the door. She didn't know whether to knock or just storm in, so she did both —knocking as she opened the door.

"What the hell is going on here?" She looked around before stopping in her tracks. She wasn't sure what she'd been expecting to find, but it wasn't this.

Derek spun from where he stood at the kitchen sink, one eyebrow raised. Becky wasn't even sure she'd surprised him. He definitely didn't look panicked or guilty. "What are you doing here, Button?"

She looked around. There was no other woman here. Hell, there wasn't much of anything in this whole house at all beyond...*art supplies*?

"What is this?" Becky walked farther into the house. Painting stuff littered nearly every surface. There was a mattress with a blanket at the corner of one room and a couch, but besides those and the kitchen table, there wasn't any other furniture.

Just lots and lots of paintings.

"Did you paint these?"

He rubbed the back of his neck, shrugging sheepishly. "Yeah."

She walked farther into the living room, studying the pieces. She didn't know anything about art. These paintings all seemed to be splashes of colors built on each other. They didn't necessarily make sense to her, but that didn't mean they weren't of artistic value either.

"Is painting something you want to pursue as, like, a profession or something?"

It wasn't a direction she would've thought he wanted to go, but that didn't mean it wasn't true. Her mind was already forging ahead. If Derek wanted to pursue some sort of artistic career, she could certainly get behind that.

He actually laughed. "Are you kidding? Look at these things. I definitely don't have any talent. No, I think I'll keep my day job."

She had to admit, that made her feel a little better. But she still didn't understand exactly what she was looking at. "Then what is all this?"

Derek moved slowly around the room. "This is my coping mechanism. This is where I go when I'm overwhelmed and other stuff doesn't help."

She turned to study him. "What sort of other stuff?"

"The stuff my therapist and I worked on. Flying. Working out. Hell, even the therapy sessions themselves."

"You go to therapy?"

He spun around to face her again. "Are you kidding? I've gone to therapy every week since I got out of that prison camp. First through the military and then private sector after I discharged."

"Oh."

"You're surprised by that?"

She shrugged. "I guess not. I just know that sometimes it's hard for former military guys to stomach that sort of counseling."

"Sometimes it feels like a lot of talking, I'll admit. But I needed it after what I went through and losing my team." He shrugged. "Although in some ways, the therapy did more harm than it did good."

He turned to look at a specific painting, so she turned to

look at one, too, that consisted mostly of different shades of green. "In what ways?"

"I guess it convinced me that I had healed more than I really had. That it was okay to be around you and that I didn't need to worry about what could possibly happen."

"Derek…" She turned back toward him. Would she ever be able to convince him that what had happened that night had been an accident?

It was as if he could read her mind. "I know. You want to say it wasn't my fault, that it was an accident."

She nodded and walked to him until she could touch his arms. "Yes, that's exactly what I want to say. Intent does matter."

He let out a sigh. "Yes and no. Yes, you're right, I would never want to hurt you. But I still did. So after what happened with you, I realized that therapy-only wasn't going to be enough if I ever wanted any chance at all of us being together again."

Derek was looking over her shoulder at one of his paintings as he said it and didn't even realize what a huge admission he'd just made. He'd wanted to fight for them even when he hadn't really understood how to do it or if it was even worth it.

He'd been trying.

"So when did this place come about?" she asked gently when his voice faded off.

"Not long after I joined helitack."

"You've had this place nearly a year?"

He nodded.

"Why didn't you tell me? Not before… I don't like it, but I understand your reasons for keeping away. But since the crash, you've come back here rather than stay with me sometimes. Why didn't you just tell me about this place?"

He shrugged again. "I mean, look at it. It doesn't make sense.

Who would possibly understand all these paintings? Plus, I was afraid you would be madder that I had been even closer than the helitack camp some of the time over the past few months."

And maybe she would've been, she had to admit. But she wasn't now.

She turned and walked around again, looking at the paintings. "This is like what your Aunt Wavy does, isn't it?"

"Yes, but I'm not nearly as talented. There will never be a market for these. This is solely for me to let off steam and express emotions in a way that I can't using words."

"I think more people would understand this than you think." She touched one of the canvases. "You say you come here when things get really bad. Have they been bad the last two days?"

She tried to tamp down the hurt the thought caused her. That he had been suffering but didn't want to share it with her or tell her about this place.

A moment later, his hands dropped gently on her shoulders, and he pulled her back against his chest. "No. I actually have been coming here to see if I could pack it up. I knew explaining all of this might hurt you and I didn't want to do that, so I was just going to quietly let it go."

She turned around in his arms so she was facing him. "No, you shouldn't get rid of this place."

"Button, I don't want it to hurt you. I don't want my being here to hurt you. I don't want the fact that this place *exists* to hurt you."

She cupped his cheeks in her hands. "We have got to start working this problem together. If this place is what you need to get you through rough patches, then you should keep it."

"You don't mind?"

She took a breath and gathered her thoughts. "I'll admit, I'd like for us to work through everything together. But thinking about it now, I'm realizing we both need to work through things separately too."

"Yes. So you keep sparring with Lilah. Maybe I'll work with her a little too so she can formulate specifics to teach you how to protect yourself against me if needed."

Becky nodded. That made complete sense to her. But when she moved in for a kiss, Derek pulled away.

"What?" she asked.

He shook his head. "Just listen to our conversation. Talking about me having a hideout and you having more self-defense training. What kind of couple does that?"

She closed the last bit of distance between them. "The kind that is committed to being together, no matter what it takes. There are plenty of couples who won't attempt to fix what's broken between them, even when it's easy stuff."

"Still…"

She pushed up onto her tiptoes so she could kiss him. "It doesn't matter. The only thing that matters is that we stand together and fight."

"I love you, you know," he said against her lips. "That never changed, Button."

"I love you too, husband."

And she always would.

Chapter 26

The next day at the Swanson ranch, Becky could barely keep the smile off her face. Not even Everett the grumpy ranch hand glaring at her could make her upset.

She probably shouldn't be so happy since she was exhausted from not having slept a wink last night due to her and Derek not being able to keep their hands off each other. Seeing the paint house and their conversation afterward had changed everything.

For the first time, she truly felt like she and Derek were going to work things out long-term. They were going to have a real marriage.

He'd even mentioned having kids.

Granted, the comment had been in passing, but it had still lit up something in Becky's heart. She wanted babies. She'd grown up as an only child and had always been a little jealous of the Bollingers' large family—three boys and a girl. Becky wasn't sure she wanted four kids, but she definitely wanted to have babies with Derek.

Of course, they would have to figure out how to make sure

Derek felt secure as a father. He'd have to feel secure as a husband first.

But it would come. For the first time since their wedding night, she felt sure that was true.

So not even Everett standing there glaring at her was going to pull the joy from her heart.

Still, she stole a glance at him from where she was treating the newborn calves. He'd basically been scowling at her for the past forty-five minutes, almost like he was some shopkeeper expecting her to take one of the calves and try to shoplift it in her pocket.

She'd ignored him as best she could and finished up with the baby cows. She hoped he'd find something else to do while she worked, but he was still there when she finished. Even worse, he was blocking the path to the barn where she needed to go next and check on Princess.

She waited until there was nothing left for her to do before packing up her med kit and heading toward the barn. Everett didn't move, didn't offer any assistance with her heavy bag as she approached. His face was even grumpier up close. Still, she attempted to at least be polite.

"Everett. Hello." She nodded at him.

"You're back again."

She barely refrained from rolling her eyes. "You know how it is. There's always going to be animals that need treatment."

"Did you drive up here this time?"

"Yes. Unfortunately, there wasn't another plane to bring me up here, so I drove."

"That was Mr. Swanson's plane that crashed."

Becky wasn't sure what the man was getting at. "Yes, it was his plane, and I'm thankful that my husband and I both walked away from the crash."

She couldn't help her smile at saying *husband*. Everett didn't know Derek and had no knowledge of their marital status or lack thereof. The man probably couldn't care less about her use of the word husband, but it still felt good to say it.

Everett was still glowering at her.

"I'm sure insurance will reimburse Mr. Swanson for the loss of his plane, so you can stop glaring at me like I did this on purpose. Believe me, I had no desire to be in that crash, even though we survived."

Although that wasn't completely true, given how things had turned out between her and Derek, but she wasn't going to make any sort of attempt to explain that to Everett. The man was still frowning at her like she was about to pull a knife on him or something.

"Things haven't been right around here since last time you visited."

She blinked, taken aback. "What do you mean? Have there been problems with some of the animals I don't know about?"

He spat a little chewing tobacco, barely missing Becky's shoe, and folded his arms over his chest. "You're causing problems."

This time, she didn't even try to stop her eyes from rolling. "I'm doing my job, trying to keep animals healthy. That's it."

"You come here, and everything falls apart. You're a problem." His voice was low and tight.

Now Becky was feeling less annoyed and more nervous. She was suddenly very aware there were no other people around, just animals.

And one man who was definitely not happy with her.

She lowered her medical kit to the ground and shifted her weight onto the balls of her feet. She didn't think Everett meant her physical harm, but if there was one thing over a year of sparring with Lilah had taught her, it was to be prepared for the unexpected.

The man looked to be in his early forties, on the shorter side, but stout. He had a strength that came from hard, outdoor work. As always, if it came down to a fight, Becky's best bet would be to use her speed and agility.

"Everett." A call came from behind Becky. "You're needed over at the bunkhouse."

Becky relaxed her stance slightly but didn't let down her guard completely at the words. At least someone else was here. She shifted so she could see and realized it was Cooper. As he walked the rest of the way over to them, Everett just grunted and turned and walked away.

"Everything okay?" Cooper asked, watching Everett's retreating back.

Becky reached down and picked up her medical bag again. "Yeah, no problem. I'm on my way to check on Princess."

"I'll come with you."

Cooper reached for the bag, and Becky offered him a smile. "Thanks. That thing is heavy."

"How are you feeling? I heard about the crash. I'm just glad you weren't hurt. It's all so crazy."

She offered him a smile as they walked into the barn. "Yeah, definitely crazy. We still don't know exactly what happened or why the plane went down."

Cooper shook his head, brows furrowed. "Becky, I'm so sorry. It should have been me in that plane with you, but something came up here, so I couldn't make it to Reddington City."

She reached over and patted his arm. "No, don't feel that way. I don't mean any sort of offense, but Derek Bollinger has the sort of pilot experience that very few civilians have. I'm not sure anybody could have successfully landed that plane the way he did. So I'm glad I was with him."

Cooper ran a hand through his short-cropped hair. "Still…"

"And I'm really sorry about the plane. I know not having it must be a hassle. I hope you don't blame me like Everett does."

"Everett is an asshole. Why would anyone blame you for a plane crash? What exactly did he say?"

She shrugged and turned toward Princess's stall. "Just called me a problem. I don't know. He doesn't like me." Maybe he didn't like anyone.

Cooper stared out the barn door, shaking his head. "Everett is always an issue."

"There always has to be someone making everyone else's life around them harder."

Cooper finally turned away from the door with a smile. "Doesn't there, though? Speaking of, Mr. Swanson was talking again about offering you a full-time position. Said last time you seemed a little more interested than when he'd mentioned it in the past. I hope the plane crash won't stop you from considering his offer."

She smiled. "The plane crash doesn't affect my decision, but I'm definitely not interested. Things have changed for me since I was last here. Oak Creek is definitely where I belong. I'll be staying there."

"Ah." Cooper shook his head. "I won't lie, I'm disappointed."

He was looking at her in a way she couldn't misinterpret. Cooper was definitely interested in her. She didn't know the man very well, but she didn't want to hurt his feelings.

"Cooper, I'm flattered, but I can't. I'm not available."

"I should have made my move sooner."

She touched him on his arm. "If it helps, it wouldn't have made any difference. I haven't been available since I was about sixteen years old."

"Then I should have made my move much, much sooner." Cooper gave a charming laugh and a wink. Becky was just glad there weren't any hard feelings between them.

"Well, let me get in here and finally check on the reason I'm here." She walked into Princess's stall.

"How are you, beautiful?" she murmured to the horse.

"She seems to be doing much better the past couple of days."

Becky nodded and walked around the horse, starting her regular exam. "I'm glad you're feeling better, Princess. Although, that's a little rude, considering I nearly died trying to get to you."

Becky continued her exam, murmuring gently to the horse as she did.

Cooper stuck around and traded out some of the old straw in Princess's stall for fresh straw while Becky was working. "Did you find anything weird about how she was acting on your horse camera?"

Becky drew a little of Princess's blood. She would run some tests when she got back to her office just to eliminate potential problems. "Honestly, I haven't had a chance to look at it, between the fire at my house and the crash." She looked up at where the camera was pointing down at the stall as it was supposed to be. "Did Everett fix it, or did you?"

"Me, of course. He never even mentioned it, except for that note I almost didn't see. I don't know what Everett's problem was. Then again, we rarely know what Everett's problem is."

She chuckled. "I'm glad he's your problem and not mine."

"Thanks." Cooper rolled his eyes. "So, how's Princess looking to you?"

"Better, for sure." But something still wasn't quite right. Becky wasn't sure what it was, but the blood work would give her more of an indication. "I'll still run some tests and look over the footage from the camera once I get back home. Make sure there's not anything I missed."

Cooper put in more straw. "I'm just glad our girl is on the mend. That's what matters. I know you have a lot of stuff on your plate right now, so if you don't get around to it, don't worry about it."

She began packing up her gear. "I'll still definitely look at the footage, but I truly appreciate your being so understanding about everything, Cooper."

He gave her a smile and a nod.

As she walked back to her car, she looked around. Working here at the Swanson Valley Ranch would have been nice and definitely financially worthwhile, but she was no longer interested at all.

Everything she wanted was in Oak Creek, and she couldn't wait to get back there.

Chapter 27

Derek stood at the mouth of the ravine where he and Becky had almost died a few days ago and stared at what was left of the plane.

"You okay?" Callum asked from beside him. "I know coming back here can't be easy."

Lincoln had already gone farther ahead of them, completely oblivious to Derek's discomfort.

"I won't lie, it's not my favorite place to be. But Becky and I both survived, and that's all that matters. It was a good landing, but not a great one."

"Oh yeah?"

Derek looked over at the older man. "Sorry, old pilot's joke. A *good* landing is one from which you can walk away. A *great* landing is one after which they can use the plane again."

Callum shook his head. "Well, according to that adage, this may only be a good landing. But looking at this, honestly, it's a fucking miracle you made it out at all."

Derek shrugged. "It was the only place around for fifty miles that was even a prospect. This was the worst possible area the engines could have gone out."

They walked farther into the ravine, where Lincoln was already examining what was left of the wreckage. Derek wasn't exactly sure why Callum had invited his cousin along, but then again, Lincoln sometimes saw things other people completely missed.

Derek had already debriefed extensively with the National Transportation Safety Board about what had happened. They found it difficult to understand how both engines had gone out, and he couldn't blame them. He had the same concerns. Looking at the wreckage now—and there was a lot less left of it than when he and Becky had examined it right after the crash—didn't make anything clearer.

Conversation faded out as they all focused on what was left of the plane. Derek wasn't sure that it was going to provide any useful intel. At this point, between the crash, the explosion, and the storm, it was basically complete rubble.

"NTSB is saying it's my fault, aren't they?" Derek asked Callum thirty minutes later when they'd all inspected what was left of the jet. "That's why you wanted to come out here. So you knew how to field their questions when they start accusing me of being at fault."

Callum kept inspecting the wreckage. "Nobody died. That's the most important thing to everyone, including the NTSB. Plus, your reputation as a pilot is stellar. Outside of you doing something completely negligent like getting in the cockpit while intoxicated, there's nothing that is going to bring down any shit on you."

Derek wasn't completely sure about that. He'd been tested for substances in his blood as soon as they'd been rescued, but someone could argue that illegal substances had faded out of his system while they were at the cabin.

Derek hadn't had a chance to talk to his bosses at helitack yet. Sam knew what had happened, of course, since he'd been part of the rescue. But one of helitack's primary pilots crashing a plane? That would need to go all the way up the chain. There would be more debriefing in Derek's future soon.

"It's all going to work out, don't worry," Callum said. "Between your statement and Becky's, the air traffic control recording of the mayday, and, like I said, the fact that both of you walked away from this relatively unscathed…it's all going to be a testament to you as a pilot."

Derek would have to worry about that when it came to it. There was nothing he could do about it now. He stopped walking around the wreckage—he wasn't going to be able to glean any more info from it. "What I don't understand is how the hell both engines went out that close to each other."

"Because it was sabotage."

Both Derek and Callum turned to look at Lincoln at his words. Derek had almost forgotten his cousin was here. This was the first thing he had said since they'd arrived.

"Sabotage?" Callum said. "Walk me through what you're thinking, Linc."

Callum wasn't surprised by Lincoln's words, Derek realized. It was probably why he had brought him to begin with.

Lincoln never got caught up in emotion. Whereas most people would look at the crash remains and have to fight not to be concerned about the people who had almost died, Lincoln didn't have that problem.

Lincoln followed the data. Always.

"The biggest suggestion of sabotage is the dual engine failure, like you said. I don't have the exact figures for the chances of that happening statistically" —he actually looked pained at those words— "but I know that it happening should have been nearly impossible. Especially in good weather, with a highly experienced pilot, and no other extenuating circumstances."

"But that doesn't automatically mean sabotage," Derek responded. "Could've just been shit luck."

"The second thing that suggests sabotage is the fact that

your plane's black box gave the wrong coordinates to air traffic control," Lincoln continued.

Both Derek and Callum tensed, glancing at each other.

"Are you sure?" Callum asked. He didn't ask how Lincoln had gotten the information. Nobody who worked in law enforcement ever wanted to know how Lincoln got his information—they were just glad he was on their side.

Lincoln nodded. "As soon as I found out that the dual engine failure shouldn't have happened, I started looking into it more fully. The black box is actually two separate pieces of equipment. Your cockpit voice recorder was fine, but the flight data recorder gave incorrect information."

This explained why there had been no flybys on the first day he and Becky had crashed. The rescue team had been looking in the wrong place.

Callum turned to Derek. "Know anybody who wants to kill you?"

Derek gave a short bark of laughter. "You mean besides my entire immediate family, Becky, and most of my friends?"

"I'm not trying to kill you," Lincoln pointed out in complete seriousness. "And if I were, I wouldn't do it via an airplane. There are much easier ways to kill someone without leaving such traceable elements. For example, I could—"

"It was a joke, Linc." Callum and Derek both said at the same time. If they let Lincoln keep talking, he would come up with at least a dozen ways of killing someone better than a plane crash.

Lincoln nodded solemnly, feelings unhurt. "Right. Joke. Got it."

"If this was truly sabotage, I don't think it's me they were after," Derek said. "I was flying the plane last minute—replaced whoever Swanson ranch was supposed to send when they couldn't make it. If we're really talking sabotage, the intended target must have been Mr. Swanson or one of his employees. Just happened to be bad luck that I was the one flying."

"Or good luck," Lincoln said. "Not many people could've made that landing."

"Okay, let me get on the horn with Swanson ranch and see what we can find out. I'll be right back." Callum walked toward the end of the ravine, leaving Derek with Lincoln.

Derek thumped Lincoln on his back. "You did some good work here, cuz. Once again spotted something most people would've missed."

Lincoln shrugged. "Just putting all the data together."

Derek was honestly not sure if Lincoln understood it was so much more than that.

"Also," Lincoln continued. "Speaking of putting the details together, I've done a little more research about that marriage issue. I did find a way to erase it completely, if that's what you're still wanting to do."

"Nope." Derek's response was immediate. "I don't want you to do anything about it." That was the exact opposite of what Derek wanted.

"I'm not sure if that means you're going to resolve it legally, or it means you and Becky are going to stay married."

"We're going to stay married. Or at least give it our best shot."

It was more than Derek had ever hoped for and definitely more than he deserved, but he was selfish enough to take it. He'd walked away from Becky once, and it had been the hardest thing he'd ever done his whole life. He didn't know if he had the strength to walk away from her again.

Especially when she was so determined to make sure that didn't happen. After she'd found out about his paint house, they had talked about more elements of his PTSD and how they were going to face them together.

Becky, being who she was, had immediately dived into

research—changes he could make in his sleep and eating habits that might possibly help. Ways *she* could become more familiar with PTSD symptoms to help.

Hell, it wasn't long before she had found there were service dogs that could use their sense of smell to identify when an oncoming anxiety attack or nightmare was changing someone's body chemistry. Fifteen minutes later, she had paid a down payment, and they were on the waiting list for a dog that could wake Derek up before he was in the throes of an incident.

God, he loved that woman. His *wife*. He couldn't live without her, and he was tired of pretending it was even an option.

"Okay," Lincoln said. "That's great news. Wait, that is great news, right?"

Derek smiled. "Yeah, cuz, it's great news. But remember that nobody else knows about it, so let's keep it a secret until Becky decides she wants to be publicly connected to me."

"Roger that."

Derek wasn't sure she'd ever want to go public with the marriage, although he hoped so because he'd been thinking about kids recently. Little Beckys running around? What could be greater than that? But he wasn't going to lie; the thought also terrified him.

They would have to take it one day at a time.

Ironically, it had been Becky who had reminded him of the "5s and 25s" expression used in the military. It was generally regarding soldiers scoping out the area around a vehicle in a potentially hostile environment. You first had to focus on the surrounding five meters—the primary and immediate threats. After five meters were clear, you turned to potential threats twenty-five meters away—the next biggest threat.

You focused on the 5s and 25s. Other threats farther off in

the distance would have to wait their turn. Derek could do that, at least with Becky's help.

When Callum walked back over a few minutes later, his face was grim.

"What happened?" Derek asked.

"I talked to Mr. Swanson, told him what we were potentially thinking in terms of sabotage, and asked if he had any enemies we should know about."

"Someone with as much money as him has to have some enemies." Derek shrugged. "He has one of the biggest ranches in the state."

"That's pretty much what he said. But he didn't feel like there were any rivals or foes who hated him enough to kill, so it might be a dead end."

"Dead ends are my specialty," Lincoln said. "Why don't you give me a couple of days on my computer, and I'll see what I can find out."

Callum nodded. "I'll take you up on that offer. But right now, I've got a bigger problem, and oddly enough, it also involves the Swanson Valley Ranch. If we're done here, we need to start heading back so I can help the Teton County Sheriff's office."

Derek took one last look at the wreckage. "I'm pretty sure there's no other information this plane is going to provide us, so I'm fine to head back."

They all started walking out of the ravine—a much different hike than when he and Becky had been trying to get out a couple days ago in the flood. But if something bad was happening involving the Swanson ranch, Derek wanted to know.

"What's going on at the Swanson ranch?" Derek asked. "Becky went up there yesterday. She was supposed to be headed back today, but I haven't talked to her yet."

Callum stopped walking. "Becky was at the Swanson ranch?"

Derek nodded.

"Get her on the phone. Make sure she made it back. I think we've got a real problem."

Chapter 28

Derek wanted to ask for more details from Callum, but that could wait until he knew Becky was safe. He pulled out his phone and pressed the button for her, his eyes locked with Callum the whole time.

Something wasn't right. The older man was definitely worried. Derek put the phone on speaker.

"Hey, you." Becky's sweet voice had everyone relaxing. "Are you guys still out at the crash site?"

"We're getting ready to pack it up now and head back to Oak Creek. Are you home from the Swanson ranch?"

"Almost. I'm about thirty minutes outside of town. Got a little bit later start home than I expected."

Lincoln was doing something on his phone, but Derek ignored him.

"Everything okay with you?" Derek asked, looking at Callum as he said it.

"Yes. Their main horse, Princess, is still not one hundred percent, but overall, a productive visit. How about for you guys?"

"Also a productive visit. I think we'll be ready for the NTSB representative when he gets here in a few days."

"Good. I'm looking forward to putting this behind us and moving forward with other stuff, husband."

Shit. He probably should've warned her she was on speaker. Callum raised an eyebrow but didn't say anything. Lincoln was still messing with his phone.

"Me too. But it's going to take us a few hours to get back, and I might need to help Callum with some things for a while."

"Anything I should know about?" she asked.

"I don't even know all the details yet."

She laughed at that. "Well, I've got to run some blood work for Princess, so I'll be working late anyway. If you want to come sleep at my house, you know you're welcome. If you feel like the paint house is better for tonight, I understand that too."

Derek knew those words were a sacrifice for Becky. Like him, she wanted them to be together all the time. But they both had to accept that might not be possible for the overall long-term health of their relationship.

One day at a time.

"5s and 25s," she whispered.

"5s and 25s," he said back. It was now almost like an endearment between them. "If I can be there tonight, I will be."

"Looking forward to whenever I can see you."

As soon as Derek disconnected the call, Lincoln spun his phone around for a second so Derek could see the screen before flipping it back toward himself.

"She wasn't lying," Lincoln said. "I used the remote version of my Prism software to check. She's about thirty miles outside of Oak Creek."

"Jesus, Linc. I didn't think she was lying."

The bigger ethical question was why he was using the tracking software he'd developed for the US Government to figure out where Becky was, but Derek decided to leave that battle for another day.

Lincoln shrugged. "Not lying and also doesn't have a gun to her head, forcing her to lie. That's really more what I was looking for."

Derek scrubbed a hand down his face. His cousin really did look at things differently from most people.

"That's good to know." Derek turned to Callum, and they all started walking again. "Okay, Becky is safe, so what's the bad news?"

"Teton County officers found a witness who saw Elena Rodriguez, the missing woman, get into a vehicle the night she went missing. Evidently, the truck belonged to the Swanson ranch."

"Shit," Derek muttered.

"Officers have already talked to everyone who works at the ranch, and no one remembers seeing her at all, much less giving her a ride somewhere."

Derek didn't like the sound of that. "So you've either got an unreliable witness, or someone at the ranch is lying."

"Bad witnesses happen—people think they see something when they really didn't. But my gut says there's some sort of brouhaha happening at the Swanson ranch we don't know about."

"Either that, or they're having the worst string of luck in the history of the world," Derek said, picking up speed. It wouldn't take long for them to get back to their vehicle, but then the drive through the wilderness would be slow and tedious. Callum was needed back in civilization.

When they made it back to the SUV, Derek drove so Callum could make whatever phone calls he needed. Lincoln sat in the back seat, mostly silent.

"Looks like I'll be headed up to the Swanson ranch tonight to help out the locals with questioning," Callum said after he hung up from his call. "They want to talk to every single ranch hand individually."

Derek nodded. "That's probably the best way to get at the truth."

"I would start with Everett Clark," Lincoln said. "He's worked at the Swanson Valley Ranch for the past four years."

Derek met his cousin's eyes in the rearview mirror. "Why do you say that, Linc?"

"I created backdoors into the financials and criminal history of every employee at the Swanson ranch."

Well, that explained why his cousin had been quiet for the past forty-five minutes.

Callum sighed and shook his head but still asked, "And?"

"There are four employees who have criminal records, but only Everett Clark's involves violence. Second-degree assault fifteen years ago. Served six years."

Callum nodded. "We'll start questioning with Everett. Meanwhile, don't tell anyone I said this, but keep doing your voodoo, Lincoln."

"It's not voodoo. It was a variation of a rootkit and a worm that could leap across multiple systems and—"

"It was a joke, Linc." Once again, both Derek and Callum said it at the same time.

"Right. Joke. Got it."

A little while later, they made it out of the wilderness and onto the road. Derek punched the gas.

"I'll be making sure Becky doesn't go back to that ranch alone, you can believe that."

Callum nodded and was soon back on the phone with his law enforcement colleagues. Derek kept driving. It would take a few hours to get back to Oak Creek.

And he'd be going straight to Becky's. He'd thought staying

away from her tonight was what he'd need, but he'd been wrong.

He needed to see his wife.

～

BACK AT HOME, Becky sipped on a cup of coffee despite the late hour, standing in her kitchen. It had been a long day, and she was sad she wasn't going to get to see Derek tonight. But it felt like they were heading even more in the right direction after their brief phone conversation a few hours ago.

Not pushing. Recognizing that this new normal for them meant they would occasionally have to give each other some space.

At one time, that would've upset Becky. She would've wanted to be there to help Derek work through any emotional hardship. Only now was she coming to understand that she might be more of a hindrance at some points than she was a help. That didn't need to hurt her.

5s and 25s.

Sometimes fighting a battle meant knowing when to lay down your sword just as much as knowing when to pick it up. She was coming to recognize that fighting for their marriage wasn't going to look like what she'd originally thought it would, and that was okay.

She took the last sip of coffee then rinsed the mug out in the sink. She had run Princess's blood sample at her vet clinic as soon as she'd gotten home a few hours ago, paying for expedited results from the lab herself. That was the least she could do for Mr. Swanson after being MIA so much over the past week. She should be getting the results on her computer any minute now.

She walked over to the small desk her parents had brought over and put in the corner of her living room since she wouldn't have access to her home office for at least another couple weeks due to smoke damage. She was thankful her home office was an add-on to the house, so the fire had been contained mostly in one area, leaving her the rest of the house.

She looked up and around, thinking about Derek and their marriage. Maybe they needed to get a new house. Something completely different and new to them both. Somewhere they could start fresh with new habits and scripts and paths of walking into the future.

The more she thought about it, the more she liked it. It wasn't that this house held bad memories, but no matter what, it was always going to be a place that was tied to their past. As much as possible, they needed to focus on things that were a part of their future.

She smiled, about to text Derek with her idea, when her computer dinged, signaling Princess's lab results were in.

Yes, getting a new place together would be symbolic of a fresh start. It would be a chance for them to tell everyone they were married and start their new life together as true husband and wife.

The smile fell off her face as she clicked on her computer and glanced at Princess's blood work results. She blinked then read them again. These results did not make any sense.

Traces of anabolic steroids in Princess's blood? That couldn't be right.

First of all, there was no reason for a horse of Princess's age and stature to be given that type of steroid at all currently.

Secondly, Becky would've been the one to prescribe the steroid if Princess needed it, and she hadn't. Had Mr. Swanson brought in another vet? Surely he would have told her if that was the case.

She thought of calling him right now and demanding answers but decided not to since it was nearly midnight.

But he could damn well bet that she would be calling first

thing in the morning. Princess should not be on that kind of drug without supervision. It would make her look healthier than she really was.

She decided to pull up the footage from the nanny cam. Maybe something had happened, requiring some sort of injection of the steroids. Hopefully the camera had caught it before it had been knocked out of place.

She accessed the online footage and allowed it to play. She watched in real time for a while, but that became boring pretty quickly. Nothing unusual was happening. Just Princess in her stall. She fast-forwarded, watching everything at quadruple the speed.

Surprisingly, it was Everett who came in and out of the stall the most. Every time he did, she stopped the fast-forward so she could see what was going on. Had Everett given Princess the steroid?

Becky watched carefully for any trace that he had, but all she found was footage of him gently murmuring to the horse and attempting to comfort the creature. She didn't find anything that suggested he was doing any harm—the opposite, in fact.

The man was definitely better with horses than he was with people.

Everett left, and Becky sped through more footage of Princess in her stall. She saw nothing that suggested any sort of foul play whatsoever. When an unknown stable hand came into the stall and accidentally knocked the camera with the handle of his shovel, Becky almost turned the footage off. That explained why the camera had been pointed in the wrong direction. Nothing nefarious about that either.

From here on out, for a couple of days, the camera wouldn't be pointed at Princess's stall, so wouldn't be helpful. But right before she hit the button to turn off the footage, something caught her attention.

A woman in the barn, dressed in a skirt and heels.

She was walking around, touching things, and talking to someone over her shoulder. The nanny cam didn't have any sound, so Becky couldn't hear what the woman was saying, but Becky let out a gasp when the woman turned enough that the camera caught her face.

Elena Rodriguez, the missing woman Callum Webb had told her about.

What was she doing in the barn of the Swanson ranch?

She slowed down the footage and watched as a man grabbed her by the arm and pulled her in for an embrace. Elena kissed him for a moment then yanked away. The man tried to tug her back into him, but this time, she resisted. She shoved at him until he let her go, then was obviously saying something scathing to the man, whose face still couldn't be seen.

Was it Everett? It was so hard to tell with the hat on.

Becky watched in horror as the man backhanded Elena, and she stumbled a couple of steps. Elena turned to leave, but the man grabbed her and spun her around, this time punching her full in the face.

Elena spat blood then yelled something at the man. This time, he grabbed her by the hair, and Becky let out a shriek of horror as he slammed her head into a wooden trowel.

Elena fell to the ground and didn't move.

Becky covered her mouth with her hands and watched the footage as one minute went by and then another. Elena didn't move.

"Oh my God." Becky was pretty sure she had just witnessed a murder.

The man bent down and took Elena's pulse, slamming his hand against the barn wall when he figured out she was dead.

He paced back and forth, still never giving a clean shot of

his face before finally reaching down and grabbing Elena's arm to drag her away.

Finally, the camera caught his face.

"No," Becky whispered.

It hadn't been Everett at all.

Cooper had killed Elena Rodriguez.

Becky stopped the footage and stood up from her chair. She needed to get this to Callum right away. She grabbed her phone so she could call him and let out a little scream when a hand covered hers and stopped her motion.

Cooper was standing over her.

"Now you know why I was going to such lengths to kill you. I was trying to make it look like an accident, but I guess that's not an option now."

Chapter 29

Becky was so caught off guard by Cooper's presence in her house that she didn't react the way she'd trained to. When he stepped back—his gun still pointed at her head, but just out of reach of her being able to attack—she knew she'd missed her best chance and was cursing herself.

Damn it. All that hard work with Lilah month after month, and when she'd needed to react most, she'd floundered.

"I can't believe it's come to this, Becky. I didn't want it to come to this."

Fighting her way out had been her best option. Now she was going to have to rely on trying to talk her way out instead. Or at least try to get Cooper to lower his guard.

It was up to her. Derek wasn't coming home tonight—something she both hated and was also thankful for. If worse came to worst, at least Derek wouldn't die here with her.

But she wasn't planning on dying either.

This was Cooper. She'd spent quite a bit of time talking to him when she'd gone to the ranch over the past couple of years. There'd been an attraction between them. She needed to foster that connection but wasn't sure the best way to play it.

She couldn't deny she'd seen the footage; he'd caught her red-handed with it. Maybe downplaying was the way to go.

"Cooper, look… I don't know what happened with that woman, but from my perspective, it looked like an accident." A complete lie, but Becky didn't care. "A situation that got out of hand. Let's just go to the police, and you can explain what happened."

"No, that's not going to work."

He was still just a little too far from her for her to make an attack. If she went for him now, he would shoot her.

"Why not? We can show them the footage, and you can explain what occurred. Or even better, we can delete the footage altogether. You can tell them in your own words."

For a second, she thought she was getting through to him. He began pacing back and forth, but he kept the pistol in his hand pointed at her.

"I'll help you explain," she continued. "Tell them that it was an accident—not something you planned. A misunderstanding between you and Elena."

His eyes narrowed. "How do you know her name?"

Becky shrugged. "She's missing. The cops were looking for her in Oak Creek too. The sheriff has been showing her picture around."

"The police are assuming she went missing during a hike. They don't know she was at the ranch at all." He nodded. "That works much better for me."

And it worked much worse for Becky. "I think you'll feel better if you just let them know what happened. You don't want to live with this. You can set the record straight. This doesn't have to weigh on your conscience."

"Actually, I don't mind living with it. As a matter of fact, if I go in and try to explain to the police, it'll be much worse for me."

252

"I promise I'll help make them listen." She would promise anything to get out of this alive. "We can make this right."

"Let's just say that even if they did listen to me, they would still start digging deeper into my past, and I can't allow that to happen."

Becky froze, staring at him. Jesus. Was he saying what she thought he was saying?

"You've killed other women?" She hated that her words came out in a squeak, but she couldn't stop it.

It was one thing to think he'd killed Elena Rodriguez in a fit of anger. It was something entirely different to know he'd also killed other people.

He let out a sigh. "Listen, I know it sounds bad, but that's not how it is. These women… I was doing the world a favor. They weren't like you. They were hussies. Trollops. They were garbage."

"*What?*" Becky whispered.

"Any woman who would go home with a man after just meeting him? Would spread her legs and lead him on? That isn't the type of woman this world needs. The world needs women like you, Becky. Classy. Smart. Pristine."

He smiled and winked at her. Funny how something so charming earlier that day now made her stomach turn over on itself.

And he was calling her *pristine?* What the hell did that even mean?

Cooper was a serial killer.

And he might have some sort of screwed-up respect for Becky as a woman, but no chance he was going to let her out of this alive. She knew too much.

There was no talking her way out of this now. She was going to have to make a physical move to get the gun.

She had to try to get closer, which meant playing a role. "Cooper, I know we talked a little earlier today about the attraction between us, but I had no idea you thought so highly of me. I'm flattered."

She forced a smile onto her face, praying it would come across as real. She took a step closer when he lowered the gun slightly.

"I tried to stop you from getting the footage," he said. "When you called and told Everett the camera had shifted, I realized what had happened. I did everything I could to keep you from watching it. I thought if I could destroy your computer, that would be the end of it."

Realization dawned. "You're the one who set my house on fire."

He shrugged. "I swear I wasn't trying to hurt you. I just wanted to make the footage go away. Then I found out it was stored online. I had hoped I could come here, get you in the plane, and then somehow destroy your phone once I got you back to the ranch."

"That wouldn't have made a difference." She took another tiny step.

He let out another sigh. "I know. Once I started researching that sort of camera, I found out that the only way to keep it from coming to light was to make sure you didn't see it at all."

"You sabotaged the plane too?"

He shrugged. "You dying in a plane crash would mean no one would see that footage, and it would look like a complete accident. But somehow, you had the only fucking pilot in the whole state who could land a plane in the middle of the Wyoming wilderness without dying."

"Cooper…"

"And now I'm going to have to figure out how to get rid of you and still make it look like an accident."

She could see him running scenarios in his mind. She was

out of time—as soon as he had some sort of plan, he was going to kill her.

But he wanted it to look like an accident. Shooting would not accomplish that. Her best bet was to rush him. She'd get shot, but maybe she could survive it and beat him in close-quarters combat.

And if she didn't survive, at least Derek would know she hadn't died in an accident. She had no doubt he would search for her killer and would eventually discover it was Cooper.

She didn't want to die here when her life was on the verge of getting restarted. But if she had to, she wanted to make damned sure her death took Cooper down as a killer so he could never strike again. That meant not allowing him to try to kill her on his timeline using whatever method he wanted.

She had to fight.

She was about to make her move and dive for the gun when the side door in the kitchen opened. Her eyes met Cooper's as Derek's voice called out.

"Hey, Button. Decided I had to see you tonight."

ONE LOOK at Becky's face as Derek stepped out of the kitchen into the living room had him instantly realizing something was wrong.

He saw Cooper Ellis a second later, the Beretta 92 in his hand pointed at Becky.

Derek had thought he'd survived the worst a man could experience, in what had been done to him in that prison camp and losing his teammates. Then what had happened between Becky and him on their wedding night.

But he'd been wrong. Seeing that weapon pointed at Becky now was ten times harder than anything he'd been through.

His first instinct was to rush Cooper. If the gun had been

pointed at him, he would've. But he couldn't take a chance with it pointed at her.

"So, you two are a couple. You weren't just her pilot. Figures."

Before Derek could say or do anything, Cooper had marched over to Becky and wrapped an arm around her neck, gun at her temple.

Derek tamped down the terror pressing at him—feelings of helplessness at seeing someone he loved being threatened. He would not let himself get swallowed by the past when he was so needed in the present.

His eyes met Becky's. Hers were clear and focused, giving him strength. But goddammit, that gun pointed at her ripped away every foundation he had.

"What are you doing, Cooper?"

The other man shrugged but didn't lower his weapon. "Your girlfriend's camera caught some footage it shouldn't have. So I'm here to tie up some loose ends since the plane crash I initiated didn't work."

Well, that explained a lot.

Derek glanced at Becky again. She didn't look surprised at what Cooper was saying. Evidently, they'd already had this discussion.

"Does this have to do with Elena Rodriguez?" Derek asked. It didn't take a genius to put it together. "If so, then it's too late. Somebody spotted her getting into a Swanson ranch vehicle with you that night at the bar."

That wasn't completely true, but close enough.

Cooper's jaw got tighter. "That makes it trickier, but I'll be able to talk my way out of that. What I wouldn't be able to talk my way out of is the footage Becky recorded."

"It doesn't have to be this way," Becky said. "I can delete the footage permanently."

Cooper pressed the gun harder against her temple, and it

was all Derek could do not to leap across the room. "I think we're well past that, and we all know it."

"Cooper..." Derek took a step closer. He didn't know what to say; he just desperately wanted that gun pointed at him rather than her.

"No, you stay back!" Cooper tightened his grip around Becky's neck. "I know all about you Linear Tactical guys and what you're capable of."

"I don't work at Linear Tactical."

"Everybody in this entire damned town is connected to Linear Tactical in some way. Don't even act like you're not trained how to fight. So stay the fuck back." Cooper pulled the gun away from Becky's head to point it at Derek.

Thank God.

"Actually," Cooper continued, eyes narrowing. "Now that I think about it, you being here is exactly what I need. You're what can make this look like an accident. Or at least something that has nothing to do with me."

"What are you talking about?" Becky asked.

"A murder/suicide situation. Your boyfriend comes in, goes a little crazy, and shoots you before turning the gun on himself."

The irony was that, given Derek's past, the situation wasn't outside the realm of possibility. Or at least, at one point wouldn't have been.

But Cooper was sorely mistaken if he thought they were just going to go meekly into their own demise. He was still too far away from Derek for him to make a move.

And that was what Cooper was counting on, Derek realized. Cooper thought he only had to worry about subduing Derek physically, not Becky. He was underestimating her, like Derek had when they'd first started sparring in the cabin.

But Derek wasn't underestimating his wife now. He was going to trust her to save both their lives.

He held up his hands in front of him. He needed to keep that Beretta focused on him and away from her so she could make her move.

"You ever heard the expression about 5s and 25s, Cooper?" Derek asked.

"*What?*" Cooper's face was almost comical.

"You're most concerned about the twenty-five, but the five is what's ultimately going to bring you down."

"What the fuck are you talking about?"

Derek's eyes met Becky's for a split second. She understood. He saw her rebalance herself on the balls of her feet.

Derek actually took a step back. It was so hard to take himself even the slightest bit farther away from the danger surrounding them, but it caused Cooper to relax slightly, thinking the threat was lessening.

This was going to be Becky's fight to ultimately win or lose. But Derek had no doubt his wife was going to win.

"Did you know I'm married, Cooper?"

Cooper laughed. "That's even better! Will give even more credence to the story of you killing Becky then yourself. An affair gone wrong."

Derek shrugged and forced himself to look sad. "I trust my wife. She's the strongest person I know."

"Are you trying to get me to feel sorry for you? It's not going to—"

Cooper didn't get a chance to finish the sentence.

Becky shifted her weight, grabbing Cooper's arm and dropping to the floor, getting away from his choke hold. Before he could even point the gun in her direction, she swung her leg around and swept his legs out from under him, causing him to fall to the floor.

Derek rushed toward them, but Becky didn't need him. Her fist shot out, catching Cooper off guard with a combination punch—fist first slamming into his face, breaking his nose, second connecting with his throat, momentarily cutting off his airway.

Cooper dropped the gun and grasped at his neck and face. Becky kicked up into a standing position, grabbed him by the collar, and threw a haymaker at his jaw.

The sweeping hook left Cooper in an unconscious pile at Becky's feet.

Derek kicked the gun out of the way then had to jump back when Becky turned on him, still ready to fight, adrenaline obviously continuing to pump through her system.

"You did it, Button. You saved us both. We're safe."

He watched as clarity came back into her eyes. She looked at him then down at Cooper, her fists lowering from a fighting ready stance.

"He killed Elena Rodriguez," she said between stabilizing breaths. "Other women too."

"Well, you've made sure he's never going to do that again. You were absolutely amazing. And a little scary, I'm not going to lie."

He opened his arms, a little concerned she might not want to be close to him right now, but she leaped into them. They held on to each other like they were never going to be able to let each other go.

Because they weren't.

Chapter 30

Six months later

DEREK PULLED up at Linear Tactical but didn't immediately get out of his vehicle.

This was going to hurt.

He didn't want to be here, but he had to. As a matter of fact, he'd barely finished signing the last set of papers closing on Becky's and his new house before taking off. He'd hated the pain in her eyes—the worry—but he'd had to go. He had to take care of this.

He'd grabbed her and hauled her against his chest right there in the real estate office. "Wait for me. We'll go into our new house for the first time together."

She'd nodded, and he'd taken off. This time, he had to do things right.

"You ready, buddy?"

He looked over at Jasper, the two-year-old service dog that had been by Derek's side since they'd gotten him a month after the Cooper Ellis incident. The border collie happily followed

Derek around everywhere. He'd even gone with Derek to the helitack base camp when Derek reported for duty. The only time Jasper wasn't around was when Derek was piloting an active mission. Then Jasper stayed in the team bunkhouse and enjoyed some time off.

Just as Becky had suggested, Jasper had been able to determine two separate times when Derek had been in the throes of a PTSD nightmare in his sleep and had woken him up before it had escalated.

Granted, after how Becky had handled Cooper the night he'd attacked, and given the amount of time she spent sparring with both him and Lilah each week, Derek no longer lived in such fear of hurting her.

Regardless, having Jasper nearby and knowing the dog could be trusted to stop things before they escalated had taken a huge weight off his shoulders.

Thus, the reason he'd been able to buy a house with Becky to start their new life and ultimately the reason why he was here right now.

He walked around the SUV and opened the door so Jasper could jump out. "Not going to lie, buddy, I'm a little bit wishing you were an attack dog right now."

Jasper was absolutely wonderful at what he did, but he wasn't the type of dog to provide much protection—he was way too friendly.

"You can at least growl or something if he takes a swing at me."

Jasper just wagged his tail and trotted alongside Derek gleefully as he walked toward the obstacle course on the north end of the property.

He could hear four men laughing, cursing, and taunting each other as they completed the course. From the way they were acting, you would think it was a bunch of teenagers rather than a group including three former Special Forces soldiers and a world-renowned extreme sports athlete.

"Of course you won. You cheated like some little bitch."

Derek looked down at Jasper. "Yep, that's my dad. Couldn't be more proud."

"Maybe if you weren't as old as dirt, you'd be a little faster," Zac Mackay responded to Finn. He'd been Derek's dad's best friend Derek's whole life.

And was the reason why Derek was here right now, rather than celebrating his new home.

Dorian Lindstrom and Riley Harrison didn't participate in the taunting. They just silently moved through the course as quickly as possible.

Boy Riley—so called because his wife's name was also Riley—didn't live in Oak Creek any longer, but Derek wasn't surprised to see him back here now. One of his sons, Tucker, worked here at Linear Tactical. His other son, Colton, had taken up permanent residency in Oak Creek after being injured in his own extreme sport stunt a few months ago.

Or at least, he said it was because of his injuries. Insisted it had nothing to do with sweet Ella O'Conner and her attention.

Yeah, right.

"Hey, look. The Linear Tactical next generation is here to challenge all of us," Dorian said from the top of the obstacle course when he spotted Derek. "Why don't you come up here and do your worst, youngster."

Derek smirked at them all. "Anytime, anywhere, old-timers. And I'm happy to bring my buddies."

The guys talked more shit and carried on as Finn descended the obstacle course and walked over to Derek.

"Everything okay?" Finn pulled Derek in for a hug. "Mom didn't send you, did she?"

"Nope. You're safe."

"Good. I'm glad you're not here to tell me I missed our anniversary."

Derek chuckled. His dad had missed his anniversary more than once.

"You here to hang out with us? I thought you were closing on your new house."

Derek sucked in a breath and let it back out. "I just finished signing the papers. Actually, I'm here to talk to Zac. Dr. Annie said he was here."

Finn raised an eyebrow but didn't ask for more explanation.

"I see." He turned back toward the obstacle course. "Cyclone! You're needed on deck."

Zac came jogging over a few moments later. "Hey, Derek. House closing go okay?"

He held out his hand, and Derek shook it.

"Yes, it did." Derek cleared his throat. He needed to get this over with. "Um, I was hoping I could speak with you privately for a few moments, sir."

Now both Finn and Zac had raised eyebrows, undoubtedly because of Derek's formal tone with the man he'd known his whole life and had called *Uncle Zac* until he was old enough to know better.

"Sure," Zac said. "I was pretty much done humiliating your dad here anyway."

"Humiliating, my ass," Finn muttered. "I'll catch you guys later."

Finn turned back toward the obstacle course.

"What's on your mind?" Zac asked.

Derek forced a breath through gritted teeth. "I need to talk to you."

"Is it about Becky?"

"Yes, it is."

Zac stiffened. "You two break up? You leaving town again?"

Derek shook his head quickly. "No, sir. I don't ever plan to leave your daughter again. Unless she tells me to go, I'll be staying by her side."

Zac relaxed a little bit. "Let's walk."

Derek nodded and walked with him away from the obstacle course. That was probably better anyway. If Zac was going to kick Derek's ass after what he had to say, it would be better if it wasn't in front of his father.

"What's on your mind, Derek?" Zac asked again once they had a little bit of distance.

"I would like to ask your permission to ask your daughter to marry me."

Zac raised an eyebrow. "If I'm not mistaken, you're a couple years late asking for Becky's hand in marriage, aren't you?"

Shit. Derek cleared his throat. "Yes, I am, actually. I wasn't aware Becky had told you we got married in Vegas."

"She didn't. I didn't know for sure until you just confirmed it."

Fuck. Zac had laid out the trap, and Derek had walked right into it. No point in withholding information now.

"Yes, sir. We eloped two years ago in Vegas. But I would like to do things correctly this time. I always wanted for everyone in the world to know that I was Becky's husband. There is nothing in my life I'm prouder of than being bound to her."

"That's good to hear."

"The wedding in Vegas was only for the two of us. We knew we wanted to be together forever, and we wanted forever to start as soon as possible. But we always planned to have another ceremony where our family and friends could be included."

"And that's what you're asking my permission for now? To have that ceremony with my daughter."

"Yes, sir."

But it was much more than that. Derek looked down at Jasper, who was still following them. He probably should've left the dog with his dad. Jasper was going to get upset at seeing Derek getting his ass kicked in just a minute. But there was nothing that could be done about any of it now.

"Becky is more than capable of making her own decisions," Zac said. "If she says she'll marry you, then you two definitely have my blessing. She's always chosen you anyway, so I'm not sure that me saying no would even make a difference."

"Thank you, sir. I promise that I will spend my whole life making her happy. But before I go any further, there's something you need to know. Something that might change your mind about offering your blessing."

Derek didn't know what he was going to do once Zac knew the truth. Taking the beating would be easy. The knowledge that Zac would rescind his permission was so much worse.

And what was Derek going to do once that happened? He already knew he wasn't strong enough to stay away from Becky. Maybe he was making a mistake even talking to Zac at all.

But he had to try. In order for him and Becky to move forward the way he wanted them to, he had to try to make her father understand.

"Do you remember when Becky ended up in the hospital two years ago in Vegas?"

Zac nodded. "Seeing my daughter lying in a hospital bed? It's not something I'm likely to ever forget."

Derek forced himself to push forward, or he was never going to get this out. "I thought she would tell you what happened as soon as you got there. I only found out later that she didn't."

"Tell us what?"

"That I was the one who put her there. I woke up in the middle of a PTSD episode and was swinging at her before my brain caught up with my body. That's no excuse," he said rapidly. "I know that. There is no excuse."

Zac was silent. Derek stared down at Jasper, waiting for the older man's response. Yelling? Cursing? Violence? All were acceptable.

"Just out of curiosity, what sort of reaction are you expecting from me right now?"

Now Derek looked up. "Honestly? A fist to the face. To start."

"And if I told you I've known this entire time it was you who put her in the hospital that night?"

Derek scrubbed a hand down his face. "She did tell you. I should've known. I don't blame her."

"No. Becky refused to speak of it completely. I had an entire group of former Special Forces guys ready to find whoever had done that to her and put him in the ground. But she wouldn't give us any information. Not even the slightest bit."

"Oh."

"It didn't take a genius to figure it out after that."

"Oh." Jesus, he sounded like a parrot repeating himself.

Zac shook his head. "Derek, I've known you since the day you were born. Your father has been my best friend my entire adult life."

"So that's why you didn't hunt me down?"

Zac turned so he was completely squared off with Derek. The other man was older, but he was still every bit the warrior he'd been back when he was in the military.

Derek might be able to take him, given the age difference and level of fitness, but honestly, he wasn't completely sure.

"If I thought you had done that to Becky out of spite or

meanness or any of the other ignorant reasons why men beat women, then believe me, you would be in the ground right now. Regardless of whether your dad is my best friend or how long I've known you, if you were a threat to my daughter, you would not be breathing."

"I see."

"I really don't think you do. Maybe it's something you can't see until you're the father of a daughter yourself, and I hope you get that chance."

So did Derek.

"I don't know exactly what happened to you in that prison camp, Derek," Zac continued. "But I can imagine. It changed who you are."

"It did change who I am. And I'm not certain that I'm not a threat to your daughter."

Zac actually smiled. "Becky is so much like her mother. Friendly and gentle and kind. Becky's whole life, I've always felt a bit on the outside of the tiny world the two of them built —I was always a little rough to their smoothness. And Becky is always going to be that way—gentle and kind—just like my Annie."

"It's one of the things I love most about her."

"And I don't blame you. But after what happened between the two of you in Vegas, Becky was forced to find a harder edge to herself. She had to dip into reserves of strength she didn't know she had. She had to become a warrior. I'd like to think that's the part of herself she got from me."

"She is much stronger than she was, but I wish that hadn't been required of her." Derek ran a hand through his hair. "And it definitely doesn't let me off the hook for what happened."

"But the thing is, Becky doesn't feel the same way. What might have broken her, instead caused her to find strength she didn't know she had. And the good thing is…that strength is now forever. And she's happy she has it, no matter what price she paid for it."

"Still…"

"She forgave you a long time ago, Derek. It's time for you to forgive yourself. I know that's easier said than done."

"I'm working on it."

Zac slapped him on the back. "And you'll be working on it until the day you die. That's okay. But to answer your question…yes, you have my blessing to marry my daughter. As a matter of fact, if you want them, I have something for you."

"What's that, sir?"

"Do you know that Becky is named after my first wife, who died years before my daughter was born? That Becky was Annie's best friend in high school, and Annie and I both loved her very much?"

"I knew something of the sort, but not the details."

"I still have that Becky's wedding band and engagement ring, and if you two would like them for whatever wedding ceremony you decide to have, I'd be honored to pass them along to you. I know Annie agrees."

Derek blinked out at him. "I—I'd be honored."

Zac reached out and squeezed his shoulder. "I've never had a son. Annie and I thought we might have more kids, but that didn't work out. So I'm happy to have you as a son now."

"Thank you."

Zac grinned. "Just don't call me Dad."

SHE'D PUSHED Derek too hard.

Becky sat outside of their new house, staring at it from inside her car. When this place had come up for sale a few weeks ago, they'd both thought it was perfect. A little outside of town, with plenty of space, plus a separate workshop Derek could use as his own painting area if he wanted.

She'd thought Derek was on board, and he'd seemed like he was. Until he'd all but run out of the office today when they'd finished closing on the house.

She'd pushed too hard. He hadn't been ready, and he hadn't known how to tell her. Honestly, she was just glad she'd gotten his text a few minutes ago asking her to meet him here.

At least he wasn't running. That was the most important thing.

She had to keep her sights on the 5s and 25s, always.

When he pulled up and parked next to her, she got out of the car.

"Hi."

He nodded, Jasper jumping down next to him. "Hi. Sorry about the office."

She wanted to go to Derek, put her arms around him, but she didn't. She'd learned in the past six months that sometimes touch—even her touch—was difficult for him. He knew it bothered her and made up for it by touching her as much as possible when he could.

"Are you okay?" she asked him, hating the space between them. "Did we move on this house too soon? Was it too much?"

She was surprised when he came over and took her hand and walked with her toward the steps that led up to the wraparound porch.

"No, it wasn't too much. But I realized there was something I needed to do before I could move in to this house with you."

"What's that?"

He led her until she was standing on the first step, then turned her around to face him. He was still a little bit taller than her, despite the assistance.

"I had to tell your dad today that I was the one who put you in that hospital two years ago."

Her eyes widened. "You did? My parents wanted to know what happened, but I never told them."

"He already had figured it out. Your refusal to tell them is what tipped him off."

"Was he mad?"

He took both of her hands in his. "He knows I would never do anything to hurt you on purpose. I wouldn't be here with my spine intact otherwise."

"I'm glad he understood."

"I had to tell him that before I could ask him for permission to marry you."

"Ask for permission? But we're already married."

Before she could figure out what he was going to do, he dropped to one knee. "Will you marry me, Becky, publicly this time? In front of God and all our friends and family. Will you do me the honor of wearing a ring that lets everyone know you're mine and allow me to do the same?"

Tears filled her eyes, and she cupped his cheeks. "Yes. I would like nothing more."

To her astonishment, he pulled a set of rings out of his pocket. "Your dad and mom gave me these—they belonged to your dad's first wife."

"Becky," she whispered. "I'm named after her."

"Both your mom and dad want you to wear Becky's rings, if you want."

She nodded. There was nothing she wanted more. Derek slipped them on her finger. They were a little big, but they could get them resized later.

She grabbed his hands and pulled him back up until he was standing. She threw her arms around him.

"Thank you. I honestly didn't know how important any of

this was to me until this moment. I want to do all of this right with you. Right and public and forever."

"Me too, Button."

He shifted and lifted her up in his arms, carrying her up the stairs and to the door. She got the key out of her pocket and unlocked it.

"We may have done things out of order, but you're the only bride I'll ever have, Becky Mackay Bollinger. I love you."

And with that, he took the step over the threshold and carried them into their new life together.

Also by Janie Crouch

All books: https://www.janiecrouch.com/books

HEROES OF OAK CREEK

Hero Unbound

Hero's Flight

Hero's Prize

ZODIAC TACTICAL

Code Name: ARIES

Code Name: VIRGO

Code Name: LIBRA

Code Name: PISCES

Code Name: OUTLAW

Code Name: GEMINI

NEVER TOO LATE FOR LOVE (with Regan Black—series complete)

Heartbreak Key Collection

Hero Forever

INSTINCT SERIES (series complete)

Primal Instinct

Critical Instinct

Survival Instinct

THE RISK SERIES (series complete)

Calculated Risk

Security Risk

Constant Risk

Risk Everything

OMEGA SECTOR (series complete)

Stealth

Covert

Conceal

Secret

OMEGA SECTOR: CRITICAL RESPONSE & UNDER SIEGE
(series complete)

Special Forces Savior

Fully Committed

Armored Attraction

Man of Action

Overwhelming Force

Battle Tested

Daddy Defender

Protector's Instinct

Cease Fire

Major Crimes

Armed Response

In the Lawman's Protection

About the Author (Janie Crouch)

"Passion that leaps right off the page." - Romantic Times Book Reviews

USA Today and Publishers Weekly bestselling author Janie Crouch writes what she loves to read: passionate romantic suspense featuring protective heroes. Her books have won multiple awards, including the Romance Writers of America's coveted Vivian® Award, the National Readers Choice Award, and the Booksellers' Best.

After a lifetime on the East Coast, and a six-year stint in Germany due to her husband's job as support for the U.S. Military, Janie has settled into her dream home in Front Range of the Colorado Rockies.

When she's not listening to the voices in her head—and even when she is—she enjoys engaging in all sorts of crazy adventures (200-mile relay races; Ironman Triathlons, treks to Mt. Everest Base Camp...), traveling, and hanging out with her four kids.

Her favorite quote: "Life is a daring adventure or nothing." ~ Helen Keller.

facebook.com/janiecrouch

amazon.com/author/janiecrouch

instagram.com/janiecrouch

bookbub.com/authors/janie-crouch

9 781950 802838